Finding Amal

Finding Amal

A NOVEL

Firyal Alshalabi

GREEN WRITERS PRESS *Brattleboro, Vermont*

Printed in the United States

10 9 8 7 6 5 4 3 2 1

Green Writers Press is a Vermont-based publisher whose mission is to spread a message of hope and renewal through the words and images we publish. Throughout we will adhere to our commitment to preserving and protecting the natural resources of the earth. To that end, a percentage of our proceeds will be donated to environmental activist groups and social justice organizations. Green Writers Press gratefully acknowledges support from individual donors, friends, and readers to help support the environment and our publishing initiative.

green writers press

Giving Voice to Writers & Artists Who Will Make the World a Better Place
Green Writers Press | Brattleboro, Vermont
www.greenwriterspress.com

ISBN: 979-8-9923988-3-0

PRINTED ON PAPER WITH PULP THAT COMES FROM FSC-CERTIFIED FORESTS, MANAGED FORESTS THAT GUARANTEE RESPONSIBLE ENVIRONMENTAL, SOCIAL, AND ECONOMIC PRACTICES. ALL WOOD PRODUCT COMPONENTS USED IN PAPERBACK BOOKS, UTILIZING EITHER CREAM PAPER ARE SUSTAINABLE FORESTRY INITIATIVE® (SFI®) CERTIFIED SOURCING.

How beautiful is night!

A dewy freshness fills the silent air,
No mist obscures, no little cloud
Breaks the whole serene of heaven:
In full-orbed glory the majestic moon
Rolls thro the dark blue depths.
Beneath her steady ray
The desert circle spreads,
Like the round ocean, girdled with the sky.

How beautiful is night!

Robert Southey
Thalaba the Destroyer, 1801

Chapter One

APRIL 19, 2019

Glass doors slide wide open for Hadeel to take her first free step into America, the land of freedom and opportunity according to the myriad of books she read in college, the land of Muslim haters according to her parents. Either case is none of Hadeel's concerns. America has never been part of her dreams or future plans. It just happens to be the land from which she received the letter that prompted this journey, the journey she can't wait to get over with and place in the deleted files of her memory.

Passengers rush around her, pushing carts loaded with luggage, shoving her left and right. She blinks. Perhaps this is not real, just a dream or the other worldliness of a computer game, one of those outrageous games she'd rather be playing right now in the darkness of her bedroom. Suddenly, fear of her father's wrath sparks up her spinal cord. What will he do if he finds out?

She's supposed to be in London for research with her pious Aunt Munira. "He will not find out," Munira assured her at Heathrow Airport when they said goodbye. Only three days, Munira promised. "Three days and you'll be back here with me to go home to Kuwait." Home, her comfort zone, hiding from the whole world, reading books and playing video games. Hadeel mumbles a short prayer, hoping her aunt is right.

Like a child pushed onto the stage against her own will, she takes a deep breath, steps forward, and tugs her small suitcase. She shakes her long Eileen Fisher skirt loose from her ankles and makes sure her blouse is buttoned all the way up to her neck. Pain in her lower back from sitting slumped for nine hours shoots up her spine. Why did she switch her comfortable seat in Club World with an old woman in Economy? Perhaps the woman reminded her of *Ydaida*, her grandmother? *Habibti Ydaida*, Hadeel mumbles as she always does when she thinks of her late grandmother. With a firm nod of her head she decides this trip should be the last in doing favors for other people, even the dearest of them. This trip, a favor for Aunt Munira, is *haram* anyway, and should not have happened. *Asteghfirullah*, God forgive me.

In the open space of the main terminal of Denver International Airport, natural light pours down through glass panels in soaring ceilings. White poles holding tall tent-shaped structures look vaguely familiar. Underneath them are leafy trees encased in huge concrete containers which make people roaming around them look small in comparison. But the most tangible difference between this airport and others Hadeel's been to around the world is how quiet it is. No noisy announcements for final calls of departing flights. No rushing passengers worried about missing flights. It's peaceful. The people standing behind a security tape in front of the arrival gates are placid, their eyes staring anxiously to spot their loved ones. Some are holding up signs with names. Hadeel looks for hers. There it is, neatly written in bold black ink. She stops.

Her eyes slowly focus on the face of the man holding the sign. The man who wrote the letter urging her to visit. The man she was forbidden to mention at home since childhood, the infidel, according to her parents. To Hadeel, he's the source of all her personal problems. Most probably the reason she's been caged at home to avoid meeting men like him. For the first time in twenty years, she's now gazing at the face of the *wahsh*, the monster, who stole her favorite Aunt's heart and stashed her away. What a wild image her childish mind had made of him, scary with fangs and evil eyes. This person seems harmless and frail. He's tall with white hair, a white beard, and wears silver-rimmed glasses. He's so thin he would be blown away by the *haboob*, the dust storms raging right now in Kuwait. He's much older than she had imagined. Hadeel reminds herself that twenty years have passed since the first time she heard of him and let her five-year-old imagination go wild. Oh well, what is she waiting for? *Bismillah*, in the name of God, she mumbles and steps forward. The wheels of her London-Fog suitcase rumble noisily behind her over the polished tiled floors.

She stops a few feet away from him. "I am Hadeel."

"Ahh . . ." he exclaims as if he's encountered a ghost. *Is that a tear slipping from his eyes? Are they blue?* "I'm Jonathan Walton. Welcome."

He offers his hand for a shake which Hadeel ignores. She's been brought up not to shake men's hands, let alone this *wahsh's* hand.

"*Hamdillah 'asalamah,*" he says in good Arabic, thanking God for her safety. Hadeel's heart softens at the familiar greeting.

"*Allah yeselmik,*" she replies, likewise. She figures he's six feet tall, three inches taller than she is.

"Can I help with your luggage?" He folds the paper with her name and pushes it into his pants pocket.

Hadeel hands him her suitcase and follows him under several signs pointing to exits and parking areas. Groups of passengers are milling around glass walls, heads bent over cell phones.

So her Aunt Amal taught him some Arabic expressions, Hadeel thinks. That's something to report to Aunt Munira, who, against all odds, planned this trip and begged Hadeel to take it as a personal favor. At the time, Hadeel sincerely wanted to help her distraught aunt, thinking of nothing else. Now she wonders about the wisdom of it. She has to stop doing favors even for her favorite aunt.

A group of dark-skinned people who look like Kuwaitis are congregating in hushed voices behind a British Airways check-in-counter. Hadeel slows down, longing to line up with them and fly back home already. Two of them, women wearing hijabs, glance at her, stirring feelings of guilt. She touches her hair and blushes deeply when one of them smiles at her. Hadeel awkwardly nods and thinks of her own hijab hidden in her purse. Those women must be brave, declaring their faith to the public. She searches for hostile reactions from Westerners towards them to justify her own cowardice but finds none. Everybody is busy with their own lives, their own journeys, their own problems. Hadeel hurries up behind Jonathan.

Outside the terminal, wind blows cold drizzle against her warm face. Goose pimples grow over her back and shoulders. Her once long, thick hair would have provided some warmth. But she chopped it off recently in a moment of depression, or was it a moment of anger? Another stupid mistake. She rushes behind Jonathan, who's swiftly weaving his way around concrete pillars and pathways in the covered garage. The weather in England was unseasonably warm for April during the week she and Munira stayed there, planning this trip. The only jacket she took is packed in the suitcase Jonathan is stowing in the trunk of his car. She hesitates next to his blue Tesla. She can't decide if she should sit in the front or back. She's never been alone with a stranger before. This is a detail neither she nor Munira had considered in their plans.

Jonathan opens the front door for her. She slides onto the cold leather seat and folds her arms around her chest for warmth. Once a decision is made for her, she rarely argues. It spares her the effort of deciding. Jonathan takes the driver's seat, buckles his seatbelt, and waits. Drifts of cold air seep through the car vents and touch Hadeel's toes, making her realize she's wearing summer sandals, no socks. She shakes her feet and watches the black nail polish on her toe nails sway like blurred words on a page. Amidst the hurried preparations for the trip, weather and proper clothing for Colorado were not priorities for her or Munira.

Drizzle changes to a downpour while Jonathan waits in his seat gazing straight ahead. When Hadeel looks at him questioningly he tugs at his seatbelt. "Fasten your seatbelt, please." Only after she buckles up does he back up and peel out of the garage area.

"How long is it to Boulder?" she asks.

"About an hour. In this weather, maybe a little longer."

His voice is serious, as if he's imparting bad news. What could be worse than what he already told her in his letter? Her Aunt Amal, his wife, "is dead due to unfortunate circumstances." Killed in a *freak* accident. What kind of accident? He did not explain. He ended his letter saying, "There are important issues that I must discuss with you. Please consider a visit as soon as possible." *No thanks,* was Hadeel's first reaction after the initial shock at the news of her aunt's death. After twenty years of absence, Hadeel did not have much emotions or desire to visit her dead Aunt's place, or discuss whatever *he* thought were important issues. His concerns were neither important nor significant to Hadeel or her family. Besides, now she has her own "important issues" to deal with. But a few days after she had received the letter, she showed it to her Aunt Munira. After an unexpected outburst of wailing and crying, Munira begged her to go.

"What?" Hadeel answered in shock. "Are you serious?"

"Yes, you have to," Munira said, still crying. "He loved her during this life. Our love for her is for the afterlife, for eternity."

Hadeel shifts in her seat and takes a furtive glance at Jonathan. He remains silent, lips drawn tight, eyes focused on the road. So this is the man for whom Amal had forsaken her family, friends, and country? Except for his blue eyes how was he different from Arab men? Or anyone her family would have approved of? What was so special about him? Why did Amal love him? Hadeel steals another look at Jonathan. She wonders if his grimness is his normal demeanor or the result of his wife's death.

The weather is not helping either, she guesses. Thunder and lightning are chasing each other as if in a game of tag. The swift wipers barely clear the torrents of rain for a second before the windshield is covered again with water. Dark clouds gather overhead promising more rain. An ache in her stomach revives doubts about the wisdom of this trip. She's regretting it to the point of tears. Why did she succumb to Munira's pleas? Couldn't she have said no, for a change? She really doesn't care if Amal ends up in Hell or Heaven. Most probably she's already in Hell. It's too late. But like all the other tasks Hadeel has carried out during her short lifetime, she's doing this as a favor. This time for the aunt who rarely asks for anything. Munira assured her she'd take the blame and responsibility if anything went wrong, or if her parents found out. *How wrong can things go?* Hadeel wonders, trembling.

"Anything can happen," a voice rings in her ears. A car accident, a tornado or a twister, a gunshot, any of the stuff she's seen in American movies. If she dies in a car accident, her parents, who think she's in England with Munira working on her Master's thesis, would possibly read about it in the newspaper. *"A twenty-five-year-old Kuwaiti tourist dead in a car accident with an old American man."* What would happen to her parents then? They'd die of shame for sure.

Hadeel shakes her feet, presses her eyes shut and recites a prayer under her breath, "*Ya Allah ya Habibi!* I beg Your Mercy and forgiveness. Please return me home safely. I promise never, ever, to displease you again. Please God forgive me, *samihni*."

"Thank you for coming by the way," Jonathan says. "I wish Amal was here to see you." He chokes up, swallows hard, and shakes his head.

Hadeel sighs and looks out of her window. What kind of a man is one who cries in front of a woman? How could her aunt love such a meek person? Should she ask him now how Amal died? Would he be able to speak without shedding more tears? She decides to wait. She's never seen a man cry before, and, for some reason, it bothers her. Besides, Munira asked her to call upon arrival. She pulls her cell phone out of her purse.

"I need to make a call," she says, dialing.

"Sure," He quickly wipes a tear with his fingers.

One phone ring and Munira's anxious voice streams in, "Hadeel!"

"Just arrived," she says in Arabic. "I'm in the car with him. I will call you from the hotel."

"Wait! Don't forget what I asked you to do. *Alheen*, right away."

"*Amma* Munira!" Hadeel leans forward. "It's raining! Really raining."

"Hadeel!" Her aunt shrieks. "I don't care! You have to . . . You promised!"

"But . . ." Hadeel's eyes well with tears.

"Hadeel!"

"*Zain*, okay. Bye."

Jonathan looks at Hadeel with concern. He must have heard Munira's piercing voice through the phone and thunder. Hadeel's whole body shakes. How is she going to explain Munira's request? She takes a deep breath, then exhales with a loud puff. What would be the best way to tell him what she promised to do? What Munira wants her to do. After all, it is the main reason she's taken this trip. Munira has never been so adamant about anything before. To Hadeel's utter surprise her reclusive aunt arranged and purchased the ticket without a moment of hesitation. She even lied to Hadeel's parents. Lied. She told them she was accompanying Hadeel to London for two weeks and would keep an eye on her all the time. They know Munira never lies, otherwise they would not have allowed the trip to London. Not only because Hadeel had never traveled alone before, but because according to her parents, she would not be able to handle it herself. Besides, had her parents known about Amal's demise, they wouldn't allow the trip, simply because they never thought Amal deserved an ounce of their affection. Hadeel's parents denounced and disowned Amal when she married the American. Hadeel's father Rashid, Amal's brother, had been especially harsh. Unlike Munira, whose love for her only sister never wavered, no matter how different they were from each other, Rashid remained unforgiving. It seemed to Hadeel that Munira's faith in this mission justified all the "wrongs" she'd committed planning it. Hadeel wished her own faith was as unwavering.

Jonathan clutches the steering wheel with both hands as another series of thunder strikes begin. To calm her nerves Hadeel plugs in her earphones, scrolls through a personal list of favorite pop artists, and stops at Zayn Malik. His song "Rear View" seems appropriate. She clicks *play* and closes her eyes. It's always easy to forget the world while focusing on Zayn's voice and lyrics. But with the tumult of the storm overhead, she just can't calm down. Her mind replays events which led to this moment. How she received the letter signed by the man now sitting next to her. How she kept it for days before showing it to Munira. How Munira wailed before announcing: "You must go!"

"Why?" Hadeel replied, horrified.

"For her sake. For my sake. Please, *habibti*, you must go. I beg you."

"Why don't you go?"

"My English is not good enough. You know that!"

"And how do you think I can go without Baba's knowledge?"

"There has to be a way. Leave it to me."

The letter had arrived in early April. If her father had known who wrote it, he wouldn't have given it to her. But since she received mail on a regular basis from Amazon, he must have thought it was part of a book shipment or correspondence for her Master's degree. The news of Aunt Amal's death in the letter shocked her. She hadn't heard from her since she'd left when Hadeel was five. That was twenty years ago. Perhaps the letter was meant for someone else. She checked the address on the envelope, then reread it again. It began, *"Dear Hadeel, I'm terribly sorry to be delivering the tragic news . . ."*

Hadeel tugs uneasily at her seatbelt and turns the volume of her music louder. She has promised Munira to do something she's not sure she can do. Should she lie to her aunt? Tell her she fulfilled her obligation? A "white lie" under such weather conditions could be justified, eventually forgiven. But lying to Munira might be more painful than the obligation itself. She lifts her head to the car ceiling with her eyes closed. "Ya *Rubbi*, My God, what shall I do?"

Would it be a sin to lie for a good reason? Munira lied to Hadeel's parents. Well, she didn't really lie, she just hid the news. But Aunt Munira is too precious to lie to. She had always been there for Hadeel whenever she needed her, especially the last two years, the most difficult time of Hadeel's life.

"By the way," Jonathan says, interrupting her thoughts.

Hadeel removes the earplugs. "Pardon?"

"You're welcome to stay in my house instead of the hotel."

Hadeel lifts her eyebrows and looks at him in disbelief. Is he serious? She brings her head a little closer to his. But of course, he is. With such a grim face could he ever not be serious?

Just imagine me staying alone in your house, I'd be as bad as Amal was, wouldn't I?

"I'm sorry, I can't." She sits upright in her seat. "But thanks, anyway."

The rain lightens up, thunder and lightning linger apart, stop chasing each other. Hadeel takes a couple of deep breaths and tries to relax her shoulders. She must complete the task she's here for.

She turns to Jonathan to explain, but he speaks first. "She spoke of you often."

"Who?"

"Amal."

"Oh."

"You still remember her, right?"

"Yes, a little. I was five when she left." She doesn't feel obliged to explain how, as a child, she was devastated at her aunt's sudden departure.

"You never answered her letters," Jonathan says.

"What letters?"

"She wrote to you constantly, at least once a month since she left Kuwait."

Rain taps on the rooftop. Hadeel wonders if Amal had actually mailed the letters or if Rashid, her father, kept them from her. She refrains from sharing her thoughts with Jonathan. It's a family matter. Twisted veins of lightning illuminate the dark sky ahead. The drive feels endless, as if time has stopped just to torture her by leaving her stranded with a man alone in a car.

Jonathan eventually slows down, takes an exit, and stops at an intersection.

Hadeel's voice shakes when she blurts out, "There's something I need to do before I go to the hotel."

"What is it?"

"Can I . . . Can I visit her?" She bites her lips hard, punishing them for uttering the words.

"You mean at the cemetery?"

"Yes. Please." A tear falls from her eye.

"Right now? In this weather?" He lets go of the steering wheel pointing to the sky with both hands, palms up.

"Yes, I must. I promised my Aunt Munira."

A vein in his forehead pulses as he turns to stare at her. "Why?"

"You won't understand. I'm sorry." She squints guiltily then reminds herself it's not her fault, it's his fault. He's the one behind this whole bloody dilemma and the problems she suffered her whole life. She was always compared to Amal every time she contradicted her parents. He is the cause of her miserable life, she now thinks. He must help her do what she's here to do. "Just take me there, please."

Thunder crashes once more above their heads. Jonathan weaves his way up onto a narrow road leading to the top of a mountain. They're so high up they could touch the sizzling white streaks in the dark sky. Once on top of the road, Jonathan lets the car roll down to the other side. Hadeel sucks in a breath and holds it until they level down on the unlit street. The area surrounding them is too dark to distinguish a tree from a ghost.

Jonathan cuts the engine but leaves the lights on, which sets off the persistent car-light alert. Surprisingly, the sound soothes Hadeel's shattered nerves until Jonathan switches the lights off and they sink into darkness. Raindrops knock hard on the car roof, as if warning her not to step out or she'll get soaked. She shivers knowing she must go out.

"I can bring you back here in the morning," Jonathan says without looking at her. "It doesn't make sense to visit at such a time."

Wordlessly, Hadeel unbuckles her seatbelt, pulls her scarf from her purse, wraps it around her head, knotting it under her chin. She straps her purse across her shoulder and places her hand on the door handle. This is why she's taken the journey. If she completes her obligation, it will be over. The trip will become a memory she can forget, forever.

She clears her throat and says, "Please, show me where she is. It will only take a minute."

"Oh well," Jonathan sighs and pushes his door open.

Outside the car a crack of thunder makes her shriek. "But it's like playing a computer game," she mumbles to calm herself, then scrambles behind Jonathan. She keeps her eyes on his white jacket, the single light object in the darkness surrounding them. In a second she is drenched in the rain. Her shirt and skirt stick heavily to her body, and she hugs her purse to her chest. Rain sloshes through the sandals and between her toes. She's having trouble getting enough air to breathe and wishes Jonathan would slow down. She's never been to a cemetery before.

Jonathan stops without warning. She bumps into him and murmurs an apology.

"She's over there." He gestures toward a grassy area surrounded by wet puddles. Strange looking sculptures and concrete slabs loom along the slippery path. Jonathan turns and pauses like a statue himself. "I'll wait here."

Hadeel shivers. "Which one is it?'

"That one." He points at a low tombstone a few feet ahead.

Hadeel steps forward and leans down to read the words on the headstone. Darkness and rain make it impossible to see the full epitaph. She waits for a flash of lightning. "This is what my . . ." There are two more lines underneath, she cannot make out the inscription, but she spots Amal's name before darkness prevails.

Resting her knees on the wet grass, she fumbles inside her purse. Why doesn't she feel sorrow for her dead Aunt? Hadeel seizes the small copy of the Quran in her purse with her fingers to figure out how much digging she'll need to do. "This has to be buried with her, *Inshallah* to keep evil spirits away." Munira had emphasized when she gave her the Holy book. "You have to bury it with her, Hadeel. I'm sure they didn't."

"Shall we go?" Jonathan urges her.

"Just one minute." Hadeel fumbles around the edges of the concrete slab searching for a spot under the tombstone. With slippery fingers she pulls grass and pokes in the dirt. Even with the deluge of rain, the grass is not easily uprooted. With muddied fingernails she reaches inside her purse for something to dig with. She grasps a pen in her palm like a dagger and digs into the soil near the tombstone.

Finally, she's dug a space big enough to force the tiny Quran under the ground. She tries not to imagine what lies further down. Has Amal been visited by the Questioner? Did she remember the correct answers? Has she been tortured? Was she scared and repentant? How does she look now? Her early memory of her beautiful Aunt remains carved in her mind even after Munira showed her a picture of a mature, serious looking woman. The eyes, which must be sealed now, had always twinkled when Hadeel thought of Amal. But, alas, no more.

"What are you doing?" Jonathan yells. "I don't think you're allowed to mess up the grave!"

"I'm sorry." She tamps the ground back in place and closes her eyes shut while reciting the verse Munira made her memorize for this task. Saying the last word, Hadeel rises, rainwater dripping from her shoulders to her toes. She searches for Jonathan. Shadows blur with rain, like a scene in a horror movie. She staggers to the car and opens the door.

"I'm done," she says shivering. "We can go."

Chapter Two

"Can I see an ID, please?" the young man at St. Julien hotel's front desk asks. He's wearing a formal blue jacket and a necktie, yet his blond curly hair is totally disheveled, covering his eyebrows.

Hadeel hands him her passport and mumbles an apology for it being wet. Her hair is still dripping over her soaked blouse. She looks down at the little puddle forming around her feet on the marble floors.

The young man clears his voice and says, "I see your stay is already paid for. But I need a credit card for incidentals, please."

Hadeel pulls a card out of her wallet and hands it to him. The hotel looks new and practically empty except for the voices of some customers in a bar far back from the lobby. A huge crackling fireplace in the middle of the reception area spreads a warmth that Hadeel's frozen limbs long for. Jonathan, waiting by the main doors of the hotel, is talking on his cellphone while keeping an eye on her. When the receptionist gives her back her documents and the key to her room Hadeel waves goodbye to Jonathan. He waves back and rushes toward his car parked a few feet away from the main entrance.

"Do you need help with your luggage?" the young man at the desk asks.

"No, thank you," Hadeel whispers, looking at the trickle of rain-water she's leaving behind, wondering if she should mention it and apologize.

He winks at her when she looks up. "I'll be here all night if you need anything."

Hadeel's face turns red at the unexpected remark. She hastens toward the elevators, her suitcase rumbling behind on the tiled floors. Inside the elevator, she pushes the close-doors button first before her floor number. *Must be the way my clothes are clinging to my body,* she thinks, seeing herself in the elevator mirrors. A sick feeling erupts in her stomach as the list of sins keeps growing in her mind with every move she makes. Showing her hair and body in front of men without hijab or decent attire must have added volumes of reasons to roast in hell. The elevator door opens to a narrow corridor leading to her room number. Canned laughter from someone's TV sounds from the room next to hers.

She walks inside her room, locks the door and makes sure the chain and all other locks are secure. She scans the tiny room, drags the desk chair to the door and props it under the handle for extra security. When Amma Munira searched for a hotel for Hadeel in Boulder she chose St. Julien on the assumption that since it's the most expensive it should be the safest. But who can guarantee safety anywhere in the world nowadays?

Hadeel finds her phone in the zipped pocket inside her purse and calls Munira. "Done," she announces. "I did exactly what you wanted me to do."

Munira's sigh of relief is audible through the thousands of miles between them. "*Alhamdu lillah. May Allah . . .* May Allah forgive her." She sobs quietly.

"Can I come back now? Why should I stay any longer?"

"Did you . . . Did you talk to him?" Munira asks between sniffles.

"Talk to who?"

"Her husband."

"About what?"

"You forgot! We're not done yet, Hadeel! But you must be tired. Call me again tomorrow." Munira ends the call with a click.

Hadeel has not really forgotten about that part. She knows exactly what Munira wants, but she is not convinced of its necessity and hopes her aunt will forgo it as well. Actually, she thinks it's ridiculous. How can she tell her grieving Aunt Munira that she doubts they can save Amal's soul from damnation by taking her body back home? It's too late, isn't it? Hadeel is still hoping Munira will change her mind after she calms down, especially now that the Quran is buried with Amal. Poor Amma Munira. Just like herself, she's now alone in a hotel room for the first time in her life. "We're doing this for Amal's sake," Hadeel repeats Munira's words to herself.

Amongst the many reasons why Hadeel is so nervous about this trip is her father's reaction should he find out about it. Besides traveling alone, which he is adamantly against, how will he react should he discover she's not wearing the hijab he pressured her to wear in public? What would he do? How would her mother handle the situation? And now, the young man's remark at the front desk added a new complication that she hadn't thought of.

After changing and performing *salat elesha*, the night prayer, Hadeel slips under the bed covers and tries to stop thinking. The time change might help her get some sleep. She shuts her eyes and tries to shrug off Amal, Munira, her parents, and Jonathan. They can wait until the next day. Right now, she's exhausted and needs rest. Flashes of the cemetery and her aunt's grave in that desolate place keep appearing behind her eyelids. Amal's laughter and voice from childhood echo in her ears. She was once full of life; she's now laying still in a grave in a foreign land. *How did she look the moment I inserted the Quran in her resting place? Would she herself approve of what I did?*

Hadeel was fourteen when death knocked at home for the first time. Grandmother *Ydaida*, eighty-two, passed away after being comatose for a week at Amiri Hospital in Kuwait. Hadeel never forgot the moment she heard about Ydaida's death. It was at sunset. Hadeel was reading under the shade of the thick palm tree in the garden. When her father walked in and announced that Ydaida had died, Hadeel could swear that at that moment the sky turned gray and the birds flew away. Nature stood still mourning for Ydaida.

Hadeel's family knew she was not coming out of the coma; still it was a devastating shock when it happened. Hadeel hid in her room all night with the pillow over her head, refusing to believe it. How could life go on without sweet Ydaida? How could Amma Munira live without her mother? Ydaida had been Munira's constant companion since the day she was born. The two were never apart a single day of their lives.

"Allah is capable of bringing the dead back to life," Aunt Munira repeated at her mother's deathbed.

Hadeel remained by her side, offering love and sympathy. She is Munira's favorite niece, most probably because Hadeel is the first niece in the family. When Amal left, Munira was eager to fill her vacant place. Out of the seven grandchildren, Hadeel was Ydaida's favorite as well.

Perhaps because Hadeel was different from her cousins. Their parents, Hadeel's uncles, sent their children to private schools and allowed them to socialize freely with friends their age. Hadeel's father, Rashid, kept her under tight control. He sent her to the girls-only public schools. As a teenager, he insisted on a female chaperone to accompany her for any social event, so most of the time she opted to stay home.

Under the tutelage of Ydaida, Hadeel performed her prayers five times a day from the age of seven. She began fasting the whole month of Ramadan at age nine. When Hadeel saw the pleasure these religious acts gave Ydaida and Amma Munira, she made them her obsession.

What else could she do to impress them? How could she make them proud of her? When Amal left, Hadeel grew closer to Munira, asking her questions about things she didn't understand.

Later, she asked why her father Rashid wouldn't allow her to join her cousins in private schools. And why wouldn't he allow her to attend her cousins' birthday parties? Munira never provided convincing answers to Hadeel's questions, and seemed to agree with Rashid. But when he refused to let Hadeel attend Haya's musical birthday party, Munira became very upset that day.

"Don't worry, Amma Munira," eleven-year-old Hadeel said. "I don't care about these parties. I'm different from my cousins. They want to be happy, but I want to be good. Just like you and Ydaida."

The morning of the first day of Ydaida's *aza*, three official days of mourning, Hadeel stepped barefoot out of her bedroom, her long black hair disheveled, her tear-streaked face unwashed. She halted at the living-room. Overnight the elegant modern salon was converted into an auditorium. The fancy sofas disappeared and were replaced by rows of blue chairs linked together with wire. Spaces between every ten chairs created an aisle for mourners to pass through. At the main doors of the salon, like busy bees, a crew of female Filipino workers in white and black uniforms were humming to each other in Tagalog, arranging small plastic bottles of water and Kleenex boxes on silver trays.

"*Yumma!*" Hadeel ran to the kitchen. "What happened to our house?"

Sipping her morning chai at the kitchen table, Hadeel's mother did not offer an answer.

She eyed her daughter's clothes warily. "You haven't changed since yesterday."

Hadeel glanced down at her blouse and sweatpants. Ignoring her mother's remark, she insisted, "What happened to our living room?"

"Your father decided women's *Aza* should take place in our house."

"Why?"

"Because Ydaida's house is too small. It won't accommodate all the women we know who'd want to offer condolences." She cleared her throat before she continued with downcast eyes. "Besides, Munira cannot handle it by herself."

How could Hadeel ever forget how distraught Munira was at the announcement of Ydaida's death? Rashid said they had to peel her away from Ydaida's corpse and drag her out of the hospital. At the house, Munira wailed and begged to be buried with Ydaida. Once she calmed down, she demanded to be taken back so she'd be the one to wash and prepare her mother's body for burial. After some argument, Munira's three brothers had to succumb to her wishes. A few hours later she returned after performing the morbid task much calmer and more accepting of the harsh reality.

Hadeel's mother placed her teacup on the table and stood up scraping the chair over the tiled kitchen floor. "Have breakfast and change," she said to Hadeel. "*Aza* will start right after the burial this morning."

"Where will the men have their *Aza*?" Hadeel asked.

"At your Uncle Nasser's house." Yumma sighed and trudged toward the kitchen door.

"Will Amma Munira go to the cemetery this morning?"

Yumma's sleepy eyes grew wide open. "Hadeel-O! Stop asking stupid questions!"

Choked with tears Hadeel sobbed. "She should go. It's the last time she'll ever see her."

Yumma shook her head. "It's not our custom. There will be hundreds of men in the cemetery, all the relatives and friends of your father's and uncles'. Besides, it would be hard on any woman to see her loved one buried, let alone Amma Munira."

The Indian cook stepped in between them and offered Hadeel breakfast which she refused. Hadeel still couldn't believe she'd never see Ydaida's gentle eyes and demure smile again. She sighed and slouched out of the kitchen.

In the living room Munira had already taken a spot at the entrance to receive condolences. The black *abaya* draped over her head covered her entirely except for her gaunt face. Hadeel threw herself on her aunt's lap and they both cried as if a rain cloud had burst over their heads. When there were no tears left, they composed themselves and Hadeel took the chair next to Munira ready to receive mourners. Yumma dropped a black *abaya* on Hadeel's shoulders and ordered her to wrap herself. "And put on some shoes," she hissed, pointing at Hadeel's bare feet.

Before Hadeel could do that, women clad in black from head to toe thronged into the house. Hadeel followed Munira's lead, stood when mourners approached, received their kisses and their comforting words, then sat back down. Soon, the living room was full of despondent women, faces pale and void of make-up. A sound system somewhere in the room played a recital of the Quran, forcing everyone to listen.

At intervals, when the flow of mourners slowed, Hadeel kept hearing Munira repeat one specific line more earnestly than any other. She'd cry harder as she begged Allah while repeating the same phrase. "*Ya* Allah, keep my mother steadfast in the face of the Questioner. Please let her pass the test. Please don't let fear divert her from the righteous path."

During the break between the morning and afternoon aza sessions, Hadeel asked Munira what she meant by asking Allah to keep Ydaida steadfast. Who is the Questioner?

"The Questioner is the Angel who visits the dead fresh in their grave," Munira answered. "Ydaida was worried about that dreadful moment all her life—the Torture of the Grave. *Allah Yerhamha,* May Allah have mercy on her soul."

Later in the kitchen Hadeel asked her mother how they could be so sure about the Torture of the Grave.

Yumma repeated Munira's words, and Hadeel shivered. "Isn't it enough we die? We also get tortured in the grave as well?" Hadeel exclaimed angrily. When Yumma's eyes doubled in size and her face grew grim, Hadeel ran out of the kitchen before her mother uttered her expected cross comments.

In the afternoon, while receiving more mourners, Hadeel noticed her younger cousins in the last row of the living room. No guests went to them to offer condolences. No kissing or handshakes. Her cousins seemed comfortable, sleepy, and bored, as if sitting in a classroom. Hadeel decided to join them the next two days of *Aza*.

"*Maskeena Amma* Munira," Cousin Haya's thick eyebrows drew together as she expressed her sympathy. "Poor thing. How is she going to live by herself now?"

"Maybe I should live with her," Hadeel offered. She hadn't thought of it before, but since she was the closest niece to Amma Munira it seemed appropriate to become Munira's new companion, even if she was only fourteen.

Fair-skinned Wafa, another cousin, whispered, "Why didn't Ammiti Munira ever get married?"

Hadeel shook her head. She had asked Munira that question before. The only answer she ever received was, "Allah did not will it."

Slim Sana, Wafa's sister said, "I heard she was madly in love with a young man, a neighbor. When Ammi Rashid found out, he got angry and refused to let them marry."

"Why?" Haya asked.

Sana shrugged. "Maybe the man was not good enough for her."

"Or he believes love is a sin," Wafa said.

Hadeel protested. "That's not true." To herself she thought, *my father couldn't be that cruel, could he? To his own sister?*

When *Aza* was over, Hadeel and her mother accompanied Munira to her house to collect a few personal things. Inside the silent house, Hadeel paused in front of Amal's room. During her lifetime, Ydaida did not allow anyone to enter the room on the assumption that Amal would return one day. The door was always locked. Hadeel now found the door ajar and slipped inside.

The room was the same Hadeel remembered from childhood. A framed picture of a man wearing the Kuwaiti *dishdasha* sat on the desk—Hadeel's grandfather. She was told he died a few months before Hadeel was born. She didn't know much about him. Ydaida grew reticent every time his name was mentioned. When Hadeel pressed for memories of him, she'd say, "We only pray for the dead and ask God to forgive them."

The double bed in Amal's room was still covered with her colorful quilt of birds and flowers. Above the headboard were five large wooden letters in English THINK. "Let's think," was Amal's favorite answer to Hadeel's countless questions. Hadeel sat on the edge of Amal's bed and thought of the times she had spent with her aunt in that very room. They played a word game with that one word, "think." Amal challenged her to form as many words out of the five letters as possible: *thin, ink, tin, in, it* and *kin*.

A notebook on the night-table, drew Hadeel's attention. Several pages inside were torn out. The remaining ones had the title "An Attempt to Translate Robert Southey's *Thalaba the Destroyer* into Arabic." It was Amal's handwriting. The few stanzas translated into Arabic began with the words that Hadeel would never forget: *Ma ajmala ellail*. For years to come Hadeel wondered if the English original words were, *How beautiful is the night? Or How beautiful is the evening?* Or simply, *How beautiful is night?* She wished she had taken the notebook or copied the title of the poem and the name of the author. But when at that moment she heard Munira's voice calling her, she jumped, dropped the notebook on the floor, and hurried out of the room.

Upsetting Munira was the last thing Hadeel would want to happen.

Back home Rashid, Hadeel's father, was waiting for them in the living room. "Of course you know, Munira, it's not a good idea for a woman to live alone."

He waited for her answer. She only nodded.

"You are most welcome in my house. But brother Nasser, whose wife is pregnant, needs help with the children. They offered you stay with them. They have a private section of the house for you. What do you think?"

Munira plopped herself on the sofa. "I can't think of anything right now. Let me be."

Hadeel, sitting close to her aunt, felt a twinge of sadness mixed with pride at her aunt's firm reply. She didn't immediately agree to her older brother's offer, which sounded more like a command to Hadeel than a suggestion.

Yumma was kinder. "We have many extra rooms you can use, Munira."

"Can you stay with me? Please?" Hadeel begged her aunt.

That night in Hadeel's king-size bed, niece and aunt tossed and turned and tried to force themselves to sleep without success. One more time, Hadeel checked Munira's eyes to make sure she was awake before she asked for a favorite story about Ydaida. Munira remained quiet, tears flowing from her eyes. She tried to say something, then turned to the other side, hiding her face in the pillow.

Hadeel placed her palm on her aunt's quivering shoulder. "I miss her too," she whispered. "But that's Allah's Will. What can we do except surrender to it?" She was repeating Ydaida's words.

Munira sighed. After a long pause she said in a nasal and fragile voice, "Moments before Ydaida died, her eyes opened. She gazed at me and said: Amal? That was the last word she ever uttered."

Chapter Three

Despite jet lag, Hadeel is grateful for the annoying ringing of the hotel phone that put an end to her nightmare. She heaves up from the damp pillow, dripping with perspiration, and reaches for the phone.

"Aloo?" she says with a hoarse voice.

"Hadeel?" a man asks.

She coughs the word, "Yes."

"You have a cold," Jonathan says more as a statement than a question.

She wipes her forehead with the heel of her hand. "Yes, I think I do."

"Well, it's two in the afternoon. I was wondering . . ."

She sits up and looks around. The four wooden bed posts surrounding her bed look like a cage. A plan for captivity? She shakes her head to get rid of the silly thought. "I'm sorry. I don't think I can see you today."

He pauses. "That's okay. But I'd like to bring something over for you to look at. Something of Amal's."

Hadeel doesn't answer. Her nightmare is still nagging, hovering over her head. The fear, the guilt, the horror of the dream is still real.

"I'll leave it at the front desk," Jonathan says.

Hadeel exhales. "All right, then. Thank you."

She hangs up and drops her head back onto the damp pillow. How could it be two in the afternoon when it's so dark? A slit between the folds of the heavy curtains allows a sliver of light, not enough to lighten the room. She shudders, remembering the nightmare, a recurring dream of late. It makes death so real and so near. This last one was more gruesome than the ones she had before. A big black raven was pecking at her pulsing heart while she lay in a desolate, open grave. The Torture of the Grave? She pulls herself up. Her cousin Haya's explanation of death is more appealing at this moment: "When you die, you die, that's the end of it. Nothing after that except silence." But Munira's and her parents' version is colder than death itself. "Pray and ask Allah for steadfastness at a moment when nothing else will help except your faith. Afterwards, you either live forever in bliss or forever tortured in Hell." Their words pierce like a cold knife stabbing her heart.

She now remembers noon prayer and jumps out of bed. Her rug is still spread open on the floor since her night prayer, pointing south-east toward Mecca. Soon it will be the afternoon prayer; she'd better hurry. Mind crammed with images of the nightmare, she splashes water over her face, reciting verses to dissipate the dark thoughts while performing ablution.

Once she envelops herself within the folds of the prayer

thoub, its soft cotton holding her face, its fabric around her body sealing her from the outside world, she feels safe and pure, surrendering in the hands of Allah. She stands tall at the foot of the prayer rug and utters the first words, *bismillah arrahman arraheem*, in the name of God, the most merciful, the most gracious. She takes a deep breath and continues with the next verse, then the ones she has repeated five times a day, since she was seven. They usually soothe her nerves and calm her down. Not today; her thoughts keep rushing back to the cemetery and the Torture of the Grave.

Some three years ago she googled the term. Several links related to the subject popped up, some accompanied by videos of bearded men, grim faces, preaching and threatening. Their looks scared her more than the words they uttered. "Why do they insist that everyone, young or old, should be at their level of worship? Degree of piety?" Hadeel had always wondered. Instead of clicking on any of them to hear their explanation, Hadeel chose a link to a theology group of Muslim Brits. They invite "logical" discussion of topics related to religion without the emotional hysteria usually attached to such subjects. But the silence that followed her request to discuss the Torture of the Grave was annoying as if she'd asked to discuss a taboo topic. None of the group members offered an opinion. Raj, the founder of the group and a Theology professor in London, welcomed her and suggested discussing the topic from the point of view of reward and punishment in all three major religions. That was how she met him. Raj, the love of her life, then became the bliss as well as the agony of her heart.

"*Astaghfirullah, astaghfirullah,*" Hadeel begs God for forgiveness out loud. She tries again to focus on the noon prayer. Uttering the verses aloud might help gather her wandering thoughts. She kneels low, then touches the soft rug with her forehead, prolonging prostrations in hope of forgiveness from Allah. These movements never failed to bring momentary peace and comfort. But once prayers end, soon after she bids her archangels farewell over each shoulder, all suspended fear and guilt descend back upon her with a weight she carries for the rest of the day.

Now, legs folded under her thighs, palms resting on her knees, she lingers on the prayer rug fervently asking Allah for guidance and protection on this journey. She especially asks forgiveness for not wearing the hijab. "*Wallah*, it's only for safety reasons," she explains to Allah. But the memory of how she wore it always comes back fresh, as if it happened yesterday.

It was the day after her fifteenth birthday party, which coincided with the last day of the school year. That day, her father announced she had to wear the hijab. She would no longer be allowed in public without it.

A week of protests and arguments did not help change his mind. Her mother, fed up with the tension at home, barged into Hadeel's room one morning while she was still asleep. She flung open the curtains, jewelry jingling on her wrists and the potent fragrance of frankincense filling the room. She was on her way to attend another of her fancy tea parties.

"Listen Hadeel-O!" She pulled the bedcover off Hadeel and shook her roughly on her feet. "I'm sick of this stupid behavior of yours."

Shocked out of her deep sleep, Hadeel tried to remember the crime she'd committed to make her mother this mad. Usually, Yumma managed to manipulate family problems into peaceful solutions with her natural cheerfulness. She was especially artful in maneuvering her way between the two worlds of restrictions and pleasure.

Hadeel, hair disheveled, rubbed her eyes and asked, "What do you mean?"

"I mean, what does it take to wear a scarf over your head when you step out of the house? Ha?" Her voice grew louder. "We all do it, doesn't hurt anyone."

"I don't want to!" Hadeel kicked her feet.

Yumma must have realized that squabbling wasn't going to work, so she tried a different strategy. "Habibti." She patted Hadeel's knee. "Wearing the hijab outside the house does not mean you cannot be modern and have fun. Look at our neighbors' daughters. They wear the slinkiest dresses at all female-gatherings under their Islamic *abayas*. I've seen them at weddings many times."

Hadeel had also seen them leave their house to the car wrapped in black except for their faces, which were covered with make-up. "It's hypocrisy," Hadeel said.

"It's diplomacy," Yumma said.

"I don't want to be a diplomat!"

Yumma shook her head in exasperation. "Be obedient then! Good daughters obey their parents. Don't they?" She yelled the last words.

Hadeel sobbed. "I know."

Her mother's face softened. "I think your father has noticed how beautiful you've become. That's the reason he wants you to cover yourself."

"I'm not beautiful! Don't try to fool me with your sweet talk." Hadeel swung her legs over the edge of the bed.

"Everyone tells me when you're with other girls, you're the one who stands out."

"That's because I happen to be the tallest one. That's all!" Hadeel snatched her hand away from her mother's.

Yuuma trotted to the door. "Why don't you sober that strong head of yours?" She turned to look at her before she left and added, "Use this opportunity. Ask for something you've always wanted. Think about it!"

As usual, her mother was right. Their life turned tranquil once Hadeel consented to don the hijab. In return for wearing it, Hadeel requested a trip to Switzerland for summer vacation instead of Beirut. Her father happily agreed.

During that vacation, amidst the Alps and the smiles of her brothers and parents, Hadeel tried to adjust to this new attire which made her scalp itchy and her heart achy. Europe that year sweltered under a heat wave. Hadeel gazed with longing at her father's and brothers' thin shorts and t-shirts. They seemed to enjoy the occasional breeze touching their bare skin while heat lingered underneath the folds of her lengthy gowns, perspiration ran down her neck under the head cover.

It's not fair, she had thought, knowing she could not do anything about it without ruining everybody's good time. So, she suffered in silence.

Her cell phone pings. *Must be Aunt Munira,* Hadeel thinks as she removes and folds her prayer *thoub*. She calculates the time difference between London and Boulder: seven hours. It's nine-thirty at night already in London. She decides against calling her. Hadeel's hoarse voice will add to her aunt's worries. Instead, she calls room service and orders a grilled cheese sandwich with fries and a pot of hot tea. In the darkness of her room, she peels off her long night gown and dons her favorite cotton sweatpants with its matching top. She draws the heavy window curtains open and the room floods with light. Mountains sprinkled with sugary powder pose majestically under a brilliant blue sky. Pine trees in varying shades of green parade around the lower hills.

What happened to the deluge of rain from last night? Just a few weeks earlier the entire City of Kuwait shut down because of a simple drizzle that caused floods in some areas. Here the streets are already dry; everything looks fresh and clean. Is this the reason Amal forgot her home and family? Can a foreign country and its natural beauty replace a homeland where one was born?

A knock on the door announces room service. Hadeel holds the door open for a cheerful teenager whose pale face is spotted with acne.

"Where would you like it, Miss?" he asks, lifting a big round tray from the wheeled cart parked at the door.

"By the window please." She runs in front of him to remove the prayer rug from the floor.

"Nice view you got here," he says as he waits for her to sign the bill.

"Yes."

"Where are you from?"

She hands him back the bill. "Kuwait . . ."

"Umm . . . Where's that?"

She raises her eyebrows in surprise. How can he not know? Instead, she says, "You know where Iraq is? Saudi Arabia?"

"Yes, sure."

"We're in between."

"Oh, okay." He says glancing at the tip she added.

"Thanks."

Hadeel locks the door and sits in the armchair by the window. She has assumed everyone in America would know where Kuwait is because of the Gulf War. But obviously not young people like him. She was born after the Gulf War but heard every detail about it from her parents and uncles. Their stories of how the people of a rich country became refugees overnight were horrifying. Hadeel tried to imagine herself going through the hardships of that time but only ended up feeling lucky she didn't live through that period of Kuwait's history.

She inserts the tiny phone earplugs into her ears and selects "Golden," by Zayn Malik, to block her rambling thoughts. Zayn's soothing music usually brings comfort, his words hope.

Now that her mission is complete, she should focus on her own life. Her future. What is she going to do after she gets back home? She gulps tea and looks up at the mountains as if they can provide an answer. Is she going to step back into her old habits, reading and playing video games, as if this trip never happened? What about the future with cousin Nawaf?

The thought of her cousin descends upon her shoulders like the flat rocks of the mountains. She's been postponing her parents' plan for her marriage to Nawaf in the hope that he gets tired of waiting and would change his mind. But sooner or later her father will insist it takes place. Then what? How can she allow her cousin, whom she thinks of as a brother, to get close to her and touch her? So far, she has successfully avoided thinking of the details. Why bother when it might not happen? But she hasn't done anything to stop it from happening except praying to Almighty Allah to do that for her. What else can she do to reverse her parents' wishes without upsetting them? She, the good girl.

Hadeel swallows the last bite of her sandwich and throws the white napkin on the empty breakfast tray. What did Amal do while living here in Boulder? How did she meet Jonathan?

Were they in love? Long-forgotten memories of Amal from childhood rush back. Happy childhood scenes with Amal before she left home, followed by unpleasant ones of family members reviling her. Hadeel was only five, but she remembers the animated faces of irate uncles discussing her beloved aunt. While the adults argued, Hadeel and her younger cousins hid behind couches and chairs and listened until they were discovered, admonished, and ordered to leave the room. Soon they were instructed by their parents never to mention Amal again. Rashid, Hadeel's father, announced that Amal did not like them anymore. "That's why she left and will never come back." He was the eldest in the family, and everyone listened to him, especially after news of Amal marrying an American. Hadeel clearly recalls a time when Ydaida tried to calm him down. He grew furious. "She ruined my reputation. She embarrassed me in front of my friends. We are a religious family; we cannot accept an infidel."

"So that's what it's all about? His reputation?" Haya once commented to Hadeel. Hadeel dutifully scolded Haya; her father is the most righteous man in the family, and they should respect him.

Hadeel had asked Munira frequently if it was true that Amal left because she didn't love them. Munira only shook her head without commenting. Being Amal's only sister, Munira was naturally the closest to her. She did not resent Amal as much as her brothers did. *It must have been hard losing your only sister,* Hadeel thinks. She often wished she had a sister instead of three brothers. "Your cousins are like sisters," Munira often told her. With time, news of Amal faded, and the girls became teenagers busy with their own lives, futures, and personal problems.

It had never occurred to Hadeel to google her aunt's name. Why didn't she think of it before? Maybe because the internet became available to Hadeel when Amal was no longer an important part of her life. Or, most probably, because she was "a slave of duty" as Haya had always nicknamed her.

Her cell announces another message. Must be a forward from her mother or friends in Kuwait. She steals a glance at it to prove herself right. It is from her mother but it's not a forward. "Call me! Now! It's urgent!"

Hadeel's heart plummets. She was hoping to avoid talking to her mother during the three days she's in the

U.S. "Only text messages," Munira has warned. "You can call the minute you arrive back in London."

Hadeel paces around the room. What could be so urgent? She talked to her mother in London just before she boarded the plane to Denver. Everything was fine then. If she texts now to ask what's urgent, Yumma will call back immediately, and she'll have to answer. Hadeel knows she's not good at keeping secrets from her mother. If she talks, she will slip about her whereabouts and the next moment her father will find out. No, she'd better wait until midnight Kuwait time, two more hours, to text. Two more days and she can call her mother the minute she walks out of the plane at Heathrow, *inshallah*.

Reading might be more successful than music to relax her nerves. She gets the only book she brought along, *Frankenstein*, by Mary Shelley. She slumps down in the armchair and tries to remember why she wanted to read this sad novel in the first place. A professor must have mentioned it at Kuwait University. "Women Authors in Nineteenth-Century England," must have been the class. The novel was not part of the syllabus, but the professor gave it as an example of how modern scientific achievements can destroy human lives. Hadeel remembers a heated discussion that followed when a Palestinian student in the classroom compared Frankenstein's monster to Israel. "Israel," the girl said, "is the monster that Western countries created amongst us, which is now going rampant killing and ruining the lives of my people."

"Why does everything have to be connected to politics?" Hadeel asked her father when she went home.

"Because it is," Rashid said. "Why do you think you're studying English literature rather than Arabic literature?"

"Why?"

"Because your mind is colonized by Western cultures."

During the brief interval that Hadeel was trying to understand her father's point, Rashid rushed to his room and returned with a book. "Here," he said, dropping a different *Frankenstein* in her lap. "Read this! It's based on facts, not hallucinations. Besides, this book won many awards."

Hadeel flipped through the pages, impressed by her father's knowledge of literature. *Frankenstein in Baghdad* was written in Arabic by Ahmad Saadawi, an Iraqi author. After reading the blurb on the book's back cover, Hadeel flung it to the floor as if it were hurting her fingers. No thanks! She couldn't read such a gruesome work. It was much worse than Mary Shelley's. Just the brief information on the book's dust jacket made her sick, let alone reading the whole thing. It was about the 2003 American attack on Iraq. The body of the novel's monster, *Frankenstein*, according to the Iraqi author, was assembled from parts and limbs of dead Iraqis who told their stories of being tortured and executed by American soldiers. Hadeel much preferred the fantasy created by Mary Shelley over the truth told by the contemporary Iraqi author. Besides, Mary Shelley's *Frankenstein* was similar to the video games Hadeel had played in the darkness of her room, knowing they were not real.

Inside the title page, Hadeel finds a quote she had copied from a reference book. The quote was from one of Mary Shelley's notes: "Idleness, rather than ill-nature, gives birth to scandal and to the observation of little incidents which narrows the mind." The quote had fascinated Hadeel more than any she had read by famous authors. After copying it down, she began observing her mother's behavior, especially when socializing with other women and relatives. After each of these gatherings, Hadeel's family had to endure Yumma's endless babbling about the women's clothes, jewelry, and cosmetics, followed by gossip and rumors. No wonder Yumma cannot follow the documentaries Rashid liked to watch on television or read any of the books Hadeel recommended to her. Is it possible that idleness led to her mother's narrow-mindedness? The quote became an incentive for Hadeel to pursue a Master's degree just to keep her mind active.

She researched Mary Shelley's personal life and got more intrigued. Mary's parents were renowned literary figures. Her father, William Godwin, wrote the much-acclaimed, *Political Justice,* and her mother Mary Wollstonecraft wrote *A Vindication of the Rights of Woman*, the first known document in support of feminism. Hadeel was shocked that although Mary Shelley and her mother were famous writers, they both had led scandalous personal lives. Would Mary Shelley and her mother, Mary Wollstonecraft, have been able to achieve what they did and become famous without those personal experiences? Hadeel decided to write her Master's thesis on "Famous Fallen Women." She would decide for herself if "Famous" and "Fallen" must tag along. And since Hadeel's father did not allow her to travel alone she settled for pursuing the degree online. Anything but idleness that leads to narrow-mindedness.

Chapter Four

"Where are you?" Yumma keeps texting every few minutes.

Hadeel tosses the phone on the bed as if it burnt her hands. She covers the phone with the bed sheets in case her mother can see her through its screen. She's always believed that her mother is capable of everything but not spying, simply because it's *haram* in Islam. Did her parents find out about her whereabouts? Does her father know she's all alone in America? Would they have contacted Munira when Hadeel didn't reply?

Heavy with worry, Hadeel rubs hard at her cheeks and forehead. It's all her aunt's fault; she is the one who made her do it; now it is Munira who should deal with it as promised. But maybe she forgot her promise and Hadeel should remind her of it. She pulls the phone out from under the cover and calls Munira. No answer. The phone is switched off. Is she avoiding her?

Hadeel texts her aunt to please call back as soon as possible. Half an hour later there's still no reply from her aunt. It's already late at night in London, and Hadeel knows she won't hear from Munira before she wakes up for dawn prayers.

In desperate need of fresh air Hadeel decides to leave the room. She slips on her sandals and pauses by the door. Should she wear the hijab? It's a habit now; that piece of cloth has become part of her attire, part of her. But Amma Munira herself recommended that Hadeel take it off during this journey for safety reasons. "With the recent anti-Islam sentiment in the West it's wise not to wear it." Munira was referring to the recent attack on a mosque in New Zealand, where fifty Muslims were murdered. "Allah will forgive you, *inshallah*."

Hadeel wraps the scarf around her neck instead and leaves the room. Downstairs, the hotel is buzzing with life. Throngs of people mill around the lobby, filling the spacious area with commotion and laughter. Hadeel glances at the reception desk. The young man who checked her in the night before is no longer there. In his place a slim girl with straight blond hair is handing a customer a pen, asking him to sign some papers. The concierge, a tall man with his hair in a ponytail, is chatting with a cheerful middle-aged couple in blue jeans and matching denim shirts. After waiting for a couple of minutes, Hadeel decides she can find the mountains on her own.

After all, their peaks appear in every direction one looks.

A cool breeze touches her scorching cheeks as she steps out of the hotel. She takes a deep breath and looks left. There they are. All she has to do is keep her eyes on them. She jogs toward them, wondering if these mountains are the same as the Rocky Mountains she learned about in secondary school in Kuwait. She still vividly remembers Abla Hafsa, the geography teacher, pointing with a ruler at a bulging spot on a large colorful map pulled over the blackboard, saying, "These are the Rockies. They span from Canada, through the U.S., all the way down to Mexico." Hadeel remembers listening to the teacher and wondering why she should care for those faraway mountains, knowing too well that her father would never allow a trip to America, the land where his sister disappeared.

A car honks while Hadeel is crossing Canyon Boulevard. She lifts her hand in apology, steps out of the way, and waits before she crosses to the other side. She searches for the mountains and finds them to her right now. But a modern structure of stone, glass, and metal-beams behind a clump of tall trees attracts her attention. The sound of rushing water under a wooden bridge draws her closer to the building. Her eyes follow the rushing white water flowing under the bridge over smooth, round rocks. It must be coming from the mountains. Hadeel pauses and looks around, taking in the view and enjoying the warmth of the bright sun that feels so close. Is that possible?

Several pedestrians, mostly in casual clothes, press on toward the building. It's Saturday afternoon; what kind of work would those people be doing on the weekend? As she joins them, a sign over the glass pyramid at the entryway says: Boulder Public Library. *Aha*, Hadeel smiles.

She lingers, speculating if the architect was trying to reflect the mountains with his roof design. It also reminds her of Denver Airport. She shudders at the recent memory of meeting Jonathan and the scary drive during thunderstorms.

Inside the building it is warm and quiet. A faint scent of books smells familiar. Colorful posters of smiling faces peeping over bookshelves add a welcoming atmosphere. Adults as well as children are fluttering around, talking in whispers. Hadeel has never seen this many people in one public library before. Back home libraries are deserted except for a few bored workers and untouched books collecting dust. Her parents told her there used to be a library adjacent to a co- op in every residential district in Kuwait during the eighties before she was born. But they were removed, most probably for the lack of readers. Yet here in this Boulder library people act as if attending a party; they look happy. Those who didn't find chairs are stretched on the carpeted floors, books open in hands, oblivious to anything else around them. She knows the feeling, the joy of reading alone. But to share such joy with like-minded people is different; it must be wonderful. What would she have done without books in her life? Hadeel stops in the middle of the lobby. A soothing sound of rippling water emerges from a circular fountain with a sculpture beneath a spiral staircase. What an awesome place!

"Hadeel?" A female voice calls from the top of the stairs, shattering the silence in the library. "Oh my God! It is you!"

Hadeel, along with several people around her, look up at the young lady who is now skipping down the steps with a huge smile. She's wearing tight jeans with torn knee gaps and a blue tank top revealing a bare belly above her belt. Her white Nike tennis shoes are mud-stained. Long, curly black hair frames a chubby face that looks familiar. When the girl lands on the bottom step, she tip-toes to reach Hadeel's cheeks for the accustomed greeting kiss.

Hadeel kisses her back and tries to remember where they could have met. "We were in school together?"

"Yes! High school. I'm Amina." She scrutinizes Hadeel's hair, then her clothes, before she adds, "You wore the hijab then. Right?"

Hadeel's smile disappears. Does Amina know any of her relatives? Is she going to spread the word in Kuwait that Hadeel is in America without hijab? She tucks a stray strand of her short hair behind her ear and shifts her eyes to Amina's knapsack. "What are you doing here?"

"Research. I'm working on a graduate degree at CU."

"*Mashallah*," Hadeel mumbles. Conflicting emotions roll over her like waves. "What are you studying?"

"Film production," Amina replies. Then adds with a chuckle, "It's time we had a Kuwaiti female director. Right? The Saudis do."

"That's true." Hadeel nods while thoughts of Raj rush to her mind. *My Oneiza*, his voice whispers in her ears. A name he liked to give her every time he mentioned an epic poem he thought should be made into a movie.

"How about you? What are you doing here?" Amina asks.

"I'm . . . I'm also working on a master's degree, but online," Hadeel says. She's groping for something to change the subject quickly before more questions ensue. "What time is it?"

The spunky girl pulls her cell from her back pocket.

"Oh my goodness! It's four-thirty already. I have an appointment at five; I should go." Then, taking Hadeel by surprise, she lifts her phone high up in front of their faces and says, "Smile!"

"No!" Hadeel says just at the very moment the selfie is snapped. She's sure that her face is in shock, her lips are puckering in a no, and her hair is a mess, but that's not why she doesn't want the selfie. Why did Amina take it? Who is she going to show it to?

Amina is already heading toward the library's main entrance. "Keep in touch," she waves. "You can find me on Instagram, Amina at CU." She makes the sign for @ with her finger in the air as she rushes out.

"Wait!" Hadeel follows her, but the girl is already a blur among the throngs of people entering the library. Hadeel freezes in a daze; people on their way in and out of the library are brushing her aside. Her picture is going to be on Instagram without the hijab. Soon the photo will be circulating on social media in Kuwait. Her family will see it. Why didn't she yell at Amina to erase the photo? Why didn't she simply speak up?

With hunched shoulders, Hadeel turns around, feeling cold. She finds a carpeted ramp with metal railing leading to another section of the library and follows it. The ramp is built over the rushing river, but thick glass walls muffle its sound. Voices become audible as she approaches a snack lounge. All tables and chairs are occupied. Hadeel buys a cup of hot chocolate from a vending machine and waits for someone to vacate a seat. She checks her pockets for her iPhone to send Amina a message about the stupid selfie and realizes she has left it at the hotel.

A man at a table by the window gathers his books and leaves. Hadeel hurries to take his place before someone else does. Watching the rushing water under her feet makes her head spin. She looks up toward the mountains and sips her drink. Jonathan mentioned in the car yesterday that she would never be lost in Boulder: the mountains are west, the rest is easy to figure out. If you face west, east will be behind you, south will always be on your left, north on your right.

There's a local newspaper on the table. She wonders if the word NEWS comes from the initials of North, East, West and South. Although lately most news comes from the middle, the Middle East. The headline in the local paper in big letters reads: "Bear Sighting in the Foothills." A black-and-white picture of two bears in a tree is posted underneath the headline.

"Can I join you?" A voice startles her. She squints up at a man standing by her table. It takes her a couple of seconds to realize it's Jonathan.

"Of course." She points at the chair on the other side of the table.

The tiny wooden chair makes him look huge. "How did you know this was her table?" he asks.

"I don't know what you mean." Hadeel squints.

"This was Amal's favorite spot in the library."

Goose bumps crawl on Hadeel's skin. She takes another look at her surroundings then traces a flower carved on the surface of the wooden table with her forefinger. There are other scratches—deep lines forming the word "why." She examines the view outside, the one her aunt must have looked at while occupying this very seat. Is Amal watching? Was she the reason the previous person vacated this chair?

"I hope you're feeling better," Jonathan says. He looks younger in the daylight despite his thinning white hair and beard. If he's Amal's age he must be in his early sixties.

"Did she come here often?" Hadeel asks.

"Every weekend."

"Oh," Hadeel says. "In your letter, you mentioned something you wanted to discuss about my aunt."

"Yes," He draws his chair closer to the table. "She had recently specified things, family possessions that she'd wanted to pass on to you."

"Like what?"

He hesitates. "I just left you some documents in an envelope at the hotel's front desk. Please take a look at them and let's discuss it tomorrow. Besides that, there are things in her home office that might be of interest to you. Family possessions."

Hadeel swallows hard to keep the chocolate drink in her stomach. The prospect of sorting through her dead Aunt's belongings makes her sick. That should've been Munira's job, not hers. Hadeel changes the subject. "Can you take me to the mountains?" She points at the window.

"Sure. Now?"

"No. I think I should rest today. Tomorrow?"

"Give me a call when you're ready." He jots down his number on the newspaper she was reading. "And please, don't forget the package at the front desk."

"I won't."

"See you tomorrow." He stands up and adds, "*Inshallah*."

Taken by surprise, Hadeel smiles. "*Inshallah.*"

Somehow that special word, "God's willing" melts some of the ice barrier she has built between them since she arrived. No, actually since childhood, when her favorite Aunt Amal disappeared from her life. Hadeel looks up, searching every corner for a sign of her aunt, wondering if Amal's ghost is somewhere looking at her right now.

Chapter Five

AMAL, 1999

Hadeel, you were only two hours old when I first laid eyes on you. Two hours since you took your first breath into this polluted world of ours. You looked like an angel, pure, peaceful, and ready to receive love and give it back with a smile. I wanted to protect you, to shield you from the evils that come with life. From vile human emotions, envy, jealousy, and biases which sometimes parents, unaware, instill in their children. But I wasn't your mother; you weren't mine. Your mother at that moment was in her maternity hospital bed frantically buzzing the nurse to take you away so she could rest. She thought her responsibility ended the moment she pushed you out of her womb.

I was attached to you, Hadeel, for another reason. I saw my father in your gentle face.

'Bu Rashid, as everyone called him, was your grandfather. His stamp of honesty and kindness was written all over your brow. That moment bonded us forever. A bond beyond unraveling. When I held you, my heart ached with sadness. Ached knowing the hardships and restrictions you as a girl would go through in life, and especially in our culture. Even more so under your father's, my brother Rashid's stiff wing.

You were two hours old, and I was thirty. At that point, I thought I'd already experienced much of the tragicomedy we call life, its bitterness and sweetness, tears and laughter. My father had died a few months before you were born. The painful loss was only soothed by your arrival.

I was considering seeking a different life somewhere far from home, which I couldn't bear anymore without my father. Then you arrived, and I decided to wait. I wanted to watch you grow and blossom, hoping to instill some of my father's traits in you—his curiosity, love of knowledge, passion for music and art. Things your father did not believe in. I had to keep reminding myself not to interfere in your upbringing. Not because I didn't want the responsibility, but because your parents' philosophy in life was different from mine. They were constantly worried about my "Western" influence on you. So, while I watched you crawl, then walk, they watched me watching you.

I felt luckier than you, Hadeel, because of our fathers. Mine, though older, was open-minded, willing to push me forward even farther than I hoped to explore in life. While yours pulled you back, kept his leash short so you wouldn't stray away from his sight. To him and my mother, your Ydaida, that was the right way to bring up girls in our society: timid, submissive, and obedient.

I wonder if anyone at home has told you the truth about me, about my being an anomaly in the family. I was so different from my sister Munira and my three brothers. Since childhood I loved books and the outdoors, while they preferred watching TV, a new invention at the time.

The pleasure they found in confining themselves within concrete walls, eyes glued to the small screen, was torture to me. I loved the desert, its vastness, purity and blowing wind. I knew then, in the depth of my heart, that nature and I were inseparable. I was never alone when my bare feet touched the ground, my hands brushed trees or plants, and my eyes roamed the deep skies. My siblings snickered when I mentioned these things. I wondered if I had happened amongst them by mistake. I used to tease my father if he had recited a poem about the love of nature in my ear at birth instead of the traditional *athan* calling for prayer. He used to laugh at that, his eyes twinkling like the stars. I marveled often if he was one of them, came down to earth to be my father before he returned to his constellation.

Baba's home office was like an amusement park for me. I was the only one in the family he allowed inside. A surge of thrill ran through my veins just gazing at the spines of tomes on the bookshelves. A collection by a ninth-century Arab poet, Abūl 'Alā' al-Ma'arrī, attracted my attention at age twelve. Imagine! Father tried to dissuade me from that selection, but I insisted. I happened upon al-Ma'arri's words: "Soften your tread; methinks earth's surface is but bodies of the dead. Walk slowly in the air, so you don't trample on remains of God's servants," and I got hooked. I believe now that those words forged my philosophy in life.

My mother, your Ydaida, belonged to a different background than my father. She was the religious pillar in the whole family; everything we did had to be according to religious rules.

When I turned seven, she decided to begin my religious education. She insisted I accompany her and Munira, who was nine, to a neighbor's house to listen to a preacher about Islam and the Quran. The *Mutawa'a*, as everyone called her, used to hold religious sessions every Thursday afternoon under a huge Sidra tree in the middle of the courtyard. During those sessions I used to lie on the floor, my head in my mother's lap, gazing at the branches and leaves of the Sidra tree. Its oval leaves were smaller and more delicate than the fronds of the palm tree in our house which I often attempted to climb. This tree was shorter, but its branches spread out like a canopy with dense leaves providing plenty of shade. While the *Mutawa'a* preached I gazed at the tree and spoke to it. I told it how much I wished to climb it and hug its leaves and branches. When the leaves moved by a sudden breeze or a hopping bird, I thought the tree was talking back to me, encouraging me to do so. I collected some of its falling leaves and inhaled their fragrance.

"Does this tree have a name?" I asked the *Mutawa'a* once after she finished her lecture.

My mother furtively pinched me on the arm for my insolence to ask questions without permission. But the

Mutawa'a smiled and said, "It's a Sidra tree. It's mentioned in the Quran."

I shook myself loose from Yumma's grasp and sprang toward the woman. "Can you show me the page?" I gaped at her Quran in wonder. Its pages with golden frames around the verses seemed like an art book. I had just started to read picture books my father gave me and developed a passion for reading words anywhere I could spot them.

The *Mutawa'a* touched my head. "Next time you come I will show you the verse about the Sidra tree in the Quran. Make sure you perform your ablution before you carry your copy over here."

Thus began my attachment to the Holy book. With my fingers tracing words I didn't understand, I searched for every reference to nature and trees. There were plenty. There were not only trees but fruits, vegetables and herbs. Therefore, to me, Islam meant Nature, revering it, protecting it, nurturing it. To my mother and Munira however, Islam meant reciting its words and performing rituals with or without understanding them because it spiritually brought them closer to Allah and therefore to Paradise. With time, the difference between my understanding of Islam and theirs widened. For me, every ritual had a purpose; for them it was just an act of worship. I saw the five prayers of the day as a schedule for Muslims to time their day, especially during the era of the Prophet in the seventh century. Dawn is the time to wake up then go to work; noon is the time to stop working, have lunch and rest at home. Socialize after evening prayer, go to sleep after night prayer. Same with fasting during the holy month of Ramadan. By feeling the pain of hunger by the poor, we should eat moderately and give the third meal to those who need it. But not for Ydaida and Munira; for them fasting made them feel hunger which would facilitate God's forgiveness of sins they might have unwittingly committed.

In middle grade, after I memorized all the verses that dealt with nature in the Quran, I began my quest in the school library. I happened upon some issues of National Geographic and got enthralled by their photography of magnificent nature around the world. At grade ten I decided to major in geography in college. At grade eleven I thought I'd rather study botany. In grade twelve I read about the history of Islam and decided to major in history. Sometimes I wonder if you will go through the same process deciding what path you'll take academically. I hope you will find a mentor to steer you according to your inclinations.

My father was a busy man. His business as a major cotton and silk importer in our region required him to travel far east and north most of the time. When he was home, I overheard the heated arguments between him and my mother regarding our upbringing. Yumma insisted on religious education, while Yuba wanted to send us abroad for liberal education. He eventually gave in to her wishes and minimized spending time with me, especially sharing philosophical books and poetry. I missed him even when he was at home and looked forward to our summer vacations in Lebanon, the only time we were together. Eventually those, too, evaporated.

During the last family vacation in Lebanon, while I was still a teenager, he took my hand and walked me to the edge of a mountain overlooking the Mediterranean. He pointed at the far horizon and talked about ships sailing down from Spain, fleeing the Spanish Inquisition when Muslims were persecuted and murdered only for being Muslims. My eyes gazed at him, my ears receptive to his words, his voice low, sad, and gentle. I internalized his words, and only later in college did I understand what he meant. I think that moment with my father in the mountains of Lebanon shaped my future.

One special summer afternoon, right after I graduated from high school Baba took me aside to his office. After expressing his joy and pride in my decision to get a university degree he suggested sending me to Egypt or Lebanon for higher education. I looked at him tongue-tied, trying to digest the unexpected offer. I finally said, "*Ommi*, my mother, will not allow it."

"Leave that to me," he waved his hand. "Do you want to go or not? Their education system is more advanced and sophisticated than ours. Kuwait University is only a couple of years old; we'll need ages to find firm grounds in scholarship and solid education. I think for now you'll get a better education abroad."

That was true. Kuwait University was as new at that time as our democracy and political system. But I was hesitant to leave home and family, especially him. I thought it over and decided to stay home and enroll at Kuwait University.

Winds of change and modernity were sweeping over our region and Kuwait was the first to embrace it.

Enrolling at Kuwait University was my first step to experiencing freedom from my mother's clutch. Strolling campus grounds with my girlfriends who wore miniskirts, which my Yumma forbade me to do in public or even at home, was as liberating as joining a protest for female rights which we heard was taking place in Beirut and Cairo. Nourishing my mind was more important to me than trimming my clothes. I was thirsty for knowledge and hungry to learn and immerse myself in cultural events of our times. Women's rights and free choice in marriage and career were pivotal issues for me and my classmates. We read Ghada al-Samman, Simone de Beauvoir, Nawal El Saadawi and discussed them in every classroom and social gathering on campus. As a junior at the university studying history, I regretted not majoring in literature. However, that didn't stop me from reading every book and novel written by those women. Oh, how I loved those days.

"Those were the days, my friend," were words in a song my classmates and I sang to each other while giggling and laughing. It did not occur to us then that one day we would be that lonely woman in the song reminiscing over those innocent days. We were young and carefree, unaware of the political and religious dark clouds heading toward us from the north.

Chapter Six

Back from the Boulder Public Library, after meeting Jonathan, Hadeel stops at the hotel's front desk. It's quiet now in the lobby. Unoccupied, the concierge nods, encouraging her to ask whatever questions she may have. But the blond girl at the front desk calls.

"Excuse me!" She pulls out a large yellow envelope from behind the counter. "Someone left you this, earlier." She slides the package across the counter toward Hadeel.

"Thank you." Hadeel grasps the package and shuffles toward the elevators. She examines the yellow package, weighing its contents in her hands—not much in it, a couple of books perhaps. Jonathan had written the word "confidential" underneath her name and room number but did not seal it. The envelope's flap is kept in place with a metal clasp.

In the room, Hadeel sinks into the brown armchair by the window and places the package in her lap. This must be the reason he asked her to visit. She bends the metal clasps, lifts the flap open, and pulls out a thin file and a couple of journals. One of them, with a hardcover, displays a colorful painting of three women, holding umbrellas, posing for the artist. One of them is smiling coquettishly, as if flirting with the artist. Small print on the back cover says, 'Women Artists in the Age of Impressionism." The artist is a woman then, Hadeel thinks, looking back at the flirting girl in the picture.

Inside, in the center of the front page of the journal, Amal wrote: *For Hadeel.* Underneath it is her aunt's full name: Amal Hamad Al Hamdeen. Although it's a given that she and her aunt shared the same last name, seeing it written stirs waves of recognition, reminding Hadeel of their blood ties, long forgotten. It also means that Amal did not change her maiden name during the twenty years she'd lived in a culture that encourages women to change their names, their identities, after marriage. Something Hadeel has always thought ironic for Westerners who pride themselves for being supporters of women's rights and individualism.

Throughout the pages of the journal only the color of ink changes, from light blue to darker shades of blue. The written pages, which occupy only half of the notebook, flow in her aunt's precise handwriting style which Hadeel remembers from childhood. The final entry was written in January 2019, approximately two months before the accident that took her life away. Sadness invades Hadeel's heart. What message did her aunt want to tell her? Did she have a premonition that the end was coming soon? She shakes the thoughts away with a head jerk. At the same time, a notification sound from her cell phone makes her jump and close the journal shut. She forgot to check her phone since she got back to the room.

In the process of shutting the journal, an old photo of herself with Amal, flies out of the pages to the floor. Hadeel picks it up with a clear memory of the time and place it was taken.

They were at their favorite beach in Salmiya, Kuwait, for Hadeel's fifth birthday. Behind them a still sea, calm and waveless. Amal was trying to explain the difference between a gulf and a sea, the Arabian Gulf and the Mediterranean Sea. But Hadeel wasn't listening, she was more interested in searching for seashells. In the photograph, Amal had both hands resting on Hadeel's shoulders, while Hadeel showed her find to the camera. The joy of being with Amal had always been a part of the memory of her lost Aunt. As a teenager, miserable and confused, Hadeel often wondered if Amal was still a fun person, or if her happiness ended when she left home.

She opens the first journal again and resists the urge to read the end, a habit of hers when starting a new book. "Knowing the end of the story will spoil the joy of reading it," a friend once told her. To which Hadeel replied, "We all know we will die at the end of our story. Does that spoil the joy of living?"

Pinned to the first page of the notebook is a folded letter, dated 2000, written by Hadeel at age five. She remembers that moment in detail, the crayons she'd used, the paper she tore from a school notebook to compose the first letter she had ever written. Some words smudged with tears she shed while scribbling with her childish fingers. She had circled the smudged words and wrote, "My tears because I miss you."

Hadeel was angry at Amal because she never received answers to her letters. She wrote several complaining to her aunt for not writing back. "How can you forget me?" She had asked Aunt Munira to help her write that sentence. "Don't you love me anymore?" Munira corrected the Arabic grammar of the last question saying, "She loves you but she's busy." Hadeel asked her father to mail her letters until he admonished her to stop writing and to never mention Amal's name again.

Inside the back cover of the journal are envelopes filled with official documents. They look old and covered with legal language. Half of the papers are written in a different language, not English, not Arabic. Spanish? Those must be the documents Jonathan wanted her to see. "*Bismillah*," in the name of God, she silently mouths the words while unfolding the papers.

Hadeel's mobile plays her favorite Kuwaiti song, which means it's her mother calling.

She sets the journal aside and grabs the phone, her heart throbbing. She really wants to talk to her mother, instead she calls Munira. This time, she answers

"Mama is calling me incessantly. Do you know why?"

"No, I don't. She called me and asked to talk to you."

"Did they find out about this trip?" Hadeel's voice shakes.

"I don't think so," Munira says.

"Then why is she persistent?"

"I don't know. She didn't tell me what it is exactly she wanted," Munira says in her noncommittal tone. "It might be important."

Hadeel tries to think of a reason. "Did she ask you why I'm not answering?"

"I told her you were in the shower. May Allah forgive me. I need to fast months to absolve myself of these lies."

"So? What shall I do now?" Hadeel's nervousness rings in her voice.

"Call her, but don't mention where you are," Munira warns her. "Only two more days and we'll talk to her together in London, *inshallah*."

Still, Hadeel can't bring herself to call. She might end up blurting out the truth. She always does, no matter how hard she tries to swallow it down her throat. No, she shouldn't call. She should send a message later when her mother goes to sleep. She checks her cell for the time in Kuwait. Her mother would still be awake. There are several voice-messages from her, something Hadeel knows her mother dislikes to do. She listens to the first one: "Hadeel! Your father wants to talk to you. He's sitting next to me right now, waiting. Call back. Now!"

It's not like her father either to want to talk on the phone. Ever since he discovered her relationship with Raj he stopped talking to her directly, as if she became someone shameful to talk to. If there are important things he wants her to know he relays them to Yumma. How would he feel now that she's in America alone not wearing the hijab? Did they see the selfie Amina took? Blood drains from Hadeel's face. What can she do if that's the case? How can she face her parents?

She listens to her mother's next message. This time her voice is hushed to a whisper. "Hadeel-O, your father just left to his *diwaniya*. He said to call him in the morning before dawn prayers. I have to tell you what's going on. You should know. Your cousin Nawaf is pressuring your father to fix a date for marriage. Nawaf said if you don't want a wedding right away that's fine, but he wants to make it official with *katb-el-kitab*, the marriage contract. Nawaf said you can finish your Master's degree while you're married to him, he doesn't mind. Of course, your father agrees with him. Nawaf wants to guarantee the marriage before you change your mind when you find out what happened to his mother."

Yumma pauses then, barely audible, she continues. "Listen Hadeel, your father does not want me to tell you, but I can't hide it anymore. Something awful happened at Nawaf's house. That's why Nawaf's in a hurry to marry you. He knows you'll change your mind when you find out. Let me say this to be fair to Nawaf, he has absolutely nothing to do with what happened. So you can't change your mind about him for that. It's his mother's fault."

Hadeel rolls her eyes and shakes her foot nervously as she waits for her mother's judgment and criticism of the woman who is soon to be her mother-in-law. "*Yallah*! Mama!" Hadeel tells the phone.

"*Elmuhim*," Yumma says, "what's important is that you should know before you get involved with this family. I'm not saying you should change your mind, it's up to you. But you should know that his mother is now in jail. Yes, you heard right—in prison, behind bars. Don't tell your father I told you! Tell him you heard from a friend. The story is all over social media in Kuwait but without specific names. Your father wants your permission to go ahead with *katb-el-kitab* without your presence. Of course, the Imam will ask him if you gave him permission to do that, and your father will not lie.

Well, let's hope he won't. *Khalas*, that's it, I vented this out and appeased my conscience. Now you must decide on your own."

"On my own? Since when?" Hadeel shouts at the phone in her hand, which is shaking violently. To marry her off without her being there? Is he mad? She resists calling her mother back. "Let's hear the whole story first!" She swallows hard and tries to calm down, her mouth feels like paper. The next voice message is a short one.

"If you still want to marry Nawaf we will be happy for you," Yumma says. "If you decide not to, I will take your side." The message ends.

Hadeel exclaims, *Oh my God.* There's a way out of this marriage? Is it true she has her mother on her side? *Ya Allah.* She paces the room, pushing her hair away from her forehead, talking loudly to herself. "I should grab this chance. I shouldn't let it slip away from my fingers. I should leave on the first flight to London tomorrow before Yumma changes her mind." Her cell bleeps. Another brief message from her mother. This time it's a text.

"Call your father. Or better, text him at night. While he's asleep."

Hadeel presses the call icon. "What shall I tell him?"

"Hadeel-O! Where have you been all this time? Why aren't answering my calls?"

Tongue-tied Hadeel tries to come up with an answer. She cannot find a good one.

"Why didn't you call your father? He's going mad!"

"What shall I tell him?"

"Tell him not to do anything until you get back home."

"Yumma, please! Tell him I don't want to marry Nawaf."

"Come back tomorrow and tell him yourself."

"I can't!"

"Why? Let me talk to Munira."

"She's not h … She's asleep."

"Why? Isn't it still early in London? Wake her up! It's important."

Distressed, Hadeel looks around the room as if her aunt is lurking behind the furniture. "She's been tired today. Yumma, please, please, I will be back as soon as possible. Tell Baba not to act on my behalf. He does NOT have my permission. And I don't WANT to marry Nawaf!"

"He won't take it from me. You must tell him that yourself. *Ma'asalamah*, I'm going to sleep now."

"Wait! Ma! Why is Nawaf's mother in prison?"

But she's already gone. Hadeel keeps the phone against her ear, her mind going wild with possibilities. It's midnight in Kuwait. At this hour her father should be leaving the *diwaniya* where he met with his male friends and relatives. She should wait another hour and text him about not wanting to marry Nawaf. Her chest brims with hope. Her mother is finally on her side. Up until now she has sided with Baba ever since the night she discovered Hadeel's plan to marry Raj. That night, the worst night in her life, Hadeel's life changed like Cinderella's at midnight.

Unlike that fairytale, Hadeel's life turned the other way round, from happy to miserable. From being a wealthy girl, to the possibility of becoming poor. Without asking her opinion, her parents accepted Nawaf's marriage proposal. "It's either you marry Nawaf or stay a spinster for the rest of your life," her mother threatened.

At first, she was convinced of the latter option. "Look

at Munira," she told herself. "She seems to be doing fine as a spinster surrounded by loving relatives." But everyone in the family, especially her brothers, insisted that her cousin Nawaf was a good catch, and that he would be a good husband. She relented, desperately hoping that something would happen and stop the marriage. Maybe Nawaf would get tired of waiting for her and find someone else in the meantime. Or, maybe she'd drop dead before it happens. None of that happened so far.

Pacing the hotel room, Hadeel remembers how she and cousin Nawaf met as adults for the first time since childhood. It was during her cousin Haya's high school graduation party.

Haya's father, Hadeel's Uncle Bader, offered to have the party anywhere Haya desired, and invite anybody she liked including male classmates on the condition that they "behave" themselves.

Haya chose the garden of their new villa in Mishref. The large swimming pool is sheltered from the eyes of neighbors by palm trees and a high stone fence.

"Would you like to come?" Haya had asked Hadeel on the phone a week before the event.

"Who did you invite?"

"All my classmates," Haya paused, "including boys. Please don't tell your parents. Uncle Rashid won't let you come if he knows, and your mother will gossip about it for the rest of her life." Haya giggled. "And don't mention it to Aunt Munira either, it'll be a shock for her naive mind."

Hadeel, seventeen at the time, remained dumbfounded. Not in her wildest dreams did she ever imagine herself in a mixed party of boys and girls.

"Hello?" Haya said. "Are you there?"

"Yes," Hadeel whispered. "I would like to come."

She hung up, not believing her ears. How could Uncle Bader allow his daughter to invite boys to his house? How can he be so different from his brother Rashid, her father? They had been brought up by the same parents in the same environment. The only difference was their college education. Rashid went to military school in Kuwait, Bader studied engineering at a university in Egypt. During the Iraqi invasion of Kuwait Rashid had to fight while Bader, according to Rashid, loitered in the streets of Cairo eating *kosheri*.

At that time, Hadeel couldn't decide if she should envy Haya's happy life or feel sorry for her because, according to Munira, she'd go straight to Hell if she didn't pursue the righteous path before the moment of death.

One thing Hadeel envied about Haya was how proud Uncle Bader had always been of her. And why shouldn't he be proud? After all, Haya graduated from high school with distinction and immediately got admission to study Medicine at a Canadian university with a full scholarship from Kuwait government. Hadeel on the other hand, majored in Arabic at Kuwait University before she switched to English Literature. She knew that no matter how successful she was academically, her father wouldn't care. The only thing he was proud of was Hadeel wearing the hijab. According to him that was an achievement worthy of reward now and in the afterlife. As usual, her mother agreed, grinning. Hadeel's feelings were not important. "You'll get used to it," her mother repeated, patting her hand, when she saw the tears in Hadeel's eyes.

The afternoon of Haya's party, Hadeel's mother insisted on supervising Hadeel's clothes and make-up. She entered Hadeel's room lugging a bundle of garments and a pair of shoes she'd purchased especially for the occasion. She spread them on Hadeel's bed, then sat comfortably in the armchair by the door.

"Try them on," Yumma said with a grin, her beady eyes twinkling.

Hadeel stared at the glittery black tank top and the red mini-skirt that would only fit her dolls from childhood. Next to them lay a fashionable Islamic abaya to wear over the slinky clothes outside the house. Hadeel jerked around to look at her mother. "Are you trying to make a fool of me?"

"Look at the tags. They're Ellie Saab, you stupid girl!"

"I don't care who designed them! They won't fit me."

"They're made of stretch fabric. Since the party is at home there'll be only women, so you can show off your beautiful body for a change. I'm sure they'll fit you, try them! Please?"

"No!" Hadeel glared at her mother, itching to tell her there were going to be men and there was no way in hell she would dress like that in front of them, or in front of any women for that matter. If she wore them to please her mother, she'd have to keep the abaya on all night and look like a bat amongst bare-limbed girls. But she'd promised not to mention the mixed party to her mother, so she had to keep quiet.

"Show me what you were planning to wear," Yumma said.

Hadeel opened her closet and took out a pink gown her mother had bought her for the last *Eid*. It had a dainty white flower design on the hem and sleeve-cuffs. "It's by Armani if that's significant for you," Hadeel snickered.

"Everybody has seen you in this dress already! We're wealthy, we can afford new clothes for each occasion!"

"So?" Hadeel hung the dress back in the closet.

Yumma sat up in the chair, her face flushed. "Stupid girl! Who in her right mind would refuse these new stylish clothes for such a gown?" She huffed out a breath and slumped back in the chair. "At least wear the shoes." She pointed at the pair of Balenciagas she'd placed at the foot of the bed.

Hadeel picked them up and examined them. They were her size but the heels were five inches high. She preferred flat shoes. "I don't need high heels."

"You do, so everyone will notice how tall you are," she grinned. Then, with a cajoling voice she said, "Try them on, *habibti*."

Hadeel inserted her feet through the straps of the shoes and stepped in front of the mirror. "They are pretty," she mumbled. "But I look like a palm tree."

"Good. I love palm trees. Now let me do your hair and make-up."

"No reason to do my hair, I'm going to keep the hijab on."

"Why?" Yumma's eyes doubled in size. "Isn't the party all women?"

Hadeel swallowed her answer and sat at the vanity

armoire, letting her mother brush her long hair. "I don't want any make-up."

"Just a little bit, please. I will make it look natural, believe me."

The pleasure Yumma displayed performing the task she took upon herself reminded Hadeel of girls playing dolls. Was that why women wanted children? To keep playing dolls during adulthood?

"You look stunning." Yumma stepped back after applying make-up and gazed at Hadeel in the mirror. She then sat down on the bed with a serious look on her face. "I wasn't going to tell you this, but maybe I should."

Hadeel swirled around on the vanity stool to face her mother. "What is it now?"

"You got your first marriage proposal a week ago. But I told your father you're still too young for that."

Hadeel let out the breath she'd held at the words "marriage proposal," with, "*Alhamdulillah*."

"Don't you want to hear more about it?"

"No."

"He's somebody we don't know. But his father came to the *diwaniya* to talk to your father. He said his wife, the boy's mother, saw you leaving school one day and thought you would be perfect for her short son. You will improve their genes with your height. They are all short people." Her mother let out one of her hysterical laughs.

"Thank you for standing up for me. I don't want to get married."

"Someday you will."

"I will let you know when I'm ready."

"No, we will let you know when you're ready." Yumma stood to leave. "I'm going to the mall this evening. I'll drop you off at your cousin's house."

Hadeel closed her bedroom door and went straight to the shower. She lingered under the hot water long enough to let the steam penetrate her face and erase the make-up. How could she ever let a stranger see her naked body, let alone touch it? How could a woman marry and sleep with someone she'd never met before? Yes, it happened to millions of women, her mother was one of them, but Hadeel would never allow it, if she could help it. Not at this time of the modern age. Shouldn't there be some attraction between couples before they sleep together? What about love?

In her mother's Mercedes, Hadeel prayed that she wouldn't barge into Uncle Bader's house. How many families kept events like this one secret? Why couldn't Uncle Bader tell his brother that he allowed his daughters the freedom they deserved? She knew the answer. Because rigid Rashid would never talk to his brother again or allow Hadeel to see her cousin. Hadeel would lose Haya, the closest to a sister she had. Maybe it was better to hide some truths?

"Don't look so sad." Her mother patted her hand at a red light on the way. "You can have a party too, you know. I'll give you the best party ever when you graduate from university. In the best hotel in town."

"I don't really care," Hadeel blurted out. "Haya is having a party because she's leaving for Canada soon."

"Really? When is she leaving?"

"In a week."

"Oh, so I have to go in and say good-bye." Yumma said as she parked the car in front of Uncle Bader's villa.

"No!" Hadeel grabbed her mother's arm. "Please don't embarrass me! The party is not for grown-ups. I'll tell Haya to come see you before she leaves."

Yumma scrutinized Hadeel for a long moment, removed her hand from the door, and pushed a strand of Hadeel's hair back under her hijab. "Calm down. Call me when you want to get back home."

Hadeel nodded and stepped out of the car. She waited until her mother drove away, exhaled, steadied herself, and moved toward the house. The heat of June felt oppressive in a long-sleeved gown and hijab, it would only get worse outdoors around the pool. She paused and wiped the perspiration dripping from her forehead with her hands, wondering how it was going to feel socializing with boys. Aside from her brothers, she'd never talked to a male her own age.

At the wrought iron gate, Hadeel could hear Haya's favorite jazz music and the male voices of the invitees. Soft shimmering lights reflected the water of the swimming pool over the large fronds of tall palm trees. She imagined herself slipping on the pool's tiles in front of the young guests, a mortification she'd never get over for the rest of her life. She bent down to take off her high heels when a voice startled her.

"Are you lost?"

Hadeel turned around quickly and almost fell at the feet of a young man. He came to her aid, taking hold of her elbow, all the while apologizing for scaring her.

She snatched her arm away and strode through the gates without saying a word, the young man following her.

"*Ahlain*," Haya called rushing towards her. "Welcome. So glad you came." She kissed Hadeel on both cheeks then stepped back examining her cousin from head to toe. Haya looked ravishing in a simple, low-cut, sleeveless silk top and a knee-high skirt showing off her buttery smooth brown skin. "Did you grow taller since I last saw you?"

"*Marhaba* Haya," the young man behind Hadeel said.

"Nawaf! Sorry I didn't see you." Haya shook hands with him and asked, "Did you two come together?"

Shocked with the insinuation, blood rushed up to Hadeel's face. *How dare she say such a thing*, she thought.

"Is this Hadeel?" Nawaf exclaimed.

Haya looked back at him with surprise. "You must have not seen each other since Hadeel wore the hijab. Hadeel, this is Nawaf, our cousin, Uncle Abdulla's son."

Hadeel covered her face with both hands. After a moment she relaxed and smiled. "I never saw him in t-shirt and jeans either."

"I think the last time we were together was when we were ten years old," Nawaf said. He laughed adding, "Sliding down Faraya mountain in Lebanon."

"Until Ahmed, my brother, broke his leg," Hadeel said, and they both laughed out loud. "You never join our family gatherings anymore," Hadeel said. "How come?"

"I started university in England a few years ago."

"Let me introduce you two to my friends," Haya said, taking Hadeel's hand.

In the company of her cousins, Hadeel relaxed and felt calm and happy for the first time since she'd been forced to wear the veil in public. She didn't mind Nawaf's admiring glances, oblivious to the intention behind them. She found out a year later.

Chapter Seven

Outside her window stars sparkle in a dark sky. Hadeel stretches her arms and legs realizing she must have fallen asleep on the armchair. What about the night prayer? The very thought sends such élan and energy through her body that makes her jump out of the chair to her feet. Something tumbles to the floor with a thump. Must be her phone. She switches on the night light by the bed and picks it up recalling the turmoil before she fell asleep. The shocking news about Nawaf's mother in jail and Yumma's exhortative voice-messages asking her to call or text her father as soon as possible. The time blinks 2:00 A.M., which translates to eleven in the morning Kuwait time. The text message she wrote for her father remains unsent. If she sends it now, he will call her back. Then what is she going to tell him if he asks where she is? She can never lie to her father. Not him.

In a few hours Jonathan will pick her up to go to the mountains. She's glad he didn't insist on taking her to his and Amal's house. What a depressing thought. Better to perform her night prayers and wait to calm down. Too wound up to go back to sleep.

After a lengthy prayer she checks her phone again for new messages. Relieved that none were sent during her sleep, she replays her mother's old voice messages to make sure she hadn't dreamt them. Life without the threat of marrying Nawaf would be wonderful, even if that thwarts her chances of getting married at all, as her mother has always threatened. She now remembers that during their last conversation Yumma said she'd take her side if she declined marrying Nawaf. She should hurry back home before her mother changes her mind again. Munira should be the first one to know of her decision.

"*Ammiti* Munira," Hadeel records an audio message. "Mama wants me to go back home today. Is it possible? You bought the tickets. Please let me know if I can change the reservation. It's very important to me to do that."

While waiting for her aunt's reply Hadeel types a message to her cousin Haya. "Have you heard what happened to our cousin Nawaf's mother?" The message doesn't go through. She googles the time in Montreal, Canada. Four in the morning. Of course, Haya would either be asleep or studying for an exam. And if Haya hates anything it's social media. "It's the poison of our modern times," Haya has often said. Oh, how she misses her, Hadeel thinks looking at her cousin's profile picture on WhatsApp. Haya is wearing a white clinical robe, a stethoscope around her neck, with a caption, *no time to waste.*

Sitting on the edge of the bed, Hadeel shakes her foot nervously, recalling the day her cousin Nawaf proposed to marry her. "It was the best of times, it was the worst of times," as Charles Dickens put it in the opening of *A Tale of Two Cities*. For Hadeel that was the time around her graduation from Kuwait University. Her mother had insisted on throwing a lavish party to celebrate the occasion. It had to be bigger and better than Haya's high-school party. She even hired an orchestra and a famous chef to prepare food for the guests. A buffet with candles and flowers would be set outdoors. They didn't have a swimming pool like Uncle Bader's, but they had a beautiful garden that can be filled with flowers imported from Europe.

"Why the extravagance?" Hadeel protested. "It's not a wedding."

"*Inshallah* your wedding will be even bigger."

Her mother even chose the date of the party. "It has to be the end of May before the weather gets really hot." Hadeel knew there was no point in arguing. Even Hadeel's father kept his peace whenever his wife insisted on something.

"It's already too hot," Hadeel reminded her mother.

"We will have fans and misters with rose water to cool the garden. We will leave the doors of the house open so the cold AC air drifts outside."

Baba and Hadeel exchanged glances, shook their heads and remained quiet. Besides, Hadeel had more important things on her mind. Finals were coming up soon. Afterwards, she'd start applying for a job. But more urgent than all that was the new fluttering of her heart. She was in love.

Despite finals anxiety Hadeel was happier than she had ever been. How was it possible that love could penetrate every cell of one's body and force a smile on one's face? She didn't know that love's glow could draw people and make them wonder about its secret. For the first time in her life, she joked and laughed with her brothers. Her parents assumed she was excited about finishing university and starting a school-free life. No one suspected the real reason. No one knew Hadeel was in love, so much in love for the first time at the age of twenty-two. Raj, the leader of the theology group she joined a year earlier, had asked her recently if they could chat privately.

"Why?" she wrote back.

"To ask you a personal question."

"Oh," she wrote back. "All right," she hesitated before switching to the personal chat site he sent.

"Would it be all right to switch on the cam?" he asked.

"No!" She blurted and reached out for her hijab draped on the back of her chair.

"Why not?" he asked. "I'm just asking to see your face."

"Why is it important?" Still, she wrapped the hijab tight over her hair.

"Wouldn't you have been curious to know how I look had my photo not been posted on my website?" he chuckled.

True, she thought, while her trembling fingers reached for the camera icon. It's only fair for a professor to see whom he's teaching, she told herself.

After several of those private cam-conversations, Raj expressed special emotions for her.

He was impressed with her intelligence, her honesty, and her faith, he said.

"Have you ever read *Thalaba the Destroyer* by Robert Southey?" he asked.

"No." She shook her head bashfully. He had referred to the poem several times during the group discussion and recommended they read it. It was his favorite British epic.

"You remind me of Oneiza." His face flushed. "At least my image of her—a refined Arab, desert girl that has not been tainted by modernity and its materialism."

Hadeel was speechless. After a long moment of silence she mumbled, "How . . . how come you're interested in . . . in . . ."

"Arabia and the desert?" He laughed his soft polite laugh.

"Yes." She nodded repeatedly.

"That's a good question, Hadeel. See, as a teenager, I grew up reading novels by a Pakistani author, Naseem Hijazi. Even though he wrote in Urdu, his novels were about the rise and fall of Islam. His main characters were Arabs and famous Muslims who lifted Islam to its glory in the Arab world and later Spain. His most famous novel, *The Shaheen of Andalus*, must have been the main influence for me to study theology."

"I see," Hadeel said, relaxed.

"*Thalaba the Destroyer* by Southey, in a way, reminds me of Hijazi's novels. I read it during the first year of college, and still is my favorite. Now, my dear Oneiza, I have a question to ask you."

When she only blushed, he asked if she'd consider marrying him. "What?" She laughed lightly as if he was joking.

But Raj was serious. "I know you didn't expect this Hadeel, but would you at least give it a thought?" he asked gently.

She said she would. *Yeseer khair*, she thought to herself, *we'll see later what good life has in store for us.*

Raj, five years older than her, spoke politely and professorially. She loved his voice, his British accent. The dimples on his cheeks didn't hurt either. He told her his mother was Indian, his father Pakistani. They lived in Pakistan while he taught at Exeter and shared his income with his parents. Hadeel never dreamed of being loved by such a handsome man, let alone being asked to marry him.

But his proposal reminded her of a "white" lie she had told the theology group when she introduced herself for the first time: that she was a poor *Bidoon*, a Kuwaiti without a citizenship, her ancestors were bedouins. At that time she had not expected to stay with the online-group for long, let alone develop a connection with its founder. She was afraid of revealing her identity or family name, since they were well-known in the Kuwaiti society and most probably among Kuwaitis in London. How would they react finding out that one of theirs was discussing her religion with westerners? A couple of years later, she forgot all about that lie until Raj proposed.

"As a smart woman, Hadeel, you will be able to get your Master's degree and teach wherever we decide to live," Raj said.

No one else told her she was smart. And the possibility of living or working outside Kuwait never occurred to her before. She told him about her dream to teach at a college level, not in an enclosed all-female high school as her father demanded.

Raj nodded, "I'm sure you can. I will commit myself to your happiness Hadeel, I promise you that."

Hadeel asked him to let her think about it during summer vacation, after finals. She had to tell him the truth about her background. Would he change his mind once he learns she wasn't as poor as she claimed to be? She wondered and worried a little until she convinced herself that there was no reason to worry. *Why should he get upset? Isn't wealth always a plus?* At that time, she was soaring over the clouds drawing future plans; it wasn't the time to let worry ruin the happiest moments of her life.

Two days before her graduation party, Hadeel drove to campus to check her grades. She found three As and two Bs. "Not bad," she told a classmate who was also checking her own grades posted on the professor's office door. "It's still worth a party," Hadeel giggled.

"What's new in your life Hadeel?" the girl asked on their way to the parking area. "You look more beautiful than you've looked all semester, *mashallah*."

Hadeel laughed. "Must be the relief from finals."

In her car, she kept thinking of her friend's comment. Hadeel wondered if Raj thought she was beautiful. They never delved in intimacies, even though she thought he was handsome. Not as handsome as Kivanc, the Turkish actor whom she idolized, but handsome enough. She smiled while she drove, even laughed at her thoughts. Halfway to her house, Hadeel became aware of a young man driving next to her and waving. He kept passing her, slowed down, then let her pass. At one point he blew a kiss and signaled with his phone. She ignored him. He honked. She sped up, watching him in the rear-view mirror hoping to lose him. A vehicle in front of her suddenly stopped at a traffic light at the moment when Hadeel was pushing the gas pedal to escape the man. She slammed into the car in front of her. The man chasing her slammed into hers. Cars honked from all directions. Hadeel fainted. When she came to, police cars and sirens sounded all around her.

"*Alhamdlillah Alsalamah,*" a policeman said with relief when she opened her eyes. "Are you all right?"

More policemen joined him at her window. Wishing what happened was a video game, Hadeel searched for a button to undo what just happened. Unfortunately, none was available: this was real. In shock, Hadeel tried to stay calm, clear her mind, and decide on what to do. The policeman at her door was asking her to open the window. She slowly moved her arms; it was painful doing just that. She tried to open the door, but it wouldn't budge. The window rolled down only halfway. She found her purse on the floor of the passenger seat and with so much pain she reached for it to get her mobile. "I need to call my family," she told the policeman, her voice shaking with pain.

"*Alhamdulillah*, she's fine," The policeman told his teammates. Then to Hadeel he said, "Let's get you out of the car first." The door wouldn't open from outside either. "We might need to pull you out from the window."

Hadeel's mother finally answered the phone. At the sound of her voice Hadeel howled. "Yumma! I had an accident."

"Where are you? Tell me!" Mother shrieked.

"I don't know," Hadeel sobbed. "There are policemen everywhere."

"Let me talk to one."

Hadeel handed her phone to the young policeman. She heard him give directions to her mother. When he handed the phone back, Yumma was frantic. "Stay where you are. We're coming to get you."

A tall policeman with a crowbar managed to break the door lock and helped her out to the street. He escorted her to the back seat of a police vehicle, gave her water and asked what happened. The officer said the man who rear-ended her car fled, but some people managed to get his license-plate number. Hadeel covered her face out of shame. How could such a thing happen to her?

Soon her mother and brother Abbadi arrived. "Take Hadeel back home," Abbadi said to Yumma. "I'll take care of police procedures. Tell the chauffeur to come back and get me right after he drops you home."

Hadeel gaped at him before she walked away with her mother. He sounded so mature, just like her father, acting somberly. Suddenly he was no longer the brother who was always cynical and laughing at silly things at home. On the way to his car, Hadeel glanced at hers. It was practically totaled; yet she was still alive. Once she sat next to her mother in the back seat, she hid her face in her mother's bosom and sobbed.

"It's an envious eye," her mother said, hugging her. "*Allah setter,* God protected you. Who would believe you can walk away from such an accident?"

"Please don't tell anyone," Hadeel cried.

"Your father must know."

"Only my father, please, Yumma."

Later in the afternoon, her father kissed her forehead and patted her shoulder.

Hadeel was touched at this rare show of tenderness. "I'm so sorry Yuba. The car is ruined."

"*Fedwa*," he said. "It's better the car than you."

"*Alhamdulillah*," Hadeel replied.

"Did you perform a gratitude prayer to God for your safety?"

"Yes, of course," she whimpered.

"Good." Before he left the room he said, "Isn't it time for your graduation gift? Maybe a new car?" He smiled.

Hadeel couldn't believe her ears. But the next surprise was even harder to believe. When she woke up the next morning there were several text messages from Raj asking her if she was all right.

Stunned, she wrote, "Why are you asking?"

"I had a feeling you were in some kind of an accident."

He texted back.

"OMG!"

"What?"

"I was!"

Her phone rang immediately. Before she could say hello, he asked, "Everything all right there?"

"I'm fine. But I can't believe you really knew! Do you swear no one told you?"

Raj sighed. "Hadeel, who would tell me? I had a strong sense of you in a horrible situation. Thank God you're fine."

"That's so amazing."

Long silence before he said, "It happens when two souls are united in pure emotions. Thank God for your safety. I must run; I have a class. Take care, Hadeel." And before he hung up, he added, "Don't forget, you're my Oneiza."

He had been calling her that since he proposed. He urged her again to read *Thalaba The Destroyer*, but she never found the time between school and video games. Also, she had a vague memory of the title from childhood but could not figure out where. But the thought had always brought back sad feelings.

For the rest of that day, Hadeel was in a trance. How incredible. That must be true love then. Raj must really love her if he sensed what happened to her. He sounded truly worried. Now, instead of doubting his love for her, she worried if she deserved his love, after lying to him. She had to tell him the truth about herself.

That afternoon, she let her mother drag her around to prepare for the party. She let her fix her hair and apply make-up to her heart's content. She even went as far as wearing sleazy clothes like the ones she'd bought for Haya's party, four years ago. Hadeel was too happy to argue.

"You look beautiful!" Haya exclaimed at the door later in the evening. She had surprised everyone by showing up suddenly in Kuwait.

Hadeel hugged her cousin tightly. "I didn't know you were here." She let go, stepped back and scrutinized her cousin. "And you look ravishing."

Haya's big smile revealed a gleaming set of white teeth. "I have great news to tell you. Come along."

In a corner of the garden that was decorated with colorful lights and balloons, Hadeel and Haya sat side by side on a marble bench. A plastic mister overhead sprayed cool mist over their warm bare shoulders, filling the air with the fragrance of roses.

"I can't believe what your mother did to this garden." Haya's eyes roamed over the green arches and gazebos in every corner of the garden, decorated with small climbing pink and red roses.

"That's not important," Hadeel said, grabbing Haya's hand. "Tell me, what's your news? Have you graduated already?"

Haya shook her head. "I still need two more years to graduate. But that's not what I was going to tell you."

"What then? Tell me, I can't wait."

"I'm getting married."

"What?" Hadeel jumped to her feet.

Haya laughed and pulled her cousin back down. "Listen! As we speak, Nat and his father are asking my father for my hand in marriage. At Baba's *diwaniya*."

"Who? What kind of a name is that?"

"Short for Nathaniel. He's Canadian. He studies medicine, same year as me. He said he can't wait till we graduate to get married."

"He must really love you to bring his father along to Kuwait."

"He does. We've been dating for a year and his family is insisting we get married now. They think we'd focus better on our studies that way. I finally gave in."

"Do you love him?"

"That's not a smart question, Hadeel." Haya squeezed her cousin's arm. "What do you think?"

"Well," Hadeel stammered. "You're talking about it very calmly, so I thought you're marrying him for everybody's sake."

"No!" Haya shook her head vigorously, strands of silky hair fell over her face. "I don't function that way. I don't do things to please other people. But don't worry, I love him very much and I am thrilled. I had a feeling we would get married the moment I met him." She winked at Hadeel with a bright smile.

"Is Uncle Bader okay with it?"

"I told Baba about Nat a few months ago. His only condition was that Nat converts to Islam, which was fine with Nat." Haya lowered her voice, saying, "Nat once said, if being a Muslim is what you are, I'd love to become one."

"How romantic," Hadeel exclaimed and hugged her cousin.

"What are you two conspiring about?" Hadeel's mother emerged in front of them. "Come," she pulled Haya by the arm. "Join us at the buffet. The chef has prepared a delicious *ghoozy*."

The girls obediently followed, inhaling the smells of saffron rice and roasted lamb meat.

They mingled and chatted with scores of women relatives and friends. Hadeel could not remember a happier day in her life. She kept glancing at Haya, itching to tell her about her own love story with Raj. How would she react? Would she encourage her to marry a poor Pakistani professor? Was that important to Hadeel? Her cousin's approval? The question faded away when Raj's words to make her happiness his priority popped into her mind. "I'd love to see those sad eyes of yours shine with happiness," he once said.

Since the orchestra included men musicians, they were asked to play inside a large tent set separate in the back of the garden. The design ensured that the invited women guests could dance free of their veils without the worry that the eyes of male musicians would roam over their bare bodies. Hadeel and Haya kicked off their shoes and danced like two women in love, swaying to the beat, dreamy eyes, imagining their partners holding them close.

"This is the happiest day of my life," Hadeel shouted in Haya's ears over the music.

"Mine too." Haya's smile grew wider. "I just got a message from Nat. My father accepted his proposal."

Hadeel stopped and yelled with joy. "*Mabrook!* Congratulations!"

"What are you congratulating her for, Hadeel?" Yumma said as she rushed toward them. She grabbed Hadeel's arm. "Come over for a minute. Someone wants to see you."

Hadeel looked at Haya who winked at her. She let her mother pull her toward the back of the house. "Where are you taking me?" she asked, getting annoyed the farther away they got from the dance floor.

"To the *diwaniya*," Yumma said, still clasping Hadeel by the arm. "Someone wants to give you a graduation gift."

For a second, Hadeel remembered her father mentioning a new car. But Baba never stayed at home when there were women guests. Must be one of her mother's lady friends who did not want to show her gift in front of other women.

At the door of the diwaniya Yumma paused, let go of Hadeel's arm and examined her daughter from head to bare feet. She smoothed Hadeel's hair, tucking it behind her ears, and straightened the straps of her tank top. "I wish you had your shoes on, but it's alright. Go in." She pushed her forward.

Hadeel opened the door and gasped. Standing in the middle of the spacious room was her cousin Nawaf. He was holding a wrapped gift in his hands.

"I'm not covered!" Hadeel turned around to leave.

With a firm grip, Yumma stopped her from leaving. "It's fine. You have my permission." She nodded at Nawaf.

"No!" Hadeel tried to hide behind her mother, but Yumma was much shorter. She searched around for a piece of cloth to cover her hair and her bare arms, but there was none.

Nawaf was more understanding than her mother. He lowered his gaze to the floor saying, "I'm sorry Hadeel. I just wanted to give you this before I leave for London tomorrow. Congratulations on your graduation." Without meeting her eyes, he handed her his gift and slipped out of the door.

Still in shock, Hadeel slammed the door shut. Eyes full of rage, she turned to her mother. "How could you do this to me? How could you! When you forced me to wear the hijab and I agreed, I also agreed to its principles. No cheating!" she screamed. "How would Baba feel about this?"

Her mother let out a snort. "According to his Imam, it's okay for a girl to be seen by someone who is seriously proposing to marry her."

"What?" Hadeel froze. Her heart turned to a piece of

ice. "What are you saying? Nawaf is proposing to marry me? Baba knows about all this?"

Yumma busied herself ripping the wrapping of Nawaf's gift. "Nawaf asked your father for your hand in marriage last week. We accepted."

"We accepted? You accepted, without asking me? Who said I'd agree?"

"Why wouldn't you agree?" mother asked, still busy with the gift.

"Why are you doing this to me?" Hadeel shrieked. "Look at me! Look at me! When I'm finally . . . When I'm . . ."

Yumma dropped the box on a chair next to her and grabbed Hadeel's shoulder. "What? When you're finally what?"

Hadeel shook her head and wiped a couple of tears that rolled down to her chin.

Yumma coaxed, "What's wrong with Nawaf? He's a good man and will be a good husband. Besides he's part of our family, and he's not in a hurry to marry. He said he needs another year to graduate. He doesn't want to lose you to another suitor while he's gone."

Hadeel pushed her mother away. Yumma shrugged and sauntered out. Hadeel sank next to Nawaf's gift, its torn wrapping at her feet. She rested her elbows on her knees and covered her face with her hands. Her own mother had just ruined the happiest day of her life. She'd tricked her into entering a room with a man unawares. Her parents had accepted a marriage proposal from a cousin without even asking her. How could she marry someone who was like a brother? He even looked exactly like her father.

Listlessly, Hadeel reached into the wrap-torn box. What had her so-called suitor given her for a gift? Through her tears she found a collection of computer games. The one on top had the title: The Headless Horseman. *Just great,* Hadeel thought wiping her tears. *He's headless alright. Doesn't even have the brain to ask if I cared to marry him.*

Chapter Eight

In front of St. Julien hotel, an enormous three-tiered fountain is flowing with flowers instead of water. In the top tier, colorful tulips stand proud, gracefully nodding their heads with the morning breeze. The lower tier is crowded with "a host of daffodils," Hadeel thinks, trying to bring the name of the British poet who wrote the lovely poem to her sleepy mind. She stoops to smell them and is surprised they actually have a pleasant faint fragrance. "William Wordsworth," she smiles and straightens up.

She draws in a deep breath and closes her eyes. What is the rest of the poem? Was it also April in England when Mr. Wordsworth came across his daffodils? She quickly dismisses the thought of the Wordsworthian flowers "fluttering and dancing . . . tossing their heads" and turns her attention to the cool breeze playing with her own hair, allowing the curls to equally dance and flutter touching her forehead and the back of her neck. She hadn't experienced this since she was fifteen; she'd forgotten how pleasing the sensation is. The immediate connection with nature, wind, and skin. Is she going to miss it when she covers herself with the hijab again?

The sun suddenly frees itself from behind the clouds and pours warmth down on pedestrians who seem happy to receive it. Whenever her eyes meet theirs, they smile or nod. It warms her heart to feel welcomed by strangers, men as well as women. Would they react the same way if she were wearing the hijab? Perhaps she'll experiment sometime before she leaves. Her friend Nabila, a popular Kuwaiti newspaper columnist who does not wear head-cover in Kuwait, wears it in Western countries to write about people's reactions. She once performed a prayer in the streets of London and wrote volumes of comments on reactions of pedestrians passing by. At the end of each article Nabila poses three questions for her readers: Is it upbringing? Education? Or civil laws that impel people, from different backgrounds, to behave in a civilized way towards each other?

Cars pass serenely by, no honking, or stopping haphazardly. Hadeel wonders as well what kind of education compels these people to follow driving rules. One of the biggest problems in Kuwait. Across the street, a few shops are open, displaying merchandise on metal racks lined along the sidewalk. Smooth sidewalks, no litter, no broken bricks scattered everywhere endangering pedestrians, something which has always bothered Hadeel back home, and made her wish for a solution. Why does it have to be like that in a rich country like Kuwait? Who is responsible?

"Hadeel!" Jonathan calls from inside his Tesla.

"Good morning." Hadeel greets Jonathan as she settles

in the front seat and buckles her seatbelt. When her father offered to buy her a new car, she asked for a Tesla instead of the Lexus he suggested. His response was, "Our country has plenty of gasoline, why bother with an electric car?"

Jonathan points at her sandals. "Don't you have a pair of sneakers?"

"A what?"

"Tennis shoes or hiking boots."

"No. I'm okay."

He shakes his head impatiently. "You asked to see Amal's favorite mountain spot which requires some hiking. The path is rocky and might be muddy from melted snow."

Hadeel shrugs. She hates wrapping her feet in socks and shoes. It's her only way of rebelling against body cover.

"There's a shoe-shop nearby. Let's see what they have for you."

She lifts her eyebrows in disbelief. Does he think he's her father? Before she can protest, he pulls into a strip mall and steps out. She trudges behind him, thinking she should've stayed in the car in protest. A potent aroma of coffee and fresh baked bread reminds her of the breakfast she skipped. Inside the small shop Jonathan points at a pair of hiking boots. "Those will give your feet ample support."

"I'd rather get these." She points at a pair of blue canvas Nikes.

Back in the car, Hadeel unfurls her toes in the warmth of the wool socks Jonathan insisted on purchasing along with the shoes. She tosses her Balenciagas on the back-floor of the car and ties the laces of her new shoes. Jonathan's heavy hiking boots make her wonder how long the hike will be and if she's fit for it. Hiking has never been part of her daily routine as there is nowhere to hike in Kuwait.

Only after ten minutes of weaving through smoothly paved streets, the car begins to climb a mountain road. A sign, "Boulder Parks," has an arrow indicating fire danger. Today it is sitting at "low." Jonathan takes a sudden turn to the left and slows down on a gravel path lined with pine trees. The road ends with a narrow dirt parking area.

"Let's go." He unbuckles his seatbelt.

Fresh fragrance of herbs and pine awakens Hadeel's jet-lagged body. Birds, hiding in tall trees, shriek down at them announcing their presence. An involuntary smile forms around her lips at the sound of rushing water nearby. Nature is a magical cure for ailing souls, she thinks.

When she studied the British poets of the Lake District, she wrote a paper about nature being the source of inspiration for the prolific literature they produced. "The Link between Nature and Creativity" was the initial topic of her Master's thesis before she changed it. Hadeel thought the topic was too peaceful for the tumultuous period of her life at the time.

She steps away from the car and turns to check if the austere expression on Jonathan's face has vanished with the beautiful natural surroundings. He's hunched over, tugging a backpack out of the car trunk. Sternly, he pushes each arm through the straps of the bag letting it rest over his thin back.

"That way," He points toward a sign. The crunching

sound of their shoes on the gravel softens as they cross to a wooden bridge.

Hadeel stops to take in the view. The wooden bridge reminds her of the one in a painting by Monet, the only colorful painting she has on the wall of her bedroom at home. She can't remember now where and why she got it. Was it from Amal?

"It's high this time of year," Jonathan nods at the rushing water under their feet. "I was afraid the recent rain, along with melting snow, would make this bridge impassable."

Hadeel's eyes absorb the dense vegetation surrounding the hiking path. White and purple wildflowers growing around the riverbank shine in the sunlight with moisture. "Was this Amal's favorite spot?"

Jonathan points at a mountain peak behind steep green hills. "Saddle Rock. It's quite a hike, are you ready?"

Hadeel nods. If he's able to do it at his age, she should bc as well.

Jonathan easily climbs a steep dirt path lined by boulders, sprinting lightly. She marches behind him copying his moves. After a few meters upward they climb log steps that must have been built to facilitate the muddy path. Gravity already begins pulling at her. Her head spins. The climb gets steeper as they ascend the rugged trail. Not more than fifteen minutes have passed when she stops to catch her breath, panting hard. Jonathan must be triple her age and yet he's moving swiftly, barely touching the ground with his heavy boots. *Mashallah*, she murmurs to herself, no evil eye.

He halts and looks at her. "Are you okay?"

She nods, but her face is getting numb. There's a buzz in her ear and she feels dizzy. "Must be the high altitude," she says. Or the extra weight she's gained recently, she thinks to herself.

"Please sit down." Jonathan points at a flat rock on the side of the path. "Coming from sea-level to six-thousand-feet is not easy on anyone."

"I'll be all right." She tries to smile.

"Have some water." He produces a water-bottle from his backpack and twists the cap open.

"Thank you." Her heart calms down after a few sips.

"I don't think we should go to Saddle Rock today. It's far, and the hike is steeper than this." He looks concerned.

Embarrassed at her frailty, Hadeel insists. "Didn't you say it's Amal's favorite spot in Boulder? Is that where she got her inspiration to write?"

He shrugs. "Maybe. But it won't be easy for you today. You need time to acclimatize. Perhaps some other day?"

She looks him in the eye and shakes her head. "I'd like to try today if you don't mind." *There won't be another time,* she thinks.

They trudge along silently. More log-steps are lodged in the ground to make it easier to climb, but some are too high to step over. Sharp turns with huge boulders obstruct the path which leads higher up the Rocky Mountains. She pauses for breath and a sip of water. A rustling sound through the dense vegetation becomes audible. Jonathan stops and points to the right. As she inches forward to see, a baby doe with shiny eyes and long pointed ears freezes, gazing at her.

Hadeel reaches in her pocket for her phone to take a photo, the same moment Jonathan yells, "Be careful!" In a flash, the deer, with bucking head, shoots off like an arrow right between them. It brushes against Hadeel's shirt sleeves. She screams.

"Jeez!" Jonathan steps back. "Are you okay?"

"Sorry," Hadeel says, shaken. "It scared me."

Behind them down the path, several hikers trudge carrying full hiking gear. Hadeel and Jonathan step aside and wait for them to pass before they resume their ascent.

"Tell me," she asks between shallow breaths, "about my aunt."

"All right." He slows down. "For one thing she loved hiking. She did it so naturally I thought your family was used to mountain hiking."

"Don't forget we are desert people," Hadeel takes another sip of water. "Except for summer vacations we rarely see mountains." She now remembers stories Aunt Munira told her of her childhood with Amal in Lebanon, how they were once lost in the mountains for hours before they were found. It never occurred to Hadeel before that her father's choice of summer vacations in Lebanon, besides it's being an Arab country, was a habit from childhood.

"Amal's other passion was the Arabic language," Jonathan adds.

"She still remembered it?" Hadeel says casually.

Jonathan knots his eyebrows, lines in his forehead grow deeper before he replies. "You really don't know much about your aunt, do you?"

Hadeel shoots him an angry look. Was that an incrimination? Is it her fault? Well, she doesn't know anything about him either. What kind of profession does he have? Where did he meet Amal? Why did he love her so much? The ringing in her ears gets louder.

"Can we rest here?" She sits on a boulder on the side of the path. *I was forbidden to ask about her,* Hadeel thinks to herself but keeps quiet.

Jonathan kicks a rock under his feet with the tip of his boot. "Did you read the lines on her tombstone?"

"Not really. I wanted to ask you about them."

"It said: 'Soften your tread, methinks the earth's surface is but bodies of the dead.'" Hadeel squints at him and waits for an explanation.

When she doesn't comment, Jonathan says, "Abul al Ala' al-Ma'arrie."

"You pronounce his name so well."

"Thank you. Did you study him in school?" Jonathan asks.

"No. He's from the ninth century."

"I think he was a genius for his time," Jonathan says. "I taught his poetry in some of my Islamic Studies classes at the university."

"So that's why you pronounce Arabic so well." Hadeel looks at him as if seeing him for the first time. A professor of Islamic Studies. No one mentioned such a significant fact before. Did anyone in her family know? Does Munira know?

"That and being married to your aunt," Jonathan says.

Hadeel stands and slowly treads up the path. "What else do you teach?"

"This semester I'm teaching *Mohammed* by Washington Irving."

She halts and turns around. "The one who wrote *The Headless Horseman*?"

"Yes, and the *Tales of Alhambra.* The original title of the book I'm teaching was *The Legendary Life of Mahomet.* You should read it."

"Wow!" Hadeel exclaims. "I never knew Irving wrote such a book!"

"Same with many Americans." Jonathan lifts his cap and smooths his hair before he puts it back on. "Irving was Amal's favorite American author . . ."

Hadeel waits for him to continue, but he turns around and resumes walking. "Wait. I have to make a note of the book to read it," she says, pulling out her phone. She notices two messages from Munira saying she will check on the possibility of changing her return date to London. In another text she wrote, "Did you ask him?"

Ask him? What does she mean? Hadeel wonders for a second before it dawns on her, and her heart sinks. She glances at Jonathan who is stretching his rangy body before he slowly turns and resumes walking. *Why doesn't Munira just get over it?*

"Who's your favorite Arab author?" Jonathan says suddenly.

Hadeel shrugs. "I studied English Literature. I liked some of the Lake poets, basically Wordsworth and Coleridge."

"What about an Arab poet?" He insists.

She tries to sift through the files of her memory to impress him. She can only think of Haya's favorite. "Ahmad Matar."

"I'm not familiar with the name. Is he contemporary?"

"Yes, he is." She's certain of that much at least. *Is he still alive?* she wonders to herself.

Suddenly a potent, putrid smell fills the air as her right foot sinks into a pile of soft dark material. She yelps. "What is this?"

Jonathan steps back, looks down. "Horse manure."

Hadeel stares at him in horror, expecting giggles like her brothers would produce in such a situation. Instead, a knot grows between his eyebrows.

Huge flies which were feasting on the manure buzz around her head and stained shoes.

Lucky she's not wearing sandals. "What shall I do?" She frantically rubs the sole of her Nikes on dirt. "Do you have wet towels?"

"No, I don't. Here, try this." He rubs off the sides of her shoes with a broken tree branch that he picked up from the path and removes chunks of horse poop.

"I'll do it." She takes it from him and rubs the muck off while thinking of her brothers. They often laughed about the poop their horses produced when they went riding at the Kuwait Equestrian Club on Sixth Ring Road. They even made bets on whose horse would poop more. If this is the stink they breathed during their rides, then Hadeel should find better adjectives to describe them than morons and stupid.

"You must be wondering why I asked you to visit in my letter," Jonathan says standing over her.

"I am." She stops cleaning her shoes and looks up at him. The reflection of the sun on his spectacles prevents her from seeing his eyes.

"You're the only family member Amal talked about all the time."

Hadeel removes the cap of the water bottle, takes a sip and waits for him to continue. He pauses, perhaps getting emotional. A trickle of sweat drips down the back of her neck.

Jonathan says, "As if by premonition, she recently mentioned things she'd like to pass on to you. Family heirlooms. Did you get a chance to look at the package? The one I left at the hotel?"

"No," Hadeel realizes she forgot about it after she received Yumma's voice messages about her marriage to Nawaf. "I'm sorry I haven't. But I noticed some official documents in a foreign language."

"Spanish."

"Do you want to tell me about it?"

"It's about real estate your grandfather gave Amal which she wanted to pass on to you."

Hadeel tries to remember something related to that from her conversations with Munira after Ydaida died. Munira has always mentioned that Amal was their father's favorite child, but nothing about real estate. In Islam, inheritance is divided according to specific rules amongst heirs.

"Let's find a spot to sit down and discuss it."

"All right," she mumbles. A feeling of resentment rises toward him for forcing her into this situation. Somehow, she now recalls the moment Amal told her that she was leaving and not taking her along. Only a child of five years, Hadeel wailed and clung to her aunt, begging her not to leave. Everyone expected Amal to get her doctorate and return home, but Hadeel must have intuitively sensed the truth.

"On the other hand," Jonathan is saying, "there are other belongings of Amal's that I'd like you to take a look at before I give them away." He removes his glasses and wipes his eyes with a handkerchief.

"I'm sorry," Hadeel says without really meaning it. She wants nothing of her deceased aunt's possessions, which at this point are meaningless. Now she isn't certain she cares to hike to Amal's favorite spot at Saddle Rock anymore.

Hadeel keeps her eyes on her feet as she falters behind Jonathan, keeping a distance between them. On top of an elevated path she pauses, barely able to breathe. A rumble behind them makes her jump. She expects to see the same fawn from earlier charging at her. Instead, two young women, in shorts and heavy gear and backpacks, skip past them.

Jonathan steps closer to Hadeel. "You have her voice. You know?"

"It's in the blood, as we say." She turns away.

"No. I mean the exact same voice," he insists.

She shakes her head. No, she doesn't know. How would she? Nobody except her parents compared her to Amal, but always in a negative way. Especially once they found out about her relationship with Raj.

Jonathan looks around searching for something. "I've packed a light lunch. Let's find a spot to eat."

Her stomach growls at the mention of food. She's always ready to eat, especially today without breakfast, but too embarrassed to admit it to Jonathan. Time on her phone flashes eleven-thirty, too early for lunch, but the steep climb is making her famished.

"This makes a good spot for lunch." Jonathan points at a flat, sandy clearing not far to their right.

With knees ready to crumple, Hadeel searches for a rock to rest on. Once she regains her breath she looks down at the canyon beneath them. The town of Boulder is spread far below, like an architect's diagram of organized streets and buildings in the open valley.

"What are all those red roofs?" she asks.

"That's the university campus. Those are tiles made of terra-cotta to give them an Italian flavor. Unnecessary feature in my opinion."

"It looks nice. And those tall yellow buildings to the right?"

"William's Village. The first student dorms outside campus." He unzips his backpack and takes out a couple of brown bags.

Jonathan's lunch reminds Hadeel of a childhood friend in elementary school who used to bring her own lunch from home, instead of eating the school's free lavish hot meals. Just like her friend's, this lunch consists of a cold cheese sandwich, fresh green pepper, vegetable juice and a dill pickle. Hadeel wishes he'd included fried potatoes instead of chips.

"Did Amal live here because of you?" She munches on the Swiss cheese sandwich.

"No. As a matter of fact I live here because of her." Jonathan snaps open the lid on his juice can. "She spent a vacation here and decided she couldn't live away from these mountains, they reminded her of Lebanon. At that time, I had just received a doctorate in Islamic History from Duke University. I applied for a job at the university here and fortunately got it. Amal and I never separated after that."

"Where did you two meet?"

"In Irvington, New York. Amal and I happened to be in the same tour group visiting Washington Irving's home. The tour began at the Washington Irving monument by the entrance of the estate. I noticed her kneeling at Boabdil's sculpture, wiping her tears. Later I learned that Boabdil was a favorite historic figure of her father's, your grandfather. But during the tour I was intrigued at the sight of a young woman, mourning someone from hundreds of years ago. I kept an eye on her. At the end of the tour, I saw her lingering in front of Irving's veranda facing the Hudson River. I followed her until she sat on a bench facing the Tappan Zee. I took a seat next to her. That's how we met." His face radiating with color as he told the story, perhaps for the hundredth time, Hadeel thinks, smiling at him.

"Have you read Irving's book, *Tales of Alhambra*?" he asks.

Hadeel shakes her head no. "How did she die?"

Jonathan crushes the juice can in his hand, then places it in the brown bag. He looks away and says, "She joined a protest in Denver in support of Muslim Americans. A man, probably a racist, rammed his vehicle into the group. Many got injured. She got killed."

"*Ya Allah!*" Hadeel gasps.

"I didn't join her that day, I had a faculty meeting." He

fiercely wipes his mouth with a paper napkin before burying it inside the brown bag.

Hadeel realizes for the first time that she and Jonathan have something in common. They share the loss of someone they both loved dearly. Her loss began twenty years ago, his loss just started.

"Did they catch the person who did it?"

"He's in jail. He claims it was an accident." Jonathan waves his hand helplessly.

"I'm sorry," Hadeel says sincerely. How terrible it must be to lose a loved one so unexpectedly. How painful to remember the last moments before they disappear from your life forever. She thinks of Munira and remembers the story about Ydaida calling Amal's name before she died. Tears suddenly fall from Hadeel's eyes. "I'm really sorry," she says, gasping for air.

Jonathan is startled by her unexpected reaction. He searches around him, pulls a napkin out of the bag and hands it to her, averting his eyes. "Me too."

She wipes her tears, wondering who she was really feeling sorry for. Herself? Jonathan? Or Amal? Or this precarious and unpredictable life? She hands him what's left of her lunch and watches him stash it in the backpack.

Jonathan points at a far dome-shaped rock on top of a mountain opposite them. She can see hikers on top of it. They look like black birds hopping around. "That over there is Saddle Rock. It will take us an hour to get there, and a couple of hours to come back. I don't think there's time to do it today."

Relieved, Hadeel exhales. "I agree."

They make sure they remove everything left of their lunch and get ready for the hike back. Hadeel follows Jonathan's footsteps cautiously downhill. The hike is easier now but dangerously slippery over loose dirt and gravel. She's grateful for these shoes he insisted on buying; her sandals would have been disastrous.

Jonathan slows down over a flat rock at the bottom of a trail and waits for her to approach. "Tell me about yourself."

She almost bumps into him. "Me?"

"Did you graduate from college?" "I did, two years ago."

"What was your major?"

She swallows the last drop of water in the plastic bottle. "I studied Arabic Literature the first year, then transferred to English Literature," she says remembering the vehement arguments between her and her father in the aftermath.

Jonathan looks surprised. "Why did you decide against Arabic literature?"

Hadeel takes a deep breath. "This is going to sound strange, but Arabic literature was difficult and alien to me. It's a long story." She doesn't want to go into details of how she enjoyed novels by nineteenth century female authors like Jane Austen and the Bronte sisters more than the didactic Arabic literature of that era. She shudders thinking of the 1914 Arabic novel *Zainab* by Egyptian author Muhammad Haykal. The book is a clear testament of how women under old traditions and family obligations were deprived of all rights while men were allowed every possible pleasure in the world. The novel made her feel malaise for days. She refused to think it applied to her, until the day all her belongings were taken away from her by her own parents.

"Do you work?" Jonathan asks her.

"No. I mean I did. Now I don't."

"So what do you do then with your time?"

"Nothing." Hadeel replies curtly. She doesn't want to mention her Online Master's degree. What if he asks about the title of her thesis?

"What kind of work did you do before you quit?"

"I taught English in a high school for a year before I resigned. My father wanted me to teach. I didn't like teaching that level. I hated the ringing of the bell after each period."

Jonathan nods with apprehension then halts in front of a steep muddy track searching for a safe path around it. "It's nice to be able to take time off for a while. Not many people are that lucky."

"Lucky?"

"Some parents in this country help their kids take a break after graduating. They travel and ponder the kind of profession they want to pursue. It costs a lot of money, not everyone can afford it."

"I knew what I wanted to do but my father wouldn't let me." Hadeel realizes her voice came out more forcefully than she intended. Jonathan stops. She bumps into him. "Sorry."

"Hadeel, listen. Let's clear things up. You may know nothing about me, but I know a lot about you, your father, and your culture. Amal and I were married for twenty years. Twenty years. We shared everything in our lives.

She wrote to you regularly, except for the last year, when she got busy with problems at work. She was sad you never wrote back."

Taken by surprise at Jonathan's outburst, Hadeel remains silent. She wonders about the letters he keeps mentioning and wonders why she never received them. Images of her father tearing them to pieces before throwing them in the trash offer a possibility.

Jonathan continues in a gentler tone, "My point is, you don't know much about your aunt. If you're really leaving in a couple of days, which I'm hoping you'll change your mind about, there's a lot for you to do."

"Actually, I might leave earlier."

"Then there's no time to waste. I think you should take a look at a few things in her office that might have a family value for you. There's also a legal issue that I need to discuss with you at home." He hustles down the path toward the parking area.

Flustered, Hadeel follows, uncertain how to respond to that. One thing she is certain about: she does not want to step inside Amal's home. It would definitely be against her parents' wishes, and most probably Munira's as well. Except for visiting Amal's grave, and asking Jonathan to send Amal's body home, Munira did not mention visiting Jonathan's home, alone.

Chapter Nine

AMAL'S JOURNAL

You're sixteen years old today, Hadeel. Happy birthday! I called Munira this morning hoping to talk to you but she told me your parents took you to the beach. That was your wish for a birthday gift, she said. I hope you had a lovely time and found unique seashells. Munira also told me that Rashid, your father, is not happy about you writing to me. That's alright. I will keep writing to you. Hopefully, one day he'll change his mind and let us meet again.

Whenever I think of you Hadeel, I think of the good old days. One special day stands out in my memory with my father, your grandpa. I'm sure nobody ever told you about that day. The day I graduated from Kuwait University. Father had a big surprise for me. He announced he was taking me on a trip with him to Spain. To my mother's utter consternation, he refused to take anyone else along. Munira and Rashid seethed with envy. "Go to university," Father told them, "and I'll give you a bigger gift than that." He explained that since my degree was in History, he wanted to introduce me to his favorite historical area, Alhambra, in Granada, the seat of Muslim civilization for eight hundred years, where Muslims passed the treasures of knowledge and science to Europe during the Dark ages.

See, against Yuba's inclinations, Munira and Rashid had only pursued two-year college diplomas instead of university education. After her college schooling, Munira preferred to stay at home doing house chores and fasting every Monday and Thursday with Ydaida. Your father, Rashid, joined military school. Baba was so disappointed. "If your goal is to hold a weapon in your hand, I'd rather it's a pen than a gun," he told Rashid. Fifteen years later, father's words were proven accurate when the Kuwaiti army scattered like a flock of birds at the first cannon shot by the Iraqis. The letters and articles written by Kuwaitis during the Iraqi occupation proved more powerful in getting help from the outside world, and eventually liberating the country.

The trip with my father to Spain was enlightening to say the least. It was like taking a blind girl to a doctor, restoring her sight, and handing her a colorful atlas of the world. We visited historical places he seemed to have read much about. His words while we were touring Europe replay often in my mind and in my dreams, "Here's your world, and here's theirs. Here's their present, and there's your past. They're moving ahead so fast; you better catch up or it will be too late. So what are you going to do? What are your plans for the future?" My head spun as I tried to understand and answer his questions.

After a week of traveling and learning I found out that Yuba's main purpose of taking me on that trip was not merely to introduce me to Granada and teach me a history lesson. That story was only a ploy to distract the family from the real reason, which remained a secret between us, until now. That deal, Hadeel, remained a secret to this day. You will be the only one in the family to know it. It will be up to you, after I pass away, to decide what to do with it. You can tell your family or keep it private as I have. It is not a world-shattering secret. It's a family token of love and freedom. Of being a human entitled to freedom and privacy. I hope you'll understand.

It was on the evening we boarded a plane for our next stop to Málaga, Spain, when Baba surprised me with another announcement. "Tomorrow, I'm going to tell you something that I'm hoping you can keep a secret between us."

"A secret from whom?" I asked.

"From everyone. Your mother, sister, and brothers, and especially Rashid."

Curiosity took the better of me. I stared at him wondering if he was about to introduce me to a private life, another wife and a family that he kept a secret. He must have noticed my agitation and anxiety because he patted my hand and smiled. "Don't worry, you'll like it."

The driver, who picked us up at the airport, seemed to know Yuba well. They exchanged a friendly chat while we drove along the ocean to an antiquated neighborhood. We parked in the middle of a courtyard surrounded by stone walls and cobblestone alleys. I stepped out of the car to find myself facing a marble fountain flowing with bubbling water. The fragrance of jasmine, the "soul dissolving scent," as Percy Shelley once described it, was intoxicating. Mixed with jasmine was the scent of orange blossoms carried by the breeze from the sea.

"Come!" Yuba tugged me toward a building with an arched green door. He looked different without his headdress. His bald head shone beneath the light bulb over the door, his blue scarf came loose and uncovered his sagging neck. From his briefcase he produced a ring of keys. He selected one to open the door and clicked a switch which shed light over an ancient curved stairway. "At my old age I would have loved an elevator, but such a convenience would ruin the historical nature of the building."

We pulled our suitcases step by step over the narrow concrete stairway. By the time we arrived on the third-floor landing, father was utterly out of breath. I fussed about his health but he hushed me. "Don't worry. There are more important things than my health, *ya binti*." He selected a smaller key from the ring in his hand and opened an apartment door.

It was like stepping into a magic box. Facing the main door, through the glass doors of a balcony, crashing waves of the blue Mediterranean welcomed us. I ran to it; sparkling white beaches were underneath us. I stood mesmerized, the expanse of the ocean ahead made me wonder what lay beyond its horizon.

"Don't you want to see the rest of the place?" Yuba asked. He perched on the orange-flowered sofa that faced the balcony.

"Of course," I said. "Can I go around?"

He nodded. Closing his eyes, he rested his head on the back of the couch.

The living room looked like a doll house compared to Kuwaiti homes I was used to. Books were piled everywhere, on side tables, wooden chairs, and built-in bookshelves. There was one bedroom and an old-fashioned bathroom with a tub. The small kitchen had a brown porcelain sink and colorful blue tiles on the counters. Surrounding the attached eating area were several musical instruments. A couple of *ouds* and a guitar hung on the wall by the round dining table. An ancient tambourine rested on a chair. I lifted one of the *ouds* and wiped a film of dust off its surface with the palm of my hand. The shiny wood revealed its beautiful Arabian ornamentation. I itched to pluck the strings but didn't want to disturb Baba. It seemed he needed the rest after the effort of climbing the stairs.

Skipping back to the balcony, I quietly opened the glass doors and stepped outside. I lifted my face, closed my eyes, and tried to distinguish the scores of different sounds of the sea waves, approaching, crashing, then withdrawing. When the sun began setting, I decided to wake my father up. Before I touched his shoulder, he flung his eyes open.

"Do you like this little place?"

"I love it! I love it!" I repeated, twirling in circles.

"Good." He sat up on the couch. "It's yours."

"What are you saying?" I dropped at his feet.

"I'll explain later," he said. "But now let's have dinner at my favorite dining place."

The ancient cafe was a short stroll from the apartment. The low ceiling with wooden beams looked like places I'd seen in movies. There were worn wooden tables and chairs crowded together making it difficult to move in between. Busy waiters and talkative customers spoke rapid Spanish. On the way to our table a few patrons recognized my father. Some stood to greet him or squeeze his shoulders. Father replied in Spanish and made them laugh.

Once we sat down, a waiter showed up at our table. That was when I had the biggest shock of my life, and my eyes grew blurry. Baba ordered a glass of wine!

"Yuba," I exclaimed. "*Haram*!"

His white eyebrows lifted over his twinkling black eyes. "Why wait till we die and go to Paradise to enjoy wine? Whatever is *halal* in Paradise can be *halal* now. Use logic Amal, you're a smart girl. Who said it's *haram* anyway, eh? Those *hadeeths* were added later by men who couldn't hold their liquor."

He kept talking. I kept getting more confused. Father faded before my eyes and got replaced by a stranger. A stranger with twinkling eyes speaking heretical words. I fought tears and the fear that my beloved father would end up in the fire of Hell.

"Is this the secret you want me to keep?" I asked, nauseated by the smell of alcohol.

"No, no. Don't be stupid." He waved his hand irritably. The Spanish waiter approached and father ordered food for both of us. When the waiter left, he pointed at the glass of wine and said, "Forget about this for a minute, can you?"

I shook my head no. How could I forget when it was right in front of my eyes? Its fermenting smell fogged my mind. My head spun as if I was the one drinking. I had been taught that alcohol was forbidden and those who partake in it would be damned forever. And now I was sure that the person I loved most in the world was going straight to Hell. Did it mean he would be tortured forever? Did it mean I would never see him in the after-life? All my childhood fears came alive at that moment. I found myself on the verge of sobbing.

"Yuba, please. I love you so much. How can you do this?"

His usual sunny features turned grim. A vein in his forehead spread all the way up his bare scalp. "I'm sorry, Amal. It didn't occur to me how shocking this would be for you." He waved again to the waiter and asked him to remove the wine from the table. Then to me, he said, "Forgive me, *ya binti*."

I looked away, astounded that this old patriarch was asking forgiveness from his young daughter.

"I will not tell anyone about it," I muttered earnestly.

A smile cheered his face again. "It doesn't matter. This is not important. Your reaction, however, is making me realize we have much to discuss to understand each other. I have a lot to tell you. But first, tell me about your goals and dreams. Have you decided about work?"

I looked at him blankly, my mind still busy sorting things out, trying to bring my familiar father, the one I've known all my life, back to the table. A sudden commotion at the entrance of the restaurant disrupted our conversation. A group of men burst in, chatting loudly. Three of them, still in their jackets and scarves, noticed my father. By the time Yuba saw them and stood to greet them, they were all over him, dragging him toward the small stage. Stunned, I watched my new father developing right in front of my eyes.

They seated him on a stool on the stage and got their instruments, a guitar, a flute, and drums. Father smiled at me, shaking his head left and right. Then he shuffled through the pages of a notebook on the music stand. After a few trial notes from their instruments, the musicians began playing. Father turned his head away from the microphone, cleared his voice and on cue sang in a pleasant clear voice. A voice full of pathos, history, and soul. He was singing a beautiful rendition of Fairuz's famous song, written by Khalil Gibran: "Give me the flute and sing, for singing is the core of existence."

I squirmed in my seat and rubbed my eyes. I thought I was dreaming. Here was my seventy-seven-year-old father, singing on a stage and cheered by fans in a Spanish cafe. How was this possible? Who was this man whom I thought I'd known all my life?

Hours later, we strolled back to the apartment. Father laughed and chatted, happier than I'd ever seen him. I asked him why he never sang at home. He told me that a long time ago, when we were still children, my mother begged him not to. "It's *haram* to make music with stringed instruments. Please, don't embarrass me and my family." He mimicked the way she'd said it. "So I didn't. I respected her feelings since she's a descendant of a well-known family of Wahhabi roots. I never performed in front of you children, or anyone else in the family." He stopped, turned to face me and grabbed my arm with his hand. "Don't let anyone stop you from doing something you believe in, Amal. Never. If your passion doesn't harm anyone, follow it. Enjoy it, be proud of it."

It was midnight. We were standing in the middle of the courtyard by the fountain, surrounded by decorative lights that cast a reddish glow on our faces. "That apartment up there," Father pointed, "is your graduation present. When you want to escape from life's troubles come and enjoy the peace here. I've done that for decades."

I peered at the building and its balconies decorated with baskets of flowers. I drew a deep breath thinking of the gorgeous sea views from its balcony. Before I could thank him, he explained that he wanted to register the apartment in my name the next day. He did not want anybody to know, especially Rashid. "If your brothers find out, they can claim the right to it for themselves after I die. They will be backed by Islamic law. But under Spanish law it will be yours. Tomorrow we'll meet an attorney to transfer ownership. I want you to have it, Amal. You are the only child of mine who will appreciate this apartment. It's been my paradise on earth." He chuckled before he added, "Who knows? It might be the only paradise I'll ever know."

My soul was soaring above the palm trees surrounding the fountain. I was twenty-one, about to start an exciting new future. My father was offering me a magical place full of 'soul-dissolving' views and books and music. My world at home under the strict rules of Ydaida and Rashid already felt like the past. When I hugged him and buried my face in his shoulder, his pointed bones reminded me with sadness of the fragility and uncertainty of life.

During the next few days, we met with lawyers and local officials to transfer my father's treasure to me. Once the legal work was complete, we took off for Alhambra. On the train, Father handed me an ancient copy of the *The Alhambra.* "The best ever written about the place," he explained. "Take care of it, Amal! It's a rare copy I purchased a long time ago from a bookshop in London."

I checked the name of the author, Washington Irving. I later learned that he was the first international American author. His name carried with it the birth of the nation. A nation that received the Torch of Liberty from a country that lit the path to democracy after a bloody revolution. I promised Yuba to cherish it and keep the book in the family.

Our visit to Granada made the grandeur of the Muslim civilization I read about in books, real. Baba had an interesting story to tell me in every corner of the enchanting palace. I was spellbound by the discovery of new facets in my father's personality. Everyone who knew him, close or distant, had revered him as a knowledgeable, wise man. But it's only when you get to know him intimately that you realize the depth of his passion for history, music, and humanity.

These discoveries of my father had laid the path to my future. My new relationship with him, bolstered by the literature of Washington Irving, provided me with a whole new colorful perspective on life and the world.

Chapter Ten

A twinge of guilt makes Hadeel stumble over the floor mat in front of the main door of Jonathan's home. Her parents, as well as Aunt Munira, would be very upset at her walking into a man's house alone. Maybe she should apologize to him, turn around, and leave? But how can she refuse a request from a grieving man? Even if he's the same infidel who seduced her aunt and stashed her away from her family and country. She shakes her head and dismisses the idea. The trip with him to the mountains has softened her heart toward him. In a peculiar way, he has become part of her world, her family even.

A familiar fragrance meets her at the entrance. She takes another step, still uncertain if she's ready to venture into this forbidden place, the one her parents were adamant in keeping a secret from her. What was their real reason? Did they believe it's *haram*? Or were they worried Hadeel would be tempted to follow her aunt's example? Leave home and marry without their permission? Either way, at this moment, it is clear all their efforts were futile.

She's at the threshold of Amal's world. Less than two years ago she almost left home on a similar path.

Jonathan is still waiting patiently by the door, staring down at his boots.

"*Bismillah*," Hadeel mutters, looking around. Just like in a computer game, she scans the place for clues to connect the pieces and solve the puzzle.

"You don't have to take off your shoes," Jonathan is saying.

"Oh, yes I do," Hadeel says, suddenly smelling the horse manure she stepped into in the mountains. She loosens the shoe laces and slips out of them, keeping her socks on.

The narrow entry foyer opens to a spacious living room with a large fireplace in the center. A huge oil painting, the same size as the fireplace, hangs over the mantelpiece. There are people in the painting dressed in old-fashioned clothes. The spotted bronze frame adds to the feel of antiquity of the scene. The leather chairs and couches around the hearth show signs of wear but look comfortable. A colorful Navajo woven rug leads to patio doors which open onto a garden. Natural light streams into the living room from skylight windows.

"Please come in. Amal's office is that way." Jonathan points to a long hallway on the right.

Instead, Hadeel shuffles towards the patio. "Is that a fountain?"

"Yes. You can take a look outside first if you like." He slides the glass doors open for her. "I've neglected the garden since Amal left. This is the time of year when she would spend hours nurturing her roses."

Hadeel steps out and finds a pair of clogs by the door.

She slips her feet into them, wondering if they were Amal's. She should let her aunt lead the way, Hadeel thinks, and heads toward the rose bushes behind the water-fountain. Some of the bushes have tiny buds at the tips of green stems already. She turns to Jonathan. "When do the roses bloom?"

He's standing by the patio doors, hands in his pockets, as if there is an invisible barrier preventing him from joining her. "In a couple of weeks. Sometime in May."

"Our roses only bloom in winter," she tells him. "They never come back after the summer heat in Kuwait."

"Luckily these tea-roses have survived the freeze of many winters. The rest," he points at tall bushes in the back by a wooden fence, "are Canadian roses. They're hardy. Excuse me," he says at the sound of a phone ringing in the house.

Mohammady, the name people at home call the fragrant tea-roses. Hadeel's mother is a big fan of them without having to soil her hands planting them. She pesters the gardener to plant them, nourish them, and cover them with gauzy fabric to shade them from the sun so they'll return the next year. They never do. The dust storms and searing dry heat of Kuwait's summers burns them down to the roots. Every winter, the gardener introduces new exotic roses with different names. But, perhaps because they're always different, her mother shows no attachment to them. After the initial introduction she stoops to catch their fragrance when passing by them on her way to her car. Here, when they bloom, the roses must look like old friends that have come back for their annual visit.

Hadeel fills her lungs with fresh air. Yes the garden is neglected yet it's buzzing with life. Bees and birds flutter around checking the early flowers and bushes. What a gorgeous sanctuary. She saunters toward the fountain. Water from the recent rain has collected in the bottom, reflecting puffy white clouds in the otherwise clear blue sky. The outside rim of the fountain is made of mosaic blue and white tile, the interior rim is navy blue with white tiny stars.

A bench under a window facing the fountain invites Hadeel to rest. She relishes the warmth of the stone seat; it must have soaked up the sun's heat all morning. Hadeel pats the bench in a silent thank you and leans back to take in the scene. She imagines Amal strolling between the rose bushes, bending to trim one and sniff another. Perhaps she looks back at Hadeel with a smile? Hadeel smiles back.

A red-breasted bird hops down onto the lowest branch of a bush nearby. Its head moves swiftly sideways, examining Hadeel from different angles. It reminds her of her favorite book she read as a teenager. *The Secret Garden.* Just a couple of days ago she was telling Munira about it in London when a robin hopped near their bench in Hyde Park. This one can't be a robin though, since it's smaller in size and gray in color. It's whistling as if asking a question. Is it asking her about Amal? Wondering where she is? Hadeel snaps several photos of the bird and the fountain with her phone for her aunt. *Ya Allah, Munira, I wish you were here to see this. To see your sister's sanctuary and perform a couple of prayers for her.*

"I made you a cup of tea." Jonathan walks towards her. "It's in Amal's office. I have to make some phone calls, then I'll join you to discuss a few things."

Hadeel grudgingly follows him. He must be anxious for her to start the loathsome task.

She might as well get it done and over with. Hopefully it won't take more than an hour. The floor creaks under their feet in the dark narrow hallway. Jonathan stops at an open door of a well-lit room and ushers her in. Hadeel draws in a deep breath and steps inside. *Bismillah*. She searches for the source of the light and finds a set of long, wooden-framed skylights in the ceiling, filling the spacious room with natural light. Built-in bookcases are stacked with tomes and journals on both sides of a rectangular window with garden views. Jonathan points to a roll-top desk in the far-right corner. "She kept personal notebooks and family items there. Take your time. Everything in this room was hers." He hesitates before he adds, "Now it's yours."

Hadeel shoots him a surprised look. He avoids her eyes and retreats. He has just dropped a heavy burden on her shoulders, a burden she did not expect and does not want. She lets out a sigh, shakes her head and moves to the middle of the room. That familiar jasmine fragrance is so potent she can lift her finger and touch it. How could Amal leave home and family to live in this faraway lonely place no matter how beautiful it is? What did Jonathan mean, "everything in this room is now yours?" She doesn't need things, she has plenty. What Hadeel really needs is love. The warmth of love from someone she can trust. Is there really love? Or is it only fiction? Was Jonathan's love for Amal real? How about Raj's love for her?

A beam of sunlight filters through the west window revealing tiny flecks floating in the air. The invisible particles eternally hanging around us, she thinks. What else is there that we're not aware of? Hadeel's eyes wander around. A set of old eyes from a large photo on the wall gazes at her. They are the eyes of an old bald man in a suit and a tie. He's seated on a stool on a stage, playing the *oud*. She draws closer. It's a black and white photograph enlarged on canvas. Could that be her grandfather? She draws nearer. The love and affection in his eyes cannot be for anyone but Amal. When Hadeel once asked Munira why Amal was her grandfather's favorite, Munira said, "I don't know. Maybe because they were both strong-headed." She said it as if being strong-headed was a negative thing.

It's the first time Hadeel has seen her grandfather in Western attire. In all family photos of him he wore traditional Kuwaiti clothes, white head-dress, and dishdasha. On both sides of the photograph are familiar artifacts: a string of ancient worry beads, an old smoking pipe, a traditional silver dagger with its ornate scabbard with arabesque designs carved in ivory. Hadeel has seen similar objects in her father's office which he had mentioned belonged to his father. She doesn't need any of them. At her age, family relics fail to bring her solace. They don't mean anything more than "ancient." She returns her gaze to her grandfather. He didn't know her, never will. Would he have given her the same love he lavished on Amal? Even though Hadeel is not as smart or as strong-headed?

A white porcelain plate with cookies sits next to a steaming cup of green tea that Jonathan left for her on the desk. Hadeel brings a cookie close to her nose, sniffs it before she takes a bite. The buttery sweet taste of the English biscuit spreads in her mouth. Must be Amal's favorites.

Hadeel savors the taste as she slumps down on the swivel desk chair. How long can she keep procrastinating the task pushed upon her? Why not resist for the first time in her life? She can walk out and tell Jonathan she's done and doesn't need any of it. "You can now give it all away." Or, simply say, "Sorry, I don't want to do this. It's painful."

A silver laptop sits still on the desk. She lifts its thin lid only to find it dead, like its owner. The wires which can bring it to life are nowhere in sight. Jonathan must have forgotten to charge it. Her hand hits a pendant with a key dangling from the key-lock of the desk's rolled top. It's the figure of a boy with a mischievous smile. He's wearing pajamas and a royal night cap, swinging from a tree branch in the middle of a colorful jungle. Hadeel wonders why she thought of the word "jungle" even though the pendant does not show it. Then a sudden recognition. It's from a children's book Amal read to her twenty years ago. It was one of their favorites about a boy, grounded for being mischievous, who lets his imagination take him on an adventure. Hadeel now recalls the laughter she and Amal shared while reading the book to each other, over and over again.

Next to the dead laptop, sits a stack of personal journals looking forlorn, as if mourning their owner. Hadeel lifts them in both hands, weighing the history hidden in their folds before she places them on her lap. Their weight on her thighs is bothersome. Who keeps journals in the age of computers? She puts them back on the desk and lifts the top one. Encased in cracked brown old leather Hadeel wonders if it belonged to her grandfather.

Inside the folds of its pages are old letters addressed to Amal from Aunt Munira. Hadeel gasps. Munira never mentioned writing to Amal after she left home. Would she be prying if she read them? But Jonathan did say everything in the room is hers now. She picks a letter from the middle, pulls it out of its faded envelope. The paper releases an odor of years gone by.

Amal, I'm shocked at your decision never to come back home! Are you sure of what you're doing? Please come back. Come back! You know you can. It's not easy to start a new life in a foreign country. Isn't it hideous being away from everyone and everything you've known since childhood? New friends can never replace family. Don't you know?

Mother misses you most and prays every day that you will return soon. I've kept your secret, even though I worry that I'm being a bad person for helping you in your folly. That's how I see what you're doing. Sometimes we have *to sacrifice our desires for more important things in life, like family and religion. What's more important to you? Happiness in this life? Or the everlasting one in Paradise? The love you seek is* haram, *forbidden. Come back to your senses before it's too late!!*

A taste of blood in Hadeel's mouth makes her realize she's been biting her lip too hard. She sucks in a breath and re-reads Munira's words, "We have to sacrifice our desires for family and religion." That concept has tormented Hadeel during her relationship with Raj. Should she have sacrificed her family for him? A stranger from a different country? To this day the question makes her restless and guilty for another reason. A question which has been torturing her since she promised her parents to end her relationship with him. Did she sacrifice her love for Raj because of family obligation or for the comfort and luxury of living at home? The lifestyle which she knew Raj could not afford. Her mother's words of living in destitution with Raj have made a deep impression on her awareness of reality. Does that make her a martyr, or a selfish girl?

Hadeel wipes perspiration from her forehead and tucks the letters back in its folder. How about Aunt Munira? Did she sacrifice love for family obligations? Is that why she wrote with authority and confidence? And why do parents assume they have the right to bring children to the world and decide everything for them? Does it ever occur to them that their children have their own feelings and desires, which sometimes are totally different from theirs? "Your children are not your children," words of Khalil Gibran that her mother forbids her to sing at home.

A ding from her cell phone interrupts Hadeel's thoughts. She pulls her phone from her pocket.

"Why didn't you text your father?" her mother texted.

Hadeel clicks on the call button. "Yumma! I will. But please tell me first, why is Nawaf's mother in jail?"

Instead of answering her question her Mother blurts out, "Text your father! Now! He's waiting for you."

"Is she still in prison?"

"Yes. Can't explain right now. I just arrived at my friend's house. Text your father. Now!"

"Not before you tell me what happened!"

Her mother sighs then blurts out in a hushed voice, "She beat up her Filipino maid, badly. I heard she tore out one of the maid's ears, I don't know the details. Somebody at the hospital called the Philippine Embassy. They got a lawyer. They might sue for millions. So your cousin is in a hurry to marry you before you hear what happened and change your mind." Her voice now gets louder. "Your brilliant father is taking his nephew's side and is asking me not to tell you what happened. He doesn't care what Nawaf's mother did to the maid. He wants the marriage to take place as soon as possible. Of course, now, without your presence, he needs proof of your approval for *katb-el-kitab* to show the Imam."

"I will not give it!" Hadeel yells.

"Text him and tell him yourself. My friend is here, I have to go."

Hadeel's heart thumps against her chest. Yumma has been adamant about her marrying Nawaf, even more than Yuba. It was all she talked about ever since that night when she discovered Hadeel's plan to marry Raj. That awful night when Hadeel's life turned from blissful to miserable.

That night, Hadeel was supposed to meet Raj at Kuwait International Airport and drive him to her father's *diwan-iya*. When her mother walked into Hadeel's room and found her ready to leave the house she demanded to know where Hadeel was going. Hadeel had to tell her the truth. She begged her mother's approval and support.

"You must be out of your mind!" her mother breathed out the words. "A Pakistani? Out of all the Arab nationalities in the world you pick a poor Pakistani? After all we've done for you, is that how you reward us? Make people think you fell in love with our cook or chauffeur?"

Hadeel froze at her mother's racist remarks. What happened to her kind, gentle mother? What happened to the Prophet's words that "no human is better than any other?" Are his words meant to remain in books? Never practiced?

Her mother's tirade didn't stop. "And how do you think you can live alone with this, this poor man? You who are so dependent, irresponsible, weak, and emotional!"

Stung by her mother's words Hadeel could only offer tears for an answer. True, she had always been dependent on her parents, never dared out of their nest. She never had to lift a finger to do housework, not even fry an egg. When she wanted things done all she had to do was push a button and maids would appear at her door. Raj was only recently appointed associate professor in a small college in England. He warned her their life might be rough at the beginning on his small salary which he shared with his family in Pakistan.

"A Pakistani? Where did you find him?"

"He's a university professor!" Hadeel hesitated before adding, "and he loves me."

"He doesn't love you. He loves your money!" Those were the most painful words her mother ever uttered.

Hadeel could have explained why she had no doubt about Raj's love for her. That when he proposed he thought she was a poor bedouin, and a bidoon without a citizenship. She could have proven his love for her by telling her mother about his dream of her car accident the same day it happened. She could have told her how Raj believed she was smart, and how they shared a passion for literature and Islam. But had she told her mother all that, Yumma would have found a way to belittle and denigrate it all to nothing.

"Open your eyes to reality!" Yumma was saying. "Stupid girl!"

"He's a Muslim!" Hadeel exclaimed. "If he or his family need help, what's wrong with helping a Muslim family?"

"If that's the reason, then we can send him charity. But not as your husband, my stupid, stupid girl!"

"You can keep your money! He'll still love me!" Hadeel cried. That's when her father walked into the room and asked what was going on. When her mother explained he demanded her car keys, mobile, and computer. The internet was soon disconnected.

Hadeel never went to the airport, never found out if Raj managed to see her father. She couldn't even apologize. A month later, when she promised not to contact Raj again, her mother returned her mobile. Hadeel found emails from him asking if she was safe. She was too ashamed to answer. Too embarrassed to explain. Besides, she had promised her parents never to contact him as a condition to get her cell, her car, and computer back. Her mother made her take an oath on the Quran. Her father accepted Nawaf's proposal to marry her.

Now Yumma is willing to help Hadeel reject the marriage. Why? Is it just a matter of reputation? Many people mistreat their house workers in Kuwait, Nawaf's mother won't be the first one. Or are there other reasons she's not telling Hadeel about yet? How will Yumma react when she happens upon the selfie Amina took of her at the library without the hijab? Would she flip back to forcing her to marry Nawaf? She must go back home as soon as possible.

Hadeel strides around Amal's office several times before she stops at one of the bookcases. Before she studies the books, she checks her phone for messages from Munira. She said she'd check on her return ticket but never got back to her. She texts her again and asks if she has heard about Nawaf's mother. But all she gets back is a notification that Munira's mobile is switched off or out of reach.

Hadeel places her cell inside her pocket and scrolls over books and artifacts on the shelves of the bookcase. Two shelves are assigned to literary journals. Each journal has a yellow post-it on its spine with handwritten notes. Hadeel reads the notes randomly: *My paper on W. Irving's letters to his favorite niece, p.73*. Another explains: *My paper on Irving's favorite childhood books, p.135*. And the next: *Irving's friendship with Charles Dickens, p.98*. Hadeel pulls that journal out: she must keep it to read later. She notices that her aunt used her maiden name in all published papers, Amal Hamdeen.

A sticker on a worn-out journal reads: *W. Irving's relationship with Mary Wollstonecraft Shelley*. "Mary Shelley?" Hadeel reads aloud. "This is definitely for keeps." A shade of a smile manages to creep onto Hadeel's somber face as she imagines her aunt's name listed in the bibliography of Hadeel's own future paper. She places the journals next to her purse and goes back to the bookshelf with the literary journals.

"Raj!" Hadeel exclaims as she reads a post-it on the next journal: *My paper on Thalaba p. 57.* Eager to make sure it's the same Thalaba that Raj has frequently urged Hadeel to read, she pulls out the journal and opens it to page 57. Sure enough, it's *Thalaba the Destroyer* by Robert Southey, the poem Hadeel never took the time to read. She sits on the floor and reads:

Thalaba: Fearless and Forgiving

By

Amal H. Hamdeen

Thalaba the Destroyer is an epic poem by the British poet laureate Robert Southey (1774-1843). At its publication in 1801, John Newman, the Catholic Cardinal at the time, described it as the most "morally sublime" poem ever written in the English language. Henceforth, the poem received mixed reviews ranging from "stunning" to "a monument of vile." However, it was a favorite poem of renowned Romantic poets, one of whom was Percy Bysshe Shelley (1792–1822). According to Percy's wife Mary Wollstonecraft Shelley, the young poet used to clutch the manuscript to his heart and recite its verses on a daily basis.

Thalaba the Destroyer told the story of Thalaba, a teenage Arab boy, who was sought by a group of sorcerers to destroy him. By doing so they would put an end to a prophecy that predicted their own demise by Thalaba's race. The sorcerers had already managed to slaughter all of Thalaba's clan, including his mighty father, the Carrier of the Sword. Only Thalaba remained. Once he got hold of the sword, the prophecy claimed, it would bring the sorcerers' doom. Therefore, as long as Thalaba was alive, the prophecy remained a threat to their existence.

With courage and faith, Thalaba managed to escape the sorcerers' traps. At age sixteen Thalaba decided to seek the sorcerers, confront and destroy them to avenge his father. But his love for Oneiza, a young Bedouin girl, purifies his soul from anger and revenge. Instead, he managed to find his father's sword, get rid of its powers and free himself with forgiveness to be united with Oneiza, "*The loveliest of Arabian maidens she.*"

Nowadays, the poem is still discussed by literary scholars. Some explain Southey's thesis as the universal message embedded in Islam's teaching: the unity of Islam and Christianity. Some ponder Southey's extensive knowledge of Islam and Arab culture, without having physically been to Arabia. Others wonder if Southey's main character is fictitious or based on a person.

This paper attempts to answer the last question. Who was the original Thalaba? Therefore, the author of this paper will discuss links between Southey's Thalaba and an actual Islamic character named, Thalaba Ibn Abdulrahman. By analyzing verses and thematic elements in Southey's poem and comparing them with the original story, the paper seeks to prove the hypothesis that the historical Thalaba Ibn Abdulrahman was indeed the original person on which Southey built his character.

Who was Thalaba ibn Abdulrahman?

Ask any knowledgeable Muslim about the name Thalaba and the story of Thalaba ibn Abdulrahman will be invoked. Thalaba ibn Abdulrahman was an orphaned child born in the city of Medina during the time Prophet Mohammed took residency there. When Mohammed heard that Thalaba lost both his parents at birth, he adopted him. He cherished the child as the son he never had. Thalaba grew up learning the principles of Islam and how to be righteous, honest and honorable. He learned about good and evil, reward and punishment.

At the age of sixteen, during one of his errands for the prophet, Thalaba paused in front of a house with an open door. Inside, the story tells , at the end of a hallway, a gentle breeze fanned a curtain open, revealing a naked woman taking a bath. In Southey's epic, the following words seems to describe the exact scene:

"So as the Servant of the Prophet stood,
with sudden motion the night air
gently fanned his cheek." Southey, 1981

Having never seen a naked woman before, the original Thalaba lingered to watch the bathing woman a little longer than his conscience allowed. He finally withdrew but guilt and shame grew with every retreating step. At the end of the day, so much guilt gathered in his heart that he could not return to confront the Prophet. Young Thalaba ran away and took refuge in the desolate hills of Medina. He hid in a remote cave for days without food or sustenance.

In the meantime, missing the young lad, Prophet Mohammed asked some of his men to search for

Thalaba. When they found him, he was on the brink of death. With his last breaths, Thalaba was beseeching Allah and the Prophet for forgiveness. The men carried him to Mohammed where the young boy deliriously spoke of his sin and fear of spending the afterlife in Hell. The Prophet stroked Thalaba's burning forehead and assured him that Mohammed will ask Allah to forgive him. The lad took his last breath with his head resting on the Prophet's lap.

This original story of Thalaba, well documented in Muslim literature, is often recited for its moral lessons: stay away from sin and live free of fear. The suffering of Thalaba because of fear of the afterlife, which caused his untimely death, is poignant. It must have touched a sensitive spot in Southey's heart to compose his most beautiful poem. Readers of the epic will sense an ingrained wish by Southey throughout the poem to bring Thalaba back to life, fearless and assured of forgiveness. Only such powerful emotions could produce an epic of such magnitude.

Awed and breathless, Hadeel hugs the paper to her heart. She sways sideways, wishing there's a way she could show it to Raj. Is it possible he's already seen it? Would he have made the connection between her and Amal? It was only after he asked her to marry him that Hadeel revealed her real last name, telling him she was a Kuwaiti citizen, not a bedouin or bidoon, as she claimed. Shocked at the fact that she lied, Raj stopped talking to her for months. "Lying is the worst of sins," he texted her. "You should know that Hadeel, our Prophet Mohammed told us so." She begged him to forgive her and understand her motives to protect herself. At that time she had no plans to get involved with anyone in the group that she lied to.

After months of apologizing and asking for forgiveness, they resumed their relationship, and she accepted his marriage proposal.

Should she send him a message now? Tell him about the paper? What about the oath she made to her parents? The promise that she would never contact him again? The fear of breaking that promise has been a yoke around her neck ever since.

Chapter Eleven

A rap on the door jolts Hadeel up to her feet. She's still hugging Amal's journal to her heart, immersed in her own thoughts and world.

"Sorry to interrupt," Jonathan says, pale as an apparition.

"It's all right." Hadeel takes a step toward him.

"My mother just had an accident. I have to check on her. I'll be back soon." He turns around to leave.

"Wait! Is she okay?"

"She fell. She said she's okay, but I'd better make sure." He quickly disappears in the dim hallway.

His mother is still alive while his wife is dead? Hadeel frowns at her illogical thought. She should know better, that age makes no difference to death. "Death is always closer to us than a brow to an eye," Prophet Mohammed had said. How old is Jonathan's mother anyway?

She waits by the door and listens to the sounds Jonathan makes before leaving the house.

Then silence. An odd phenomenon in Hadeel's life at home, where there's always someone talking over the TV noise, or a video game blasting away. She looks down at the journal in her hands and determines to keep it. She'll decide later whether to send it to Raj or not. She hasn't contacted him for exactly one year, seven months and a few weeks. To receive something from her all of a sudden would seem like she's asking for another chance. Is that what she wants? And would he care at this point? Is he still available?

Hadeel adds the journal to the stack of books next to her purse on the floor and speculates about the coincidence that both Raj and Amal were captivated by *Thalaba the Destroyer*. Is it some kind of a sign? If she tells Raj, maybe he can explain. She sighs and walks out of the room.

On the way to the patio Hadeel pauses at the fireplace. The oil painting displays six people in old fashioned clothes standing around a fountain like the one in Amal's garden. The two women in the painting look familiar. Hadeel guesses one of them is Amal. Is that Jonathan standing to her right? But Amal seems more affectionate toward the man to her left. She actually has her arm around his shoulder. All six figures are looking back toward the artist as if they were caught by surprise. In the far-right corner of the painting sits a man on a bench with a small animal at his feet. The fountain seems to be the centerpiece in the painting as it is in the house. Is there a connection?

Outside, the sun is still high, tilting toward the west over mountain peaks that can be seen from the patio. It's warmer outside than it is inside the house. She halts in a sunny spot and relishes the warmth. "Spring is the time of year when it is summer in the sun and winter in the shade,"

Hadeel recites Charles Dickens' words. He once was her favorite British author before she read *Little Dorrit.* She loved the lengthy novel until a couple of pages toward the end where he slams Arabs with bad language. Shocked at the unexpected nasty remarks, Hadeel slammed the book shut. "How can a well-respected author be hateful and racist?" she asked her professor. "They're not necessarily his own thoughts," her professor argued in defense of Dickens. "He might have been repeating British society's views of Arabs at that time. Or," he added with sudden insight, "it could have been inserted later by someone else, an editor or a publisher." Hadeel got more irritated at her professor's placid reaction. How can he accept a distasteful comment about his own people from an outsider, even if he were his favorite author? But she herself wished the professor's latter explanation was true to keep reading Dickens. She now wishes she could discuss the subject with Amal. Why do Europeans hate Arabs and Muslims? And most of all, how can we separate the art from its artist?

The red-chested bird she noticed earlier plunges and alights on the fountain ledge. Hadeel waits under a tree and watches it wagging its tail up and down while it sings, as if dancing to its own tune. His song is long and more melodious than a robin's. Is he going to dig a hole in the ground, like in The Secret Garden? Show her a key that leads to her aunt's hidden secret? The bird hops to a higher branch and disappears.

Hadeel recalls giving her precious copy of *The Secret Garden* to her brother Abbadi years ago. She told him the boy in the novel reminded her of him because of the way he used a commanding language and tone when he talked to the house maids. Abbadi snatched the book from Hadeel's hand and, to her utter horror, he tore it to pieces, page by page. "Now you see how much I care about what your book says!" The shock at the sight of her favorite book being destroyed still shakes her. She should have known better. All three of her brothers hated reading. They believed it was a girlish thing.

She draws closer to the fountain. There are two rectangular tiles on the opposite ledge of the fountain she hasn't noticed earlier. With raised blue glazed Arabic script, one says: *La ghaliba illa Allah,* no victor but God. The other one, *There is no victor but the Truth.* Everyone in Hadeel's family assumed Amal relinquished her native language and religion. Some even claimed she'd converted to Christianity. But *La ghaliba illa Allah* offers a different reality.

Hadeel steps back and snaps a photo of the fountain and its crescent moon shining in the sun from the waterspout.

She rests on the bench under the window. The stone is now cold since the sun slid behind the mountains leaving the bench in the shade. *La ghaliba illa Allah*, No victor but God. Why did Amal choose those words for her fountain? Hadeel flicks away an insect hovering near her ear and leans back on the wall behind her. She could relax here all day long, facing this fountain, breathing fresh mountain air and listening to birds chirping, but she cannot hide from her thoughts, her past. Can one forget the whole world and its problems while hiding in this beautiful place? Can one overcome the longing for the company of family and friends?

Hadeel's cell announces a message. A text from Munira says: "I checked on changing your return ticket. The fee is exorbitant. You might as well buy a new ticket."

Entranced by her surroundings Hadeel wishes Munira were with her at the moment to see her sister's abode. But Munira only cares about the afterlife. Hadeel once dared ask her, "Who can prove that there's really a Hell or a Paradise in the afterlife?" Irate Munira insisted Hadeel should fast for a week to ask God's forgiveness for her blasphemy. "It's written hundreds of times in the Quran. Hadeel, how can you even ask such a question?"

Munira sends a new message. "Did you talk to him about sending Amal's body back?"

Startled, Hadeel stares at the words. She was hoping Munira would let go of this request after the grief over her sister subsides. After burying the Quran in her grave. How could receiving a dead body make any difference? How would Jonathan react to such a request?

"No," Hadeel writes back.

Munira texts right away. "You should ask, and soon. You don't have time."

"I don't want to ask," Hadeel writes.

The phone rings. "Just tell him I will pay for it. He won't mind if you tell him that!" Munira's voice is unbecomingly loud and agitated.

"Yes, he will mind!" Hadeel answers vehemently. "You don't know him. He loves her more than you ever did." She tries to calm down, surprised at her outburst. She takes a breath and waits for her aunt to say something, to reprimand her for her ill-manners. "Hello?"

Silence persists. Munira has terminated the call. Hadeel checks the screen on the phone. The battery signal is now on red, she hopes it's the reason the call ended. She calls Munira back. No answer.

Hadeel paces around the garden. This is the first time she ever snapped at her aunt, let alone belittled her love for her only sister. Munira has always been the model of goodness and righteousness. Hadeel never argued with her, always acquiesced to her wishes. What has just happened?

Doors slam and loud footsteps from inside the house force Hadeel to shrug off thoughts of Munira's call. She sees Jonathan through the glass patio doors. He's grim faced and hunched over. Her heart aches with sadness.

Jonathan steps out into the patio, carrying a large brown bag. "Hi," he says when he spots her walking toward him.

"Is your mother all right?"

He places the bag on the patio table. "Yes. She said she'd like to meet you."

"Is she here?" Hadeel tiptoes to look over his shoulder toward the living room.

"No, no. She's ninety years old, doesn't go out much. She's hoping you don't mind visiting her before you leave."

"When? Now?" She would rather visit someone alive than rummage through her dead aunt's possessions.

"Tomorrow morning?"

"Oh, Okay," she says. Her plan to leave for London the next day isn't happening anyway.

Jonathan places paper plates, napkins and plastic forks on the table. He pauses and looks at her questioningly. "Chinese okay?"

Hadeel inhales the aroma of Oriental spices floating out of the paper bag. "Sure," she sits on the bench facing him. "I saw the tiles with Arabic writing on the fountain."

"*La ghaliba illa Allah,*" Jonathan says in perfect Arabic, correctly emphasizing the last two words. "It's Amal's own handwriting, you know."

"How did she do it?"

"She took a pottery class when we designed the fountain. You know where the sentence comes from, right?"

"I'm not sure." Hadeel peers at the food on her plate.

"*Alhamra,*" Jonathan says, dropping the B in the word the way Arabs do when referring to Alhambra, the Moorish residence in Granada, Spain. *Alhamra* meaning the red one, in this case the red castle. "The sentence is written on tiles all around the halls of the palace. You've never been there?"

"No. We keep postponing that trip." Hadeel thinks of her mother's objections toward old historical places. She prefers shopping, especially in modern air-conditioned malls like the ones she's used to in Kuwait.

"The sentence meant a lot for Amal and her father. She told me they used to spend hours discussing the philosophical aspects of it." Jonathan looks at Hadeel and proudly says, "She did a great job replicating it, don't you think?"

Hadeel nods and gives him a sympathetic look. "What are you going to do?"

"What?"

Surprised at her thoughtless question, Hadeel tries to change the subject. He's still waiting for her to explain. "I mean, what are you going to do without Amal?"

"I don't know. I ask myself the same question all the time." He shakes his head, takes a deep breath then adds, "But I know I'll be busy for a year or two on a lawsuit Amal and I started shortly before the accident."

"A lawsuit?" Hadeel asks, not sure if she understands correctly.

"A professor at Amal's department libeled her, claiming her research was false and that she was trying to promote Islamic Sharia Law. We don't know his real motive, maybe it's Islamophobia, or sexism, or both. Whatever the reason, he impacted Amal's career and caused the denial of her tenure. Well, it's too late for that now but I'd like to restore her academic reputation. I'm working with a lawyer to substantiate Amal's work and prove that her research was original. We want to prove that she wasn't trying to spread Sharia or anything of that sort. She was simply uncovering truth that was concealed for a long time."

"Can I help?"

"Yes, as a matter of fact I'm hoping you will. Amal had many papers published in Arabic by accredited Arab literary journals which we were going to use as proof of the background of her literary discovery. You can help by listing the sources of these papers with a summary of the subject matter and the dates when they were published. That professor began assailing Amal with unfounded accusations after she published a paper on Percy Bysshe Shelley's Revolt of Islam.

Amal told me she published that paper in Arabic hypothesizing that Shelley might have converted to Islam, which was why some critics called him an infidel and an atheist. I'm hoping you can translate the paper into English."

"Of course," Hadeel says. "I'll do my best." Raj's name flashes into her mind as one of the sources in that area. "Why was Amal interested in Southey's *Thalaba the Destroyer*?"

"Because it was Percy Shelley's favorite poem."

Hadeel reshuffles information in her mind, trying to connect Percy Shelley to Washington Irving. "Wasn't Washington Irving Amal's favorite author?"

"Yes, he was. His book *The Legendary Life of Mahomet* led Amal to the Shelleys, and then to Robert Southey. It's like connecting pieces of a puzzle. That whole time-period is fascinating, especially how Islam was viewed in Europe."

"Wish I could take your classes." Hadeel smiles at him. Jonathan smiles back at her, but it's a sad smile.

Chapter Twelve

In Jonathan's car, as they drove back to the hotel, a text message appears on Hadeel's cell's screen just before the battery dies and the phone goes blank. Hadeel was able to read the first line of the message before it disappeared: "Come to my presentation tonight at 7 pm." It's from Amina.

"Is campus far from here?" Hadeel asks him.

"Not really. A couple of minutes by car. Would you like me to take you there?" The time on his dashboard says 6:08 pm.

"I'm not sure," Hadeel hesitates. "No, thanks, it's okay."

"I'll pick you up tomorrow morning at nine." Jonathan reminds her of his mother's visit as he stops in front of St. Julien's main entrance.

"*Inshallah*. I'll be out here." She jumps out of the car.

In her room, Hadeel plugs the phone into the charger. Once the device gets some life back she finds Amina's Instagram site. There she is looking happy and hopeful in her profile picture. Hadeel scrolls recent posts and blogs, searching for the one of them together.

The most recent post was the day before, a picture of Amina in a classroom with the tag: My First Video Clip, Tomorrow, 7 pm.

Hadeel puffs out the breath she held and checks the time again. If she attends, she'll have the chance to ask Amina not to post their selfie taken at the library. "Do it and get it over with," she tells herself. She picks up the hotel phone and presses the concierge button. "Is it possible to take a taxi to the University?"

Twenty minutes later the cab driver stops in front of a modern-looking building on the old campus. It's like being in Leicester Square. Digital screens crowded with colorful pictures and video clips show teachers and students in classrooms busy with various activities. The Atlas, Amina called the building where she takes her classes. Hadeel steps out of the car and inhales a unique sense of freedom. Somehow being in the middle of scores of young people rushing around with purpose liberates her fogged up mind. She longs to be with them, and one of them.

"Hadeel?"

Not expecting to be recognized Hadeel freezes. She looks in the direction of the voice and exclaims happily, "Amina! I came to attend your presentation," she says in Arabic.

"Wonderful!" Amina replies in English. "Come along. I'll introduce you to my professor. He's very nice." She's wearing a black t-shirt and tight-fitting jeans. Her wild hair is loosely tied to the back with a colorful cotton scarf. On her shoulder is a knapsack that looks heavy.

"So this is your department?"

It's one of them." Amina smiles at someone and waves. "CU offers a program for film production which is a mix of courses from different departments."

The two girls weave their way through the giant doors. Inside the building the aroma of coffee fills the air. Students, walking out of a small cafe in a corner, carry large cups as they hurry down the halls. More digital images flicker on the walls between lecture rooms.

"This way," Amina points at one of them.

Hadeel slows down and lets Amina proceed a few steps ahead of her. The large lecture hall is an auditorium with wide steps that descend to a podium with a wall-to-wall screen. A young casually dressed professor behind a stand smiles at the girls when they approach.

"Are you ready for your presentation?" he asks Amina.

"Yes, I am. Professor Bryant, this is my friend Hadeel. She'd like to attend class today. I hope you don't mind?"

"Of course not. Are you also from Kuwait?"

"Yes I am."

"Great." He spreads his arms. "You're welcome to stay."

"Thank you." Hadeel steps away to give space to students who are already queuing behind them to confer with their professor.

"I'll sit in the back," she tells Amina.

"Let's have dinner together after class. Okay?"

"Sure." *That would be a perfect time to ask her to delete the selfie,* Hadeel thinks as she heads to the back row.

Professor Bryant knocks on the microphone announcing the beginning of the lecture. A sudden hush reigns in the auditorium. "All right!" he says. "Today we have four students presenting their first professional video clips.

These are: Sean, Suzanne, Justine, and Amina, in that order. As with previous presentations, the topic is still, 'A Unique Aspect of the City of Boulder.' We'll take fifteen minutes after each presentation to discuss the work. We'll focus on how relevant the clip is to the topic, the messages implied, and the effect of these messages on the audience. So, let's begin. Sean!"

Hadeel notices how everyone seems alert, interested, and engaged. The air of seriousness and adroitness feels different from that of her experience in every classroom she's attended in college at home. Must be the subject matter, she thinks. Who wouldn't be excited to watch videos? Or is it because it's a graduate class? She wishes she can experience such an atmosphere; it's been one of her daydreams ever since she started her Master's degree online.

The first presentation is about the outdoor facilities and Open Space in Boulder. When Sean's video clip is over a lively Q&A takes place. At the end students suggest ways to improve the clip from the point of view of cinematography.

Soon, it's Amina's turn. Hadeel sits up, anxious for her friend to do well. As with the three earlier presentations, the fifty-some-students in the auditorium watch the screen with expectation.

Amina seems relaxed and confident as she sets her laptop on the table and hooks it to the media outlets. Hadeel wonders if she'd be as relaxed in front of a big audience waiting to discuss and judge her work.

"Here it is," Amina says into the microphone. "Hope you like it."

The video begins with the sound of laughter as the camera pans young happy faces.

Amina's voice begins narrating as the picture moves onto a long path leading to a yellow brick building. "When I arrived in Boulder to study at CU, I assumed that Boulder was a haven only for young people. I was looking for a place to stay when I noticed this building. I liked it because of its proximity to campus."

The camera slides into a reception area and focuses on the face of a middle-aged woman at a desk. The lady smiles and nods. Amina's narrative continues. "I asked for a room here and was told this residence is only for senior citizens. Half of them need medical assistance. Since I had never heard of such a facility outside of a hospital, I asked permission to look around. Here's what I saw."

The next shot looks like the surface of a tree trunk. But when the camera zooms out the viewer begins to realize it's the grooves, veins, and lines of an old face. The face of a woman who smiles gently and waves hello with a hand blue with bulging veins and scars. "She reminded me of my Ydaida," Amina's voice says in the video. "Ydaida means grandma in the Kuwaiti dialect. Like most old people in Kuwait my Ydaida lives with us at home because she needs our care and attention. We do not have such facilities in Kuwait. Arabs think it's shameful to send one's grandparents to places like these instead of caring for them in their own homes. As I looked around this place, I wondered how Ydaida herself would feel living here."

The video scans the recreation room, then the swimming pool with four elderly people doing laps with their trainers. In the communal area a few people sit comfortably watching TV. In the library a group chat quietly, and a couple played board games. The camera moves through a long hallway then enters an apartment displaying a living room, a bathroom, a small kitchen, and a couch facing a wide window. The picture moves outside the window showing garden views and the foothills beyond. Young people run around the fields laughing and throwing Frisbees. Amina's voice concludes: "After this visit I realized that Boulder is a place for both young and old, a unique aspect of a university town. Although I'm not sure if senior citizens in Kuwait would prefer living in a similar home rather than with their families, I wish we have similar services. I would love to have such a choice when I'm that age." The video ends with a Frisbee disk soaring in a clear blue sky before it is caught by a senior woman.

"Okay!" Dr. Bryant says, joining the rest of the class with applause.

Memories of her own Ydaida and Aunt Munira crowd Hadeel's mind while Amina's classmates discuss her presentation. How would Munira react to the idea of an assisted-home- living like this one? How would she herself feel if she ends up an old spinster like Munira? A constant warning from her mother when Hadeel objects to marrying and having children.

"Why isn't there something like that in your country?" a student asks Amina.

"Because a basic ethic in our culture and religion is to take care of the elderly. When an older person cannot live independently, families take them in and care for them."

"I like that," one student says.

"What if that person doesn't have a family?" someone else asks.

Amina chuckles. "That's a good question. I've never heard of a case like that. Have you Hadeel?"

All heads turn toward the spot Amina pointed. Hadeel shrinks at the sudden attention and only shakes her head with a 'no'.

"Let's discuss Amina's work from a technical perspective," the professor suggests. "How's her message delivered? Yes, John, go ahead!"

John, a blond student in the front row discusses different shots in the clip, using technical words Hadeel is not familiar with. A new admiration for Amina captivates Hadeel as she gazes at her friend. Way down there at the auditorium's podium Amina looks so small and trifling, yet she has managed to attend a foreign university, produce an important project, and stand with confidence participating in a discussion about her culture and people. Hadeel enthusiastically joins the class applauding Amina's work at the end of the discussion.

"Let's go eat," Amina says, standing by Hadeel's seat a few minutes later. "I'm starving."

"Where shall we go?" Hadeel gathers her bag and jacket and follows her friend out of the classroom.

"At the C4C. We need to hurry before they close in half an hour." Weighted down with her laptop and bag strapped over her shoulder, Amina darts out of the building.

Trying not to lose her friend through buildings and hallways Hadeel bumps into students rushing in different directions. "Is it always busy at this time of day?"

Amina pulls open a gigantic glass door and holds it

for Hadeel to slide through behind six other people. "It's campus, yes. This way," she points at another crowded lobby.

"This looks like a new building." Hadeel stops to admire the design of open ceilings and wide staircases.

"It is." Amina reaches in her back pocket for a card. She lines up in a short queue at the entrance of a dining area. "Two please," she says to the attendant who takes the card. She pulls Hadeel by the arm saying, "It's on me, they don't take cash."

Inside, she heads toward stacks of trays and silverware containers. She picks up a set for each of them and zooms toward the food area. "What kind of food would you like? Persian, Chinese, Lebanese, or traditional? Take your pick. Over there is the dessert buffet, all included."

"Ya Allah!" Hadeel exclaims looking around the crowded dining area. "Where are we going to sit? All tables are occupied."

"Let's get food first, then worry about a place." Amina rushes toward the Persian kitchen and asks for chicken kebab with saffron rice. The young worker who seems to know Amina takes his time serving her while engaging in a conversation about classes. When finally he finishes piling her plate with food he turns to Hadeel.

"I'll have the same, please."

The two girls carry their trays to the seating area which seems more crowded now than earlier. They stop in the middle of the hall.

"Amina!" someone calls from a corner table. "Come join me over here." Amina giggles and winks at Hadeel. "It's Dr. Bryant. I can't say no."

The professor is sitting at a round table that has just been vacated by a group of students. "This place is crazy busy, but the food is good."

"What did you get?" Amina asks while she places her tray on the table and drops her bag on the floor.

"The usual,' Dr. Bryant points at his plate. "Humus, falafel and tabouleh." He looks at Hadeel and asks, "What's your name again? Can't remember, forgive me."

"It's all right. Hadeel."

"Does it mean anything? I know that Arabic names always mean something." Amina laughs. "Not always, but in both our cases they do mean something. Tell him Hadeel."

"Mine means the cooing of doves."

Dr. Bryant nods while chewing his food. He swallows then says, "That's really nice." He turns to Amina and says, "And you're the trustworthy one, right?"

"Right," she giggles. "Do you remember what it would be for a male?"

"Mmmm," the professor closes his eyes and thinks. "Wait, don't tell me. Ameen."

"Wow! That's correct. You remembered." She gives him a thumbs-up.

He smiles. "It's interesting. Well, good job on your presentation today. You captured a spirit in Boulder that many ignore. People forget that thousands of professors who taught here when young like to retire in the same place."

"Thank you Professor Bryant, I appreciate it." She's suddenly holding her phone in her hand. "Can I take a photo of you with Hadeel?"

Before Hadeel can protest, Dr. Bryant leans toward her and the picture is snapped. Hadeel's hand which was holding a spoon towards her mouth freezes midway. Her lips are saying *No*. Next moment, while Hadeel's mind fogs up with fear of yet another photo, Amina and her young professor engage in a serious technical discussion of documentary art and filmmaking.

Chapter Thirteen

AMAL'S JOURNAL

There are things better not told. Shameful, disgraceful, stupid things. Yet when I think of my folly I wonder if I could possibly get over it once I put it down in words. To this day, fifteen years later, I still find it hard to fathom. How could such a thing happen to me? How did I fall into such a pit? I used to think I was a smart, determined, and rational woman. A feminist, no less. Besides, religion was still a pivotal part of my life. I wasn't as devout as Ydaida or Munira, but I diligently performed my daily prayers, fasted the month of Ramadan, and read the Quran. So how did I let a horrid thing happen to me?

I convinced myself for a while that it was the result of losing Baba. His death was so sudden it devastated me, still it should not have been an excuse for my folly. Baba was a good man and I should have learned that from him. He and I became close friends after our trip to . We spent many hours of every evening together in his office discussing books and poems he transposed into songs. He played the *oud* and taught me how to sing along, teaching me about the human voice, the "best instrument on earth." We even managed to take a few weekend trips together to Beirut, once the "Paris of the Middle East."

Before Baba died, I had grand plans for my future. I was offered a teaching assistant position from the History Department at Kuwait University, the first step toward a doctorate scholarship. I had dreams of being a professor at the department and changing the world. Yes, I was young and naive, but with father's encouragement I was optimistic and diligent, and believed that everything was possible. I attended seminars given by international intellectuals, such as Nawal El Saadawi and Edward de Bono who coined the term "Lateral Thinking." Lateral thinking, I thought, was what we needed in our Arab countries to move forward.

Mingling with professors and highly educated colleagues was a thrill those days. Trips to remote parts of the Kuwaiti desert and islands organized by my department introduced me to my country's history and archeology I did not know existed. My deeply ingrained passion for my hometown grew with my knowledge of it, along with the desire to improve it. Therefore, living away from Kuwait had not presented itself to me. Not yet.

During those department trips I met and became attached to an older professor. He was erudite, well known on campus for his intellectual contributions to his field in Political Science. We shared the passion and zeal for Kuwait and hopes to ameliorate its position in the region and the world. I introduced him to my father during one of the department functions, and the two acted like good old friends. That friendship saved me briefly during the hardest day in my life, the day my father died, and my world crashed.

My father's empty spot was immediately filled by this colleague (I will refer to him from now on as Professor X). I spent most of my work hours in his office, taking his opinion and advice to heart, just like I did with Baba. I trusted him and told him about my apartment in Malaga. He admired my independent thinking, encouraging my future academic plans to earn my doctorate. We discussed politics, religion, and philosophy. Not once did I ask him about his personal life. His intellect was all I cared for, his friendship all I needed.

He applauded the topic of my Master's thesis, which was inspired by my father: "The Spanish Inquisition against Islam and Muslims started by Isabella and Ferdinand in the 1500s has never stopped, and continues to the present day in different forms." In the proposal I explained how the fear of Islam encroaching on Christianity in Europe is still alive and is evident in Western media's demeaning of Islam. That was the reason, I explained, why Western leaders to this day support Muslim leaders and Arab dictators who encourage repugnant religious authorities to rule the Arab masses and smudge the shining spirit of Islam.

With the encouragement and enthusiasm of Professor X and other colleagues, I finished my Master's degree in a year and a half. Since Kuwait University did not offer doctoral degrees then; the next step was to apply to Universities abroad. During that time, without Baba's protection and support, pressure at home to limit my freedom increased. Mother nagged me about wearing the veil, Rashid pestered me about accepting marriage proposals from some of his friends and relatives. My hours at work became longer to avoid such a gloomy and disheartening environment at home.

Only once after father died did I manage to escape to my hideaway in Malaga. That beautiful place! It contained all the elements that a sanctuary could offer: Books, music, and beautiful views of the Mediterranean. The memory of Yuba's presence in the tiny apartment was so tangible and was all the company I needed. I read and reread Irving's Tales of Alhambra, along with books about Arab philosophers and scientists during the Muslim civilization in Spain.

I found out that Irving and my father had much in common. They both came from large families and studied and earned law degrees. Instead of pursuing a career in law they shifted their attention to literature. They both traveled and lived overseas for years, during which they established a name for themselves and their countries, gaining fame and respect. They were both devoted family men. Having no children of his own, Irving provided for his brothers, sisters, and their children. I fell in a spiritual love with Washington Irving and read everything he wrote.

When I shared my thoughts and feelings with professor X, he laughed long and loud. He then recommended I focus on Washington Irving for my doctoral degree.

"Arabs and Muslims owe much to Irving for preserving an invaluable historic site such as Alhambra," he told me. "It was Irving who pulled the palace out from the rubble and made it shine again for the world to enjoy."

I was ecstatic. Those would have been my father's exact words. I took his advice to heart, Washington Irving became the topic for my Ph.D. thesis, and the focal point in my studies. His home in Irvington, New York, became the choice of my next destination. I had to go there.

I applied to universities in New York to do my doctorate. And while I waited for an admission, my brother Rashid pressed another offer of marriage on me from one of his military friends. He threatened if I didn't accept, he would prevent me from pursuing my doctorate. "How could he?" I asked Ydaida. Silence was her usual answer. "My father would never allow it!" I yowled, but she only shook her head. It wasn't clear if she agreed with me or my brother.

When I complained to Professor X about my problems at home he stared at me silently.

Sometimes later, I'd catch him gazing at me, his eyes wandering over my hair, my body, my youth. At those times, thoughts of being married to him flashed in my mind. I found myself wishing he'd ask to marry me and rescue me from my brother's candidates. Instead, Professor X said, "I'd like to see your apartment in Malaga and look at your father's books."

"How?"

He laughed. "By visiting while you're there. When are you going?"

"I don't know," I said. "It's not easy for me to travel alone."

He studied me for a moment longer. "There's a conference in Madrid, during our Winter Break, this February. Why don't you apply and come with me? After the conference we can visit Malaga together."

I was taken by surprise. Traveling with a male colleague sounded outrageous to me, even though many of my female colleagues had been doing it. Some in my department mentioned attending the conference Professor X recommended. It was a chance for them to get a paid vacation. Islamic History and Politics was the main topic of the conference, so I could apply and get some benefits as well. But I didn't. I planned a vacation instead and told my family I was attending the conference, a white lie, I thought, shouldn't hurt anybody. Besides, being in my apartment in Malaga would be like attending the conference. Professor X was the only person I told about it. He asked for my phone number, said he might find the time to visit me there.

A day before my vacation was over, he called. He happened to be at the beachfront hotel in Malaga and wanted to see me, he said.

"Now?" I asked. It was late in the afternoon, I had just finished packing and cleaning the apartment, ready to leave early next morning.

"Yes! Give me the address."

In half an hour he was at my front door. We shook hands.

"You look lovely," he said. He was carrying a brown paper bag in his hand.

I straightened the straps of my dress over my shoulder and let him in. "Please have a seat. How was the conference?"

"Just like any other conference, a lot of talking, no action." He walked straight to the bookcase and began examining titles on book spines. "This is a good one, read it." He pulled out a book and handed it to me. It was by Taha Hussain, a criticism of Ibn Khaldun.

I sat on the couch facing the balcony and placed the book in my lap. The sun was sinking behind our building casting golden light over the sea. Frothy waves rushing to the shore faded with tiny bubbles once they touched the sand. I tried to convince myself that the man standing at my bookcase, talking nonstop, was my father. But I couldn't. My father was never domineering or bossy like Professor X was suddenly acting. Why was he here anyway?

"What are you thinking of?" He asked sitting next to me, too close.

I pulled away to the other end of the couch. "My father," I said with emphasis.

"What about him?" He reached for my hand and squeezed it.

I shrugged and snatched my hand away.

"You have a nice view of the Med here. But not as good as the one from my hotel room. You should come and see it."

"No thank you. This is good enough for me."

"Do you have something to eat? Or shall we go out to dinner?"

"No. I have some food." I stood up. Before he arrived I had thought of taking him to my father's favorite restaurant. But I changed my mind. A repugnant feeling toward him took over me, I did not want to share my father's memory with him anymore. I stomped to the kitchen.

He followed. I rummaged through the refrigerator looking for the cheese I almost trashed before he arrived.

"I'm assuming you have two glasses for us?" He raised his paper bag and produced a bottle of wine.

"I don't drink alcohol," I said, blood rushing to my face.

"Good. You should try it then." He twisted open the metal cap of the bottle.

"No thank you." I snapped open a can of Pellegrino and took out a box of crackers along with the cheese. I placed them on the dining table which I'd cleared before he arrived and pointed at the chair across from mine. "Please, have a seat." I sat down.

"You're acting like a peasant," he said, still holding the bottle in his hand.

"Why?"

"You didn't even offer me a glass for my wine."

"I'm sorry."

He set the bottle on the table and placed both hands on my bare shoulders, pushing me gently on my chair. "It's okay, stay. I can find the glasses."

He whistled while looking through my kitchen cabinets. The touch of his warm hands on my shoulders still radiating over my skin, making me want to find a shawl or a sweater to cover up my body. Was I giving him the wrong idea with the way I was dressed? Was it my fault he was flirting with me?

"I can tell you're a neat person," he said, bringing two glasses from the cabinet.

I tried to smile and look relaxed but I couldn't. How would he react if I suddenly ran for a jacket? He'd sneer and jeer for sure, calling me a peasant again. But why should I be forced to do something I didn't want to do?

He poured blood-red wine into the two glasses and placed one in front of me. "Try it."

"No. Thank you."

"Cheers." He clinked his glass with mine, and with fat fingers he helped himself to cheese and crackers. He chewed, drank, and talked at the same time. Instead of listening to him, I watched crumbs and droplets float in the air from his mouth before settling down on my table. "Did you get admission from a university yet for your doctorate?" he asked.

"Not yet." Then, without thinking I asked, "Are you married?"

His sleepy eyes shot open. He smiled and acted casual, but it was obvious he became tense. "Why are you asking?"

I raised my voice. "To see how faithful you are." I looked at his fingers again, no wedding band.

"Even If I were married, why would I be unfaithful?" He poured more wine into his glass. "We're not doing anything wrong, are we?"

"True," I said, encouraged by his edginess. "Still, I'd like to know."

He took a big gulp of his drink and swallowed it down. "You just reminded me of an old friend of mine. He wears a wedding band even though he's not married. He wanted to test if his girlfriends truly loved him or just wanted to marry him." He chuckled stupidly.

"Are you married?" I insisted.

"If you take a sip of wine, I'll answer you."

"No." I jolted up. "You don't have to answer. It's not important anymore." I headed toward the main door. "Please leave. Now."

" No." He waved his hand and headed to the balcony. "You don't mean that. You're just upset because I didn't answer your question. Come on."

I folded my arms and stood behind the couch, glaring at him. "Come join me out here. There's a nice, cool breeze."

He leaned back on the balcony railing behind him, smiling. It was the first time I saw him without his headdress. His hair was silver on the sides, thinning on top, revealing a bald spot.

Gray hair invaded his trimmed mustache. He looked older than I'd previously thought. "You look ravishing by the way," he said, coming toward me.

I looked around for something to cover my bare arms. "Please leave now!" I stepped around the couch when he drew closer, as if we were playing cat and mouse.

He placed his empty glass on the dining table, checked the empty bottle, and came toward me. Slurring his words he said, "This Spanish dress really becomes you, with your raven hair and fiery eyes. I'm sure you know but are acting modest." He grabbed my arm and tumbled on the couch, pulling me with him.

"Stop it!" Shaking my arm free I steadied myself up on my feet. "Please leave!" I was trembling all over. What would a liberal woman do in such a situation?

"Come, sit, relax," he said and rested his head on the back of the couch. Out of breath, and with mouth open, he fell asleep.

I watched him for a couple of minutes before I stealthily slid away to the bedroom. I closed the door, and blamed myself for what happened, for not giving a thought to how I was dressed for his visit. I should have known better, I thought, looking for a sweater to don on before I'd wake him up and make him leave. I spotted a woolen-shawl on the clothes hanger behind the door. I was reaching for it when he suddenly pushed the door open.

"Here you are!" professor X slurred.

"How dare you!" I exclaimed in disbelief.

"Don't be afraid. I won't harm you." He drew nearer.

Feeling cornered, between the bed and the door, tears flowed down my face while I still tried to look brave. "You are shameless. How dare you barge into my bedroom?"

"I want you. I love you; don't you know that already?" he said, his breath all over my face. "Isn't that why you gave me your address and invited me over?"

"I did not invite you," I said, pushing him away.

"Oh yes you did, calm down." He wrapped his arms around me.

I struggled and screamed while he tried to hush and lull me. Even though old and drunk, X was strong and determined. Strangely enough, the image of a little bird striving to escape the claws of a street cat filled my mind at that moment. The bird would flutter for life and freedom against the vicious cat while I fought for my dignity and honor. At the end, It was a futile fight.

To my utter horror, signs of what happened began to appear a month later. In disbelief, I hid myself at home for another month, hoping it wasn't true. How could this happen to me?

What was I going to do? How can I handle the situation if I got pregnant? But my period refused to show up. Devastated, I walked into his office on campus one day and asked him to do something before my family found out.

"What do you want me to do?" His face drained of color; deep wrinkles lined his wide forehead.

"Marry me," I forced myself to say, nauseated. He was the last person on earth I wanted as a husband at that moment.

He looked at me in horror. "I'm already married. I have five children."

I collapsed in one of his office chairs, hiding my face in my hands. "How can you do such a thing?"

He rushed to the door, closed it, came back, and sat in a chair opposite mine. "Please. Listen to me, Amal."

I lifted my head and stared at him. Bile rose to my throat seeing how old, ugly, and terrified he looked.

"Listen." He drew his chair closer. "I'm willing to marry you as a second wife."

"Your second wife?" My mind was already muddled with absurdities, this was not one of them yet.

"Yes, as soon as you wish. Before this," he pointed at my stomach, "before this becomes apparent."

I looked down, my hands in my lap, violently shaking. I swallowed, pushing down the nausea rising to my throat. "A second wife?"

"My wife is religious and understanding. I'm sure she wouldn't oppose my request to . . ."

I snatched myself up in a sudden movement that prevented me from containing my sickness. I threw up right there, over his face, over his white dishdasha, over his shiny shoes.

"*Ya hmara*!" he cussed in shock.

I ran out of his office, slamming the door shut.

An admission letter to Columbia University in New York for my doctoral program arrived the next day. I was supposed to begin the fall semester, but I knew I had to leave right away. My Mother was already giving me suspicious glances and Munira was pestering me with questions about my health. I couldn't tell anyone about my shame. It would have killed Yumma, and devastated my family. I had to leave. I had to get an abortion.

Chapter Fourteen

Loud laughter, cheers and whistles drift through the vents of Hadeel's room through, as if it is the middle of the day. She gives up trying to sleep, tosses the pillow she has placed over her head and calls the front desk.

A sleepy male voice asks how he can help.

"What's all the noise?" She tries to keep irritation from her voice. "It's impossible to sleep."

"I apologize Miss. There's nothing I can do about it."

"What is it?" she asks irritably.

"It's tango night. Sometimes young people get carried away with fun," he chuckles annoyingly. "Maybe you should join them. Or, if you prefer, we can change your room to a quieter one."

"No, thank you!" She slams the receiver back down, more piqued than before she called. Is it really the noise that's annoying her or is it her failure to ask Amina not to post her photos on Instagram? So chatty over dinner with her professor, Amina discussed her presentation and her future plans nonstop. Hadeel couldn't interject with, "Please don't post my photos without my hijab on."

It would've been embarrassing in front of the professor. And she couldn't have one minute alone with Amina since Dr Bryant offered to give Hadeel a ride back to the hotel. Now she's worried and irritated at herself, at her weakness, at her fears.

No new messages from home or London. Munira is refusing to talk to her since the last conversation they had at Jonathan's house. Hadeel sits on the edge of the bed and contemplates her situation, away from home and the sedation of her video games. She tries to look at her life from a new perspective. A twenty-five year-old with an unclear future. Options offered to her by her parents are not satisfying, while what she wants is precarious. Her mother's recent reaction regarding marrying Nawaf brings a glimmer of hope. But how will her father react? He usually allows her mother to have her way in trivial things like furniture, food, and summer vacations. But when it comes to major family issues, he is the one who makes the final decision. And Raj, would he still want to marry her? After she stood him up the day he was to ask her father for her hand? Has he found someone else? Could she be happy unmarried, an old spinster like Aunt Munira?

She's tired of being manipulated like a puppet moved around with strings by its puppeteer. One day, she doesn't know when, she must take things into her own hands. Maybe she should start right now and do something about the noise outside.

Hadeel opens the curtain and searches for the source of the noise. Right underneath her window, colorful lights twinkle on wires hung between rows of trees. Three couples are doing the tango in front of cheering people sitting on the grass. She examines the dancing couples. The physical closeness and movements of the dancers are obscene. Are they feeling each other's body heat, inhaling each other's odor? Only lovers should be that close to each other, and privately, for that matter, Hadeel concludes.

She drops the curtains and shuffles toward the bed when the cheering and clapping gets louder. There's no way she can get any sleep. Without any idea of what she's going to do, she pulls off her pajamas, slips on a pair of leggings and a t-shirt. She picks up her cardigan from the armchair, brushes her hair with her fingertips and marches out of the room. Her Aunt Munira paid a hefty amount of money for the hotel, she shouldn't have to put up with this noise.

Downstairs, she turns toward the front desk and recognizes the young man who checked her in the night she arrived. She steps backward before he gets a chance to see her. Her shabby appearance might add ridicule to his previous insulting comment. Turning around toward the elevators she runs into a rowdy group of young people dashing across the lobby toward the courtyard. When they open the back doors, the cheering reaches a feverish pitch. Hadeel follows the crowd. A young man holds the door open for her. She steps out without looking at him.

Under the covered patio a cool breeze soothes her nerves. The words: "How beautiful is night," come to her mind. Who said that? Hadeel wonders, repeating them. But it is a beautiful night, despite the noise. The night breeze carries a faint fragrance of pine and perfume. There's a big crowd of people seated around wrought-iron tables, while others stand on the grass. Barefoot, Hadeel steps onto a mound where she has a better view of the musicians and dancers. There's only one couple now dancing in the middle of the circle. The woman in a low-cut black dress, is swaying sensually to the music. With one arm around her waist the man keeps her close to his body. Their legs intertwine, then kick forward and backward in unison to the music. Hadeel marvels at the couple's precision. It's something she has never experienced in her life.

"Would you like to tango?" a voice whispers in her ear. Its warmth over her earlobe gives her the shivers. She pulls away.

"I'm sorry I scared you," a young man says.

Hadeel stifles a gasp upon seeing his face. It's impossible, she thinks and swallows hard. Her eyes piercing at his face. She wraps her cardigan tight over her chest, looks down at her bare feet and tries to leave without bumping into him.

"I didn't mean to scare you," the young man persists.

She shakes her head then peers again at him. She couldn't resist asking him, "Are you Kivanc?" His honey-colored hair and blue eyes and eyebrows are exactly the same as the Turkish actor. So are his eyebrows she and many other girls and boys on social media tried to copy for years, thin in the middle and wider toward the ends.

"Who?" The young man asks, knitting his eyebrows. His neatly trimmed mustache and beard cannot hide his baby face. The face she, and millions of female TV-viewers around the Middle East gazed at every night watching the Turkish soap, "Muhannad and Noor."

"Never mind." Hadeel mumbles, while blood rushes to her neck and face.

"I love your British accent," he's saying. "Are you British? I thought you were Spanish." Hadeel shakes her head and turns away hoping her eyes won't reveal too much.

"I bet you can tango." The Kivanc-double follows behind. "Wanna give it a try?"

"No." She pushes on and finds herself in the middle of a gaggle of young people. She has to escape from this seductive situation. If she turns around to leave, he might follow her to the room. Then what would she do? Would she scream for help? Is it really possible he's the same Turkish actor Kivanc Tatlitug from the TV show but denying it?

Close around her, more couples flow into the dancing area when the musicians announce the last song for the night. Hadeel rushes toward the lobby, ready to sprint and hide inside the elevator.

"Excuse me!" He calls.

His voice sounds threatening. She halts and turns around.

"You dropped your room key." He's holding up the plastic card between his fingers.

Hadeel pushes her hands into the tiny pockets of her cardigan, the key isn't there. That must be hers. The handsome smile on his face grows bigger. She remembers how nice Muhannad was to Noor in the TV show.

"Here you are." He hands her the keycard. "Who's Kivanc?"

"Never mind," Hadeel says and shakes her head.

"Hope he's a nice guy."

She laughs. "He is." Taking a deep breath she adds, "Thank you for the key, I really appreciate it. Good night."

She hurries toward the lobby without looking back, wondering if he's following her. Should she have taken his picture. She can easily claim she'd met the one and only Kivanc Tatlintug, the actor thousands of women in Kuwait rushed to the airport with flowers to meet upon his arrival. She would've gone to the airport as well if she had different parents.

"Would you like to join me for a cup of coffee?" he asks while she waits for the elevator.

Ignoring his question, she squeezes inside the crowded lift. To her relief there's no room for an extra person.

"Nice meeting you," he waves as the elevator doors slide close.

Hadeel lets out the breath she held for the last minute or so. Crammed into the compact space, she cannot reach the button for her floor. A young couple, lost in a passionate kiss, block the call buttons. Hadeel looks away. They kiss like this in public?

"Excuse us!" People behind her yell drunkenly when the elevator doors open. It's the fifth floor, she needs the third. Hadeel steps aside for them to leave, hoping the kissing couple will leave as well. Instead, they moan and grope each other. The elevator doors are about to close leaving her alone with the ardent lovers. She sprints out.

She waits for the next elevator going down and tries to shake off the image of the kissing couple from her mind. She's only seen couples kissing like that in Hollywood movies. She can't believe it actually happens in real life, in public.

The elevator finally arrives, and she waits for the people to get out. "It's you again," Kivanc's double says. He opens his arms, blocking her from entering the elevator. "Are you waiting for me?"

Stunned, Hadeel groans with frustration. For some reason, tears gather in her eyes. How can she explain how upsetting this is? She realizes she's acting like a helpless idiot. No wonder her parents forbid her to travel alone.

"What's the matter?" the young man asks with concern.

She pushes the button to recall the lift that has just left. "Leave me alone. Why are you following me?"

"I'm not! This is my floor."

She wipes the tears with the heels of her palms and glances at him. His hair is disheveled but he is still the most handsome man she's ever seen.

"You don't believe me? Come let me show you my room." He waves his room key, grabs her wrist, and pulls her toward the hallway with his other hand.

"No!" Hadeel shrieks, freeing her wrist from his grasp.

He stops and lets go of her wrist. "I'm sorry."

She steps back and wraps her arms around her shoulders and looks away. "Just wanted to prove I wasn't following you."

She nods. "It's getting late."

"It's almost morning. I can make you a cup of coffee in my room."

Hadeel laughs, surprising herself. How can he be so persistent? If he really is Kivanc Tatlitug, would she say no? She finds herself saying, "Can you wait here? I'd like to bring my mobile to take a picture of you."

"Why?" His smile vanishes.

She has to explain. "You look exactly like a famous actor."

"Oh, this Kivanc you mentioned? What kind of a name is that?"

"Turkish."

"Nobody ever said I look Turkish before. Is that where you're from?"

"No. Can I bring my phone?"

"Only if you promise to have coffee with me. Wait, I have a better idea." He pulls his cell from his pocket. "Let's take a selfie and I'll forward it to you."

Hadeel giggles. "No, it's okay. I have to go." She reaches for the elevator call-button.

"Wait. You look so familiar."

"I don't know how?" She removes a hair strand from her eye and turns around. "I've only been here for two days."

The elevator produces a single ring before the doors open. Hadeel finds herself glued to the carpet staring at him. "Where are you from?" she asks.

"California." He then points at the elevator doors that are sliding close again. "Are you leaving or staying to guard the elevators for the rest of the night?"

Hadeel pushes the elevator button then says, "I think I'll have that cup of coffee you offered."

"Really?"

She turns around. "Yes, but you should know I usually

wear the hijab and I don't stay with men alone in the same room." *What a stupid thing to say, Hadeelo!*

He laughs. "Okay. I don't mind. Here's an idea. Since you seem to like standing by the elevators, I'll go make the coffee and bring it over here."

Before she can reply, he's jogging down the hallway. Hadeel has heard many stories about how friendly Americans are but never imagined them this friendly. The elevator chimes again, she sighs and steps away. Spotting the room Kivanc disappeared into she walks toward it and sits on the floor next to the open door. She leans her head against the wall, pulls up her knees, and closes her eyes. Besides the clicking sounds inside his room, the hotel is finally quiet. She guesses it's around four in the morning. Jonathan said he'd pick her up at nine to visit his mother, but she'd rather be with young people her age. It felt so natural being on campus with Amina and her classmates earlier, and now this nice young man.

"Here you are." He steps out of his room and hands her a black mug of steaming coffee.

She takes it with both hands. "Thank you."

"It'll be more comfortable in the room. I have a balcony with chairs."

She smiles. "Do you have mountain views?"

"Come and see for yourself."

"No, it's okay." She takes a sip of coffee, then rests her head against the wall.

"What's your name?" He sits next to her on the carpeted floor, balancing his coffee cup on his knees.

"Hadeel."

"Where are you from, Hadeel?"

"Kuwait? Probably you've never heard of it before."

"Of course, I have," he says with confidence. "Actually, my father liberated your country from Saddam in 1991."

"No way!" She sits up. "Are you serious?"

"I am." He takes a sip of coffee. "He told me so many stories about those days, some are funny."

Hadeel cast her eyes down. "All the stories I've heard are very sad."

"Yes of course, I understand. But sometimes in the midst of disaster a bright moment happens. My Dad said a few days after liberation he was walking with his battalion combing the streets of Kuwait City, making sure no more Iraqi soldiers were hiding. A group of Kuwaiti men and women rushed toward them. My Dad thought they were going to be attacked. Instead, the men hugged and kissed them in gratitude."

Hadeel nods, thinking of how grateful her mother has always been to Americans, wishing she could meet an American to thank him in person. "If it wasn't for America," Yumma's favorite tag since the invasion, "We'd be maids and servants for Iraqis."

"Then what happened?" Hadeel asks anxiously.

"A pregnant woman approached my father and asked his name. She said she would name her son the same."

"What's your father's name?" Hadeel asks as he starts laughing. "Why are you laughing?"

"My father's name is Chris, you know, from Christ."

"Oh, I get it." Hadeel smiles.

"My father and I still wonder if she really named her son Chris."

"Instead of Mohammed," Hadeel joins him in laughing. "That is a funny story. What's your name by the way?"

He takes another sip of coffee before he says, "Kevin."

"Are you serious?" She looks at him to see if he is joking. "Yes, why?"

"Because Kevin is almost like Kivanc."

He sighs. "All right, let's take a look at this Kivanc you're so enamored with." He sets his cup on the floor and pulls out his cell. After he switches it on he finds a search engine. "How do you spell his name?"

Simultaneously, as she spells the name a picture of the Turkish actor fills the small screen. "That's him!" Hadeel taps the screen with her finger.

Kevin zooms on the photo. "Hmmm, he does look like me." He touches the screen.

Hadeel suddenly sees herself, head close to his and realizes he's snapping a selfie. "There you go," he says. "Now you can tell your friends you met your favorite Turkish actor in Boulder, Colorado, out of all places."

"Out of all places." Hadeel sighs glaring at her smile in the picture. This is probably the first real sincere smile in a long time, but it's the third selfie she'll worry about.

Chapter Fifteen

"Hell does *not* exist!" a man on the radio announces as Hadeel belts herself in the front seat of Jonathan's car. "Yes, you heard right folks," the radio announcer says cheerfully. "That's what the Pope recently revealed, 'Hell doesn't exist!' How about that?"

Hadeel looks at Jonathan in astonishment. "Is that possible?"

"What?" Jonathan is weaving his way out of the hotel's driveway. Nine in the morning and it's already busy with people checking out of the hotel and others standing in line waiting for their cars delivered by sprightly valets. Must be the Tango audience, Hadeel thinks, furtively searching for Kevin in the crowd.

"Sorry I didn't hear your question," Jonathan says when he finally exits onto Broadway, heading south.

"Can the Pope decide if there's Hell or not? Isn't it already written in the Bible?"

Jonathan waves his hand. "The Vatican has already refuted this statement. They said the Pope didn't really mean that."

Hadeel thinks aloud. "If bad people are not punished in Hell, then what keeps them from sinning? Doesn't the negation of Hell encourage crime and bad behavior?"

Jonathan gives her a questioning look before he focuses back on the road. "I don't think fear of Hell prevents many people from committing crime."

"What then?"

"Good upbringing? Teaching compassion and responsibility towards fellow humans at a young age?" He shrugs.

"According to the Pope," the man on the radio is saying, "bad people's souls disappear after death. Whoosh! Just like that. Good people's souls get to live in paradise forever. I like that, how about you?"

Hadeel shakes her head in disbelief. She had many discussions with her theology group about Christianity, how flexible their rules are since the Bible has been rewritten a few times. On the other hand, Quranic rules are unchangeable since it's the word of God. But Hadeel likes the concept that Hell does not exist. Wouldn't it be nice to live free of fear of torture in the afterlife? Torture of the Grave or walking the straight path on Judgment Day, balancing on a thin line while below you, sinners are roasting in Hell? There is no argument about Hell and Heaven for Muslims. The Quran contains plentiful descriptions of each.

Hadeel shudders and peers out her window. The sun, pouring through the glass, fails to warm the chill in her heart. She has already committed too many sins since she arrived in this paradise, this beautiful place. Despite Munira's assurance it's not haram to drop the hijab for safety reasons, Hadeel feels guilty. Sitting close to Kevin on the floor without her hijab must have added a ton of weight to the scale of her sins, tipping her over closer to hell fires. She also lied to Kevin, claiming she's married. The list keeps growing and she's only been in America a couple of days. Perhaps she should stay in her room fasting and reading the Quran to keep from sinning. She shakes her foot nervously.

She takes a deep breath. Visiting Jonathan's ninety-year-old mother might help. Perhaps she, who is closer to death, can provide insight to the concept of Hell and Paradise. That would be a good conversation if there's nothing else to talk about. Hadeel imagines the old lady wrapped in a shawl, hunched over on a couch, speaking gently and softly. In other words, like Ydaida and many other grandmothers at home.

The talk on the radio continues. Between jokes and laughter with callers discussing Hell, the host plays what he calls an "appropriate" song. Hadeel listens carefully. A male voice moans: I'm just a soul whose intentions are good, Allah, please don't let me be misunderstood.

Hadeel exclaims, "Oh my God! Did he just say Allah?"

Jonathan listens for a moment. "No, no. He says, Oh Lord."

"You know this song?"

"It's an old song by a group who call themselves the Animals."

"Funny name." At home it's an insult to call someone an animal.

At a traffic light on Baseline, Jonathan turns the radio dial to a classical station. Soothing tunes of piano and violins stream out of the speakers.

The streets are buzzing with energy. People, young and old, are either walking, jogging, or bicycling. Flowers are blooming at every corner. Construction workers block the traffic. To her right, mountain peaks pop in and out of view behind buildings. Signs leading to campus are everywhere, as if it's indicating roads to Mecca. In Kuwait, almost everybody knows and talks about this university town, Boulder. Many people obtained degrees from CU, as they call the university. Soon, Amina will as well. Hadeel never thought it would be a place she'd visit, let alone attend a presentation in one of its classrooms. The mere mention of the subject would have brought an angry scowl to her father's face.

"Those are William's Village University dorms." Jonathan points at tall yellow brick buildings as he drives along the buildings. Students hover like a swarm of busy bees in front of the dorms. Some are waiting to take buses to campus, a couple of the vehicles resemble school buses in Kuwait. Hadeel wonders how she'd feel if she were one of those students going to CU.

"Did your mother go to this university as well?" she asks, realizing that everything in Boulder is connected to the university somehow.

"She was a professor of Comparative Literature there before she retired."

"Really?" Her picture of his mother wrapped in shawl on a couch changes to a lady wearing a professional suit. "Did Amal teach at CU?"

"No. Amal taught at a university in Denver. My mom and Amal were very good friends, by the way. They shared many interests, especially related to women's issues."

"That's nice," Hadeel says, looking out of the window.

Jonathan slows down to enter a parking area in front of a high-rise red brick building. He finds a spot and parks. "Let's go."

Outside the car Hadeel stretches her arms and back then follows Jonathan across the wide lawn to the main doors. He touches a keypad with a card similar to her hotel key. The door clicks and unlatches for them to enter. Inside, a strong cleaning-solvent smell assaults her nose. She sneezes several times while passing through a lobby with dilapidated furniture. Jonathan pushes an elevator button and waits. The doors slowly open. Jonathan presses number seven, the top floor. After a jerk and a shake, the elevator begins carrying them upward. The image of the kissing couple jumps into Hadeel's mind.

She quickly turns to Jonathan. "Does your mother live alone?"

The elevator stops with a disconcerting rumble. "She does. This way," Jonathan says pointing to the right.

Like an apparition, a very tall thin woman stands at the end of the dimly lit corridor. She looks like an old mannequin in a yellow cashmere turtleneck and gray stretch pants. Her stark white hair is cropped short around her narrow pasty face. She eagerly eyes Hadeel over Jonathan's shoulder as they approach. "Ah, there she is. Welcome. I'm Dorothy."

"Good morning." Hadeel offers a hand, but Dorothy pulls her in a tight hug. "Come in. Did you have breakfast?" She steps aside for her guests.

"Yes, thank you." Hadeel passes through the foyer. The living room is wide, spacious, and flooded with daylight. A balcony with glass doors wraps around the west walls, offering incredible views of what the locals call the Flatirons. Hadeel treads lightly over the beige carpet toward the balcony. "Quite the views you have here."

"Yes. Thank you Hadeel. Do you know you have your aunt's voice?"

Cacti-goosebumps grow on Hadeel's neck. "I'm just learning that." She glances at Jonathan who looks away.

"You also have the same accent she had when she first arrived. Some sort of a British accent. I used to admonish her not to let us corrupt her English." Dorothy smiles and points at a leather chair near the balcony. "Please have a seat."

Dorothy wobbles to an opposite chair with legs that don't seem to work in harmony. "Thank you for coming to see me."

Hadeel settles into the offered chair. "You're welcome."

"Jonathan tells me you're leaving soon. Is there a possibility we can convince you to stay longer?"

"No," Hadeel says emphatically. "My Aunt Munira is waiting for me in London. We're hoping to get back home before my father finds out I came here on my own." She bites her lips wondering why she's revealing this information.

"It's amazing he let you go to London without a muhram in the first place!"

Hadeel's eyebrows rise in astonishment. How does she know the word for a male chaperone? Did Amal find it significant to explain such a minute detail? "Did she also tell you about the positive things in Islam as well?" She says without thinking.

"Who?"

"Amal!"

"I'm not sure I understand what you mean." Dorothy turns to Jonathan for an explanation. He ignores her inquiring eyes, slides the glass doors open and steps outside to the balcony.

Hadeel finds herself compelled to defend her culture and religion. "Did Amal bother to tell you the benefits of a muhram and family protection?"

"Please," Dorothy waves her hand. "I read so much about Islam and your culture, you have no idea."

"But you didn't practice it to know the serenity of the word 'surrender.'"

As if she hasn't heard Hadeel's words, Dorothy says, "I want you to know I miss Amal more than I miss my own daughters. She was a brilliant woman. She gave me company and solace during tough times when my own daughters didn't have time for me. I guess that's a positive aspect of your culture, isn't it? Respecting and caring for the elderly."

Hadeel stares at the old woman, not sure if her aggressiveness is worthy of respect or caring. She prefers the docile version of Ydaida.

Dorothy continues. "I also wanted you to know that I am going to establish a foundation in Amal's name. It will be for the education of women who cannot afford higher education."

"That's very nice of you," Hadeel says, slowly absorbing the woman's affection for her aunt.

"Now, please tell me about yourself."

Taken aback by the unexpected question, Hadeel ponders what to say. She then tells her she's working on a Master's degree in London.

"I didn't know that!" Jonathan steps in from the balcony. He slides the glass doors, shutting out the traffic noise.

Hadeel nods. "I'm in the middle of finishing my thesis."

"What's your thesis about?" Dorothy asks rather loudly.

Hadeel hesitates swallowing hard. She has avoided discussing work on her degree with Jonathan because of the subject matter. Now she's about to impart the information to the wrong person. She glances at her watch, her mind searching for a way to reword the title of her research. "It's about Mary Wollstonecraft and her daughter Mary Shelley."

"Oh My… Did you know that, Jonathan?"

"No." He slumps on a footstool before realizing he sat on a pile of magazines. He removes them and places them on the floor with a thud. "No, I didn't."

"Does she know about Amal's papers?" his mother asks. Jonathan looks at Hadeel without saying anything.

"Some of them," Hadeel offers.

Dorothy addresses Hadeel. "Mary Wollstonecraft was a formidable woman. Does the time period of her life remind you of Muslim societies nowadays? It would be the best subject matter for women in your country."

Hadeel gets more unsettled at Dorothy's words. "First off, what Wollstonecraft said about Islam was totally wrong! Second, I'm trying to prove that no matter how brilliant feminist women are, they ultimately become the victims of their own emotions and the weakness of their nature." Hadeel takes a breath and waits for a negative response. But the old woman keeps her gaze level expecting more explanation. Hadeel continues, "The powerful and intellectual personality of Wollstonecraft, which everybody admired, was shattered when she fell in love with a married man, then tried to commit suicide. Basically acting like any foolish, ignorant woman would act."

"That's fascinating," Dorothy says. Her pale blue eyes move between her son and Hadeel. "Aren't you going to discuss Wollstonecraft's A Vindication of the Rights of Woman as the first book written for women's rights?"

"I will. However, the first chapter of my thesis deals with Wollstonecraft's wrong views and misinterpretations of Islam. But it is her scandalous style of living, along with her daughter Mary Shelley, and Claire Clairmont who was Mary Shelley's half-sister, which will occupy the largest part of my thesis."

"Oh my!" Dorothy's fingers begin to play a silent tune in her lap. The lines between her eyebrows deepen. "What's the title of your thesis?"

Hadeel hesitates. She's dealing with a shrewd woman and there's no way to back track now. She has to face the devil, she thinks before blurting out, "Fallen Women."

Dorothy's crackling laughter stabs Hadeel deeply in the guts. Her blood curdles with resentment. She bites her lower lip recalling Munira's words of advice about controlling anger with strangers. "An instant of tongue wagging might lead to lifelong regret," she used to tell Hadeel. "And when you argue with nonbelievers, our Prophet said, 'argue gently and with the best of your logic.'"

"I can't believe it," Dorothy says and wipes tears of laughter. "You are skipping over those women's important achievements to harp on their personal affairs? What exactly is your thesis trying to prove?"

Hadeel tries hard to keep her voice steady. "My hypothesis is that no matter how strong women think they are, they should acknowledge the weakness of their nature and surrender to it, which justifies Islam's requirement to defend and protect women. It also proves the validity of the Islamic law that requires women to dress decently." Another piece of information Hadeel did not need to add.

Luckily, Dorothy seemed not to hear very well. "Surrender to what?"

"Surrender to their docile nature and their role in society, which is to nurture the young and keep families together."

"What about men?" Dorothy's sonorous voice belies its source, a very old lady who seems harmless but is proving otherwise. "Are they allowed to follow their nature? The multifarious emotions and desires which fit their strong constitution? Is that why men in your culture can marry four wives?"

"No one does that any more!" Hadeel's voice rises. "That was for a time when there were reasons for it. Personally, I believe that it's better for a man to marry more than one woman legally, than to have several illegal mistresses and illegitimate children. That's why Islam allows more than one wife. Because of the insatiable nature of men!" Hadeel stands up, ready to run from this interrogation.

"Sit down," Dorothy orders. "We're not done yet. Please, tell me more. Who's your target audience? Your professors? Or perhaps your parents?"

"That's enough, Mom!" Jonathan says, sounding as irritated as Hadeel feels.

"Don't take me wrong, Hadeel." Dorothy holds on to both arms of her chair and struggles to lift herself up. "I find your research interesting but you need more focus. Don't forget that the freedom women enjoy today is the result of the hard work and sacrifices of those brilliant 'fallen women,' as you call them."

"I'm not sure about that," Hadeel murmurs.

Dorothy limps toward Hadeel and rests a hand on her shoulder. "Don't let personal experience divert your search from the truth. The nature of men and women is different, that's true, but similar in many aspects. That's why we need to work together to create a better society for everyone." She brings her face close to Hadeel's. "If a woman decides to go awry, it's her choice, she's responsible for her own actions. But she should be free to make her choices even if they become mistakes. Society should not force her into a corner as a punishment. There are different kinds of suffering, but the worst is the kind imposed on us by other people."

Dorothy's words cut through Hadeel's defenses. It's as if the woman sees right through her. She steps back, wanting to escape, yet finds herself saying, "Still a woman doesn't have to make her family suffer so she can be happy."

"Are you saying she's better off miserable in the family's golden cage? While they're happy, rejoicing over her forced obedience?"

Hadeel can't think of a rejoinder. She's been asking herself the same question for years. When she fell in love with Raj, she knew it was almost impossible her father would consent to such a marriage. Not only because Raj was a foreigner but also because he was not of the same social status as Hadeel's family. She wished, at that time, someone would tell her if she should give up her love for her family. Which decision would she ultimately regret more?

Under Dorothy's glaring eyes Hadeel manages to keep her voice level as she says, "I wish I know the answer." Her own eyes, however, betray her by filling up with tears.

"Okay, Mom!" Jonathan says firmly. "Hadeel has a lot to sort out in Amal's office. We have to go." He places his arm protectively around Hadeel's shoulder.

"Wait! Just a second." Dorothy shuffles over to a bookshelf in the foyer. She runs a finger over the stacks of tomes, pulls out one and hands it to Hadeel.

"Please accept this as a gift. This is the best book ever written about Mary Shelley and her mother Mary Wollstonecraft, *Romantic Outlaws*. It's a relatively new publication."

Hadeel hesitates, wondering if she should accept it. She finally takes the book and mumbles a thank you.

"I hope I will see you again." Dorothy hugs Hadeel tightly. "Please keep me informed of your research. I'm very much interested."

At the door she makes another piercing statement. "By the way, to the best of my knowledge, Amal was happy here, despite the fact she might have been labeled a 'fallen woman' by your family. She was an honest and hard-working woman, gave a good example of your people. The way her life ended was horrible. It should never have happened."

Hadeel turns around only to see the tears fogging the old woman's eagle eyes.

Chapter Sixteen

Anger wells up as Hadeel traipses behind Jonathan to the elevator. The unexpected altercation with Dorothy has taken them both by surprise. Jonathan steals glances towards her but does not offer a word of consolation. They remain silent, keeping a distance between them as they head to the car. Dorothy's words stir emotions which Hadeel has tried to ignore for a long time. Her situation with her family, her freedom, their control, choices in education and marriage were kept under the lid of religion. Now they're rising, brewing into resentment.

Wind rustles tree leaves and branches over Hadeel's head as she waits for Jonathan to unlock the car. Just like bringing her to visit his old mother, now he's dragging her back to Amal's office. Why is she obeying him like a mute sheep? This whole trip should not have taken place. She should have said "No" when Munira suggested it. She pulls the door open and throws Dorothy's book on the seat. Then, as anger shoots up to her head, she slams the door shut without getting inside. She swiftly takes to her heels toward an opening in the hedge-fence of the parking lot. Luckily, the path leads to a long winding trail.

"Hadeel!" Jonathan calls. "Where are you going?"

"I don't want to go to your house!" she shouts back.

"Fine! I'll take you back to your hotel."

"No!" She starts running. She wants to get away from him, away from his mother, away from the ghost of Amal. She's had enough of them already. If Munira doesn't change her return ticket to leave this evening, she will buy a new one for herself. She'll charge it to her credit card.

When her father gets the bill to pay it, she'd already be at home and will then explain. She'll tell him everything, everything. She will tell him the truth. She'll explain about this trip, about not wearing the hijab, about meeting the infidel and his mother.

She runs faster, her strides wider. The path circles behind the apartment building toward a small lake. Before she turns at a bend and out of sight she glances back. Jonathan stopped in the middle of the road, a helpless look on his face. Good, she thinks and runs faster. She heads west on the edge of the lake toward the mountains. She doesn't know where the path will take her and she doesn't care.

Dorothy's words, 'are you writing your thesis for your parents?' ring clear in her ears. "None of your business!" Hadeel shouts the way she wishes she did to Dorothy's face.

'Amal was happy here,' Dorothy had said. "Well, good for her!" Hadeel yells. "But she's dead now. Dead!" Hadeel cries at the sky.

It's obvious the old woman loved Amal. But was that

enough to replace the love of her family and friends? If Amal made the choice that Hadeel made and sacrificed love for family, wouldn't she have avoided her violent death? Wouldn't they be together now?

The tops of the yellow buildings Jonathan called Williams Village appear in the distance. She hurtles toward them, through narrow streets and winding paths among churches and houses. She finally gets closer to the dorms and slows down. On the west side of the tall building fewer students are lined up for the next bus. Out of breath, Hadeel joins them and stops behind the last person in line. She asks if she can take a ride to campus.

"You have to show an ID," the girl says showing hers, dangling on her chest from a band around her neck. "Sometimes the drivers don't check, though." The girl smiles.

Hadeel falters away. There are several shops and restaurants across the street where she can rest until she decides how to get back to the hotel.

"Hadeel!"

Hadeel halts. It sounds like Amina, she wishes it's Amina.

"Right here," Amina waves from the passenger seat of a red Mazda idling at the curb. "Come on, we can give you a lift."

Without hesitating, Hadeel rushes to the car and slides inside the back seat. "Thank you so much," she pants from exhaustion and realizes the driver is a male. She shrinks back a little in her seat. "Hi," she says.

The young man turns his head and his somber face breaks into a wide grin. "*Hala wallah,*" he answers her greeting.

"Yousef," Amina says. "This is Hadeel from Kuwait. Hadeel this is Yousef from Saudi Arabia."

"Are you also a student here at CU?" Hadeel asks him.

"Yes, electrical engineering. How about you?" He slows down through jammed traffic before he turns left on Baseline. "You must be new, haven't seen you before."

"I'm just visiting," Hadeel says.

Amina turns to look at her from the front seat. "Where would you like us to drop you?"

"Anywhere. I don't mind walking around campus. Are you going to the Atlas building?"

Amina giggles. "We're actually going to the Boulder Falls. Have you been there?" "No."

"You're welcome to join us," Yousef says, glancing at her over his shoulder.

Hadeel looks at Amina and Yousef back and forth wondering if it's appropriate to join their private outing. "Is it far from here?"

"About twenty minutes or so," Yousef replies.

"You should come," Amina insists. "It's gorgeous. You'll love it."

"Okay," Hadeel exhales. She sits back and relaxes her shoulders.

"Great!" Amina says happily. "I'm working on a new project for my class. I'm thinking the Falls would be a nice opening scene."

"You said you're visiting Boulder?" Yousef asks.

"Yes, I'm leaving tomorrow," Hadeel says with obvious relief.

"*Hasafa!*"Amina complains. "That's too bad."

"Are you also a graduate student, Yousef?" Hadeel changes the subject.

"No, undergrad, but I'm graduating this semester. I'm hoping I can extend my scholarship to do my Master's degree so I won't have to leave."

"Inshallah," Hadeel says. "You must like it here."

"Oh yeah, I love it. Who doesn't? Look at this." He slows down on a narrow curvy road surrounded by high mountains on both sides. "I will miss this, wallah."

"Me too," Amina says holding a Nikon camera in both hands and snapping pictures left and right.

Hadeel remembers the selfie Amina took at the library and wonders if she can take her aside and ask her not to post it on her Instagram. It's embarrassing to ask a liberal girl like Amina for such a favor, but it would put her mind at ease.

"Look at the river to your right," Amina points.

"It's so beautiful," Hadeel mumbles. She watches the water flowing swiftly over smooth rocks, and how it twists and turns as they drive alongside it.

"Careful. The parking spot is coming up soon," Amina points at a gravel area on the left side of the road.

"Okay. No cars behind us. Hang on," Yousef says, swerving to the left and hitting the brakes. "Sorry," he says as he stops the car.

The sound of the Falls becomes audible the second they step out. Amina, in denim shorts and a white and black striped t-shirt slings the camera over her shoulder and smiles at Hadeel. "I'm so happy you've joined us."

"Not a lot of people for a change," Yousef says, locking his car.

Amina holds the straps of her camera while studying Hadeel's sandals. "Are these Balenciagas?"

Hadeel lifts her eyebrows in amazement. "Yes. How'd you know?" She eyes Amina's smudged Nikes and wishes she was wearing the sneakers Jonathan bought her. Her chest tightens at the thought of Jonathan.

They wait for a passing truck before they scramble across the road towards the Falls. "I know how comfortable they are," Amina points at Hadeel's sandal. "But be careful on the rocks, they can be slippery." She hollers at Yousef ahead of them, "Hey, wait for us!"

"Amina," Hadeel whispers. "About that selfie you took . . ." Hadeel's voice is drowned out by the sudden roar of the falls.

"What?" Amina shouts. "Look at that." She points at the cascading water rushing down just a few meters away. She lifts her sunglasses to the top of her head and squints through the viewfinder in the camera.

"Allah!" The height and pounding rush of the water makes her lightheaded. She exhales letting go of her anxiety. Mist sprays her face. "This is reminding me of Lebanon," Hadeel tells Amina who kneels down to take more photos.

"Come on!" Yousef calls. "The view is better up here." He's standing on a rock some fifty feet from the falling veil of water.

Beneath them, a stream formed from the falls flows with force under the bridge they just crossed. A handful of people are scattered around. A young couple sit on a flat rock facing the falls. Others wade around boulders in the river.

Amina, busy with her camera, stops at various spots on the trail shooting photos from different angles. How wonderful it must feel to do something you really love, Hadeel thinks, watching her friend. With her mobile, Hadeel clicks a couple of photos of Amina. She'll forward them to her later.

"Go ahead," Amina says when Hadeel stops next to her. "It will take me a while to get the right lighting."

Yousef, standing on top of the highest rock, is waving his arms and saying something.

Hadeel carefully climbs towards him. With each step the sound of the water becomes deafening, and the spray more frequent. Enjoying nature, someone wrote, is not a luxury, it's a necessity for the soul. Hadeel cannot remember the author, but she believes the words. She already feels free- spirited and happy. Dorothy's resentful words evaporate in thin air.

Yousef waves at her from the highest point of the trail. Hadeel studies the path, looking for flat stones to step on. The rocks leading to where he's standing are wet but the proximity to the falls is mesmerizing. She has never been so close to a waterfall before. She shrieks with laughter when a powerful spray splashes over her.

"Give me your hand," Yousef says, his arm stretched out to help.

Hadeel clasps his fingers. The moment she lifts herself up she glances back to see Amina who is aiming her camera at them. A photo of herself holding a man's hand posted on Instagram flashes in Hadeel's mind. She lets go of Yousef's hand. The next moment she's falling backward. With left leg bent, she hits a flat boulder. Seconds later the pain is so excruciating, she blacks out.

Chapter Seventeen

AMAL'S JOURNAL

Even in a liberal city like New York, getting an abortion was not easy. It took several weeks to find a clinic and a doctor. There were rules, requirements, and restrictions. Besides, I was alone, and had no friends or relatives to accompany me for such an emotional procedure. But I was determined. I wanted to pull that folly out of my body and bury that horrible mistake behind me. I was eager to forget and start over.

But the doctor insisted I take time to reconsider my decision. "Remember there's no turning back after this is done," she said sympathetically. "It will have a lasting impact on your life." She made me listen to the fetus's heartbeats and showed me how it looked on an ultrasound screen then recommended I talk to a therapist.

I was devastated. Up until then, I hadn't thought of it as a living being growing inside of me. I'd thought of it as a mistake, as proof of a crime a man with no conscience had forced on me. I was certain, before I saw the doctor, that I wanted the thing erased, scraped off. But now seeing it helpless with a beating heart, I faced a real dilemma. Also, at that stage of pregnancy was I about to commit a crime? I did consider consulting with a therapist, but I knew they couldn't determine for me.

I took the doctor's advice and decided to wait a week before the procedure. During that time, I planned a trip to Irvington, New York, the home of Washington Irving. There, alone, tormented by my plight, I roamed the grounds of Sunnyside, clutching my father's book The Alhambra to my heart. I was hoping to sense my father's and Irving's presence, to ask them for help in making a decision.

Tired from walking I sat on a bench facing the Hudson river. The bench was shaded by trees that Irving had planted with his own hands. I closed my eyes and earnestly pleaded for help. Suddenly a voice broke through my meditation. A kind and gentle voice. I opened my eyes expecting to see Irving or his apparition. Unlike Irving, this man was tall and thin with blond hair and blue eyes.

"Can I join you?" he asked, a book clutched under his arm. I nodded.

He sat down and pointed at the river. "Irving used to call the Hudson his little Mediterranean."

His words brought a smile to my face. "That's what I was just thinking." I peered at the title of the book he placed on his lap, The Tales of Alhambra. I lifted my copy to show him.

"I'm Jonathan," he said, offering his hand. "Glad to meet a fellow fan of Irving."

Before we knew it, we had spent the whole day together. We discussed our mutual admiration for Washington Irving and his writings. We strolled around Tarrytown and paused over the bridge where Irving's story, Sleepy Hollow, and the "Headless Horseman" were supposed to have taken place. At the end of the day Jonathan and I exchanged phone numbers.

The friendship that ensued between us saved my life. I told Jonathan about my plight and asked his opinion. "Whatever you decide I'll be there for you. You can count on me," was his reply. He told me about his personal problems. He had recently broken up with a girlfriend he'd dated for years. They were already planning their wedding when he found out he could not have children. He was up front about it and told her the truth. Crying, his girlfriend told him that her life-dream was to have lots of children, six or seven. They canceled the wedding.

I decided to keep my baby. I would try to live a normal life, if such a thing was possible. That decision made Jonathan happy. So happy he promised to be there for the birth of the child. Our friendship grew stronger. For months we met every Sunday. He would either come to New York, or I'd go to Durham, North Carolina, where he went to school at Duke University. He was getting his doctorate in Islamic Studies, another topic that filled the hours of our days together. I couldn't stop telling him about my father, his poetry and music. Jonathan couldn't stop reciting poems by Abul al Ala' al-Ma'arrie that he memorized by heart. The only thing we never discussed was what we were going to do after the baby arrived.

One day, in the middle of a class, during the seventh month of my pregnancy, I went into an unexpected labor. Someone called an ambulance and I was rushed to the hospital. I gave birth to a still-born child. When they placed him in my arms, an image of the first baby I ever held and loved deeply flooded my mind. Hadeel. I thought of Yumma and how she must have felt holding me in her arms when I arrived. I thought of my only sister Munira, and my brothers and drowned with emotions of remorse and guilt. Before I buried my baby I named him Hadi, the tranquil one. Then I went into intense depression. I'd failed all the people who loved me, my mother, my sister, brothers, and my culture. I failed Hadi. He must have sensed how unwanted he was. He must have sensed my dread of seeing his father in his face, my shame and guilt, so he just left, quietly.

Without Jonathan by my side, I don't know what would have happened to me. For months I did nothing more than gaze at the walls of my dorm-room, at a sheet of a large-printed paper Jonathan gave me. Desiderata. I had pasted it next to my bed and recited its words before I slept and first thing in the morning. The words became the pulse in my veins and a positive force during the day. "Go placidly amid the noise and haste and remember what peace there might be in silence . . . Nurture strength of spirit to shield you in sudden misfortune . . . Beyond a wholesome discipline, be gentle with yourself . . ."

Eventually I went back to my classes with an injured soul. Life was not the same anymore. The guilt of actions I'd taken in my life was a heavy burden which I dragged along with me wherever I went, getting heavier with the recent event.

Then one day, during my research through Irving's biographies, I happened upon an epic poem that once used to be a favorite of mine. I actually tried to translate it into Arabic but never finished it. It's by the British poet Laureate Robert Southey: *Thalaba the Destroyer.* What a find! It was a gift from God sent to me in time of need to revive me. I inhaled the poem as a drowning person inhales air when coming out to the surface. For some reason, the words of Southey became a balsam for my injured soul, "A dewy freshness fills the silent air, no mist obscures, no little cloud breaks the whole serene of heaven . . . How beautiful is night!"

Southey, in his beguiling poem *Thalaba the Destroye*r, had indirectly addressed the same thesis I worked on for my Master's degree: the conspiracy against Islam since the Spanish Inquisition. Or at least, that's how I saw it. Soon, researching the poem led me to a literary breakthrough—the original real Thalaba on whom Southey based his fictional character. With Southey, Thalaba Ibn Abdulrahman, Irving and Jonathan by my side, I went back to work. My professors encouraged me, firmly believing I'd come up with a valuable literary discovery no one else had found. My own healing discovery was the theme of my research: Forgiveness. Forgiveness of self and others.

In the meantime, Jonathan and I became inseparable. Our mutual literary interests and research strengthened and enriched our relationship. Secretly, I was convinced that Washington Irving sent Jonathan to me along with my father's blessings. Three years later, after we both earned our doctorate degrees Jonathan invited me to visit his mother in Boulder, Colorado. Then, standing on top of a twelve-thousand-foot rise in Rocky Mountain National Park, Jonathan asked me to marry him.

There was no doubt in my mind that Jonathan was the only man I would ever truly love and marry. Yet I hesitated. I was considering going back home and getting Ydaida's blessing for the marriage. But the thought of stepping into the past frightened me. It would be like poking a wound that had healed and making it bleed again. Besides, during the last three years in an academic environment like Columbia university, I felt my world moved ahead while my family remained stagnant in the pool of old traditions and religious rituals. I told Munira, my only connection to home, about Jonathan's proposal and asked her to gently break the news to my mother and get her blessings. I doubt if she ever tried. Instead, she wrote me a long reprimanding letter.

So I called Yumma over the phone one day and told her about my plan to marry Jonathan. For the first time in her life, she got cross with me. "No! Never! No daughter of mine would do such a thing!" Those were the last words I heard from her. I never saw her again.

Chapter Eighteen

Hadeel jolts out of unconsciousness, dazed, with a piercing pain in her leg. She lifts her upper body up on her elbows and finds herself stretched on a metal hospital bed in a tiny square room with white-washed brick walls. Standing nearby is Jonathan with a crestfallen face. His white hair seems scarce under bright neon lights, his skin paper pale, his blue striped shirt wrinkled. He's looking at his feet.

A door opens and a doctor in green scrubs rushes in with x-ray pictures in his hands. He clips them on a board with a lit background and casually says, "Well," he clears his voice. "This doesn't look good."

Hadeel presses a button on a remote control hooked to a wire and comes to a sitting position. She struggles to keep from screaming. The pain in her left foot is unbearable but what hurts most is this unexpected situation. She's in a hospital, in a foreign land, without family, one day before she's supposed to go back home. And the only familiar face is Jonathan's. Her fingers hover over the remote wishing she can rewind to the moment before she fell. The moment she held Yousef's hand. In the new version, instead of looking back at Amina, she would jump to the top of the rock next to Yousef then look down at Amina. She lets out a deep sigh.

The doctor is pointing at a gray line in a white bone structure in the black x-rays. "There are two fractures on your ankle. One is deep and I'm afraid needs surgery."

"She's flying to London tomorrow," Jonathan says.

"Well, we can't do surgery anyway until the swelling goes down. So she can have it done in London if she prefers. But I recommend she doesn't move her foot much during the next couple of days."

"I have to leave," Hadeel snivels.

The doctor shrugs. "It's your choice. Too much pressure on the foot might misplace the muscles around the fracture, which would result in a more complicated surgery." He takes a close look at her foot. "We need to put a cast on your swollen ankle to keep it from moving. The cast must be changed soon when the swelling subsides," He hums while examining her feet. "Probably in three days."

Hadeel cringes and turns to Jonathan who is staring at the x rays. She wishes he'd tell her what he's thinking.

The doctor walks to the door. "Any questions?"

"I'm in pain," Hadeel moans.

"The nurse will give you a pain killer to relieve the pain. I'll be back to construct the cast in a few minutes."

Jonathan hides his hands in his trouser-pockets and looks at Hadeel. "I'm so sorry," she says, avoiding his eyes.

"Yeah. Me too."

"My Aunt Munira is waiting for me tomorrow at Heathrow."

"I know," he says.

"I don't know what to do," she says in a small voice. Most probably he's thinking how childish and stupid she is. How unlike his brilliant wife, how disappointing she turned out to be.

Jonathan suddenly clears his voice and says, "I think you should stay for surgery. You can't leave like this."

"I can't stay," she says.

"I understand your reasons, but you're my responsibility now. If you leave and God knows when you'll get to do the surgery, you may ruin your ankle forever."

She wipes a tear. "I'll take responsibility."

"And live with a limp?" he asks, looking at her in the eye.

A knock on the door ushers in a middle-aged nurse pushing a wheelchair. "Hi," she says cheerfully. Except for the name tag on her upper right chest, nothing else indicates her profession. She's wearing a casual beige shirt tucked into black slacks, her light brown hair tied back in a ponytail. "I have to move you to a different room where the doctor will put the cast on your foot." She takes the bed-remote and lowers the mattress to the wheelchair's level. "Shall we?" She smiles as if she's offering Hadeel a fun ride in an amusement park.

Hadeel slowly slides into the wheelchair. Her swollen ankle looks like an alien limb attached to her leg. Her head spins as the nurse rolls her along a narrow hallway over gray linoleum-tiled floors. They turn left into a larger room that smells of anesthetic and burnt plastic. The nurse helps her up to a firm gurney and carefully lifts her legs in front of her. She hands Hadeel a tiny paper cup with a blue pill inside it and a cup of water. "This is for the pain. The doctor will be here in a minute."

Hadeel looks around for Jonathan.

"Your uncle is in the waiting room," the nurse says. "Would you like me to call him? It might be a couple of minutes before the doctor shows up."

"My uncle?" Hadeel panics.

The nurse reads from a board attached to the wheelchair. "Jonathan Walton."

Hadeel exhales and waves her hand. "Oh. No, it's okay." His distress oppresses her more than her own. She needs to call Munira and tell her what happened. Hadeel's heart tightens when she remembers her last conversation with her aunt, "I'll see you tomorrow at the airport." Her voice was harsh and reproachful, a different tone coming from her gentle aunt, just because Hadeel refused to ask for exhuming her aunt's body. Now Hadeel has a new decision to make; to stay until the swelling subsides which means her father will find out her whereabouts, or leave and live the rest of her life with a limp? Live with a limp, or cause both Munira and herself a world of trouble from her family?

The nurse leaves the room and shuts the door. There are no clocks on the walls to tell the time. Hadeel searches her pockets for her mobile. Not there, neither is her purse. She tries not to panic; they must be with Amina. She recalls calling Jonathan while waiting with Amina and Yousef to be admitted to the Emergency room. When the hospital staff took her in, Amina left, and promised to call her back after her evening class.

"Are you okay?" Jonathan asks at the door.

"I need my phone."

"I have your purse right here." He lifts the hand holding the her purse.

"Thank you. I'll take it."

"Excuse me." The doctor glides into the room. "This will only take a couple of minutes."

Jonathan nods and leaves with her purse. She wonders why he feels responsible for her when it was her own fault. After all, She ran away from him.

"Ready?" The doctor asks. He sits on a stool and pulls a metal wheeled cart towards him. "This shouldn't cause more pain than what you're experiencing right now. Remember to change the cast when the swelling goes down. Especially if you're not doing the surgery right away."

"How complicated is the surgery?"

"Let's put it this way, it will be more complicated if you wait and the fracture becomes large."

"But you said I can wait a few days?"

"You can. But I recommend you don't wait too long. What color would you like?"

"Excuse me?"

The doctor points at three different rolls of bands on the table. "White, pink, or blue?"

"Blue," Hadeel says half-heartedly. Why does it matter what color it is?

"I expected you to say pink." The doctor must have noticed the puzzled look on her face.

He adds, "Matches your pink shirt."

"Oh." She leans back and tries to keep still and let him wrap her aching foot and calf with the blue gauze. After a few minutes a buzzing sound emanates from a little device he's using on the cast, it smells like burnt plastic. She sits up on her elbows to watch.

"This little machine hardens the gauze and makes it stiff to keep your ankle in place." He stands up and asks her to bend her knee.

Pain shoots up her leg at the attempt. "It hurts," Hadeel squeaks.

"I'll write you a prescription for pain killers. What pharmacy do you use?"

She wipes her eyes. "I don't know. Please talk to . . . my uncle, he's waiting outside."

He picks up his iPad and reads, "Hadeel? Did I say it right?"

"Yes, you did." *Is there any other way to say it?*

"Does it mean anything?"

"It means the 'cooing of doves.'"

"Oh that's nice. Well good luck, Hadeel. Take care."

A few minutes later, the cheerful nurse helps her into the wheelchair and rolls her out to the lobby. Jonathan asks them to wait by the main doors so he can bring the car closer. "It's very windy out there," he says, stepping through the sliding doors.

"We usually lend patients crutches for a few days," the nurse tells Hadeel. "I think you'll need them."

Without waiting for an answer, she disappears and returns in a few minutes with a pair of crutches. "Give this receipt to your uncle. There'll be no charge if he brings them back within a week."

Hadeel sets them over her legs. Charge? So far, she hasn't thought of costs for the medical services. In Kuwait, all medical services are free unless you choose to be treated in a private clinic. She wonders which kind is this one.

Outside, the wind is blowing from all directions. Tall tree branches move like waves in the sky, their leaves rustling like water. Jonathan's car appears in front of the main doors. He holds the car door open so the wind won't slam it shut. The nurse helps Hadeel into the front seat. She buckles Hadeel in and pats her on the shoulder.

"You'll be all right sweetie, don't worry," she says before retreating inside.

"I got your prescription," Jonathan says, taking his seat. He hands her back her purse and a white paper bag. "The doctor said to take one every six hours or when the pain is too much to bear."

"Thank you." She fumbles for her cell inside the purse.

"I'd feel better if you come home with me," Jonathan says moving the car toward the exit. "Just in case you need help moving around."

"No!" she wails. "Please take me to the hotel." The thought of him helping her to the bathroom makes her stop breathing. "I'll be all right, don't worry."

"I'm sorry but I can't leave you alone in a hotel in this condition. Let me at least call a friend of mine to stay with you tonight. A lady," he adds when Hadeel glares at him.

"No need," Hadeel shakes her head. "I'll call my friend Amina, who brought me here.

I'm sure she won't mind staying with me." She pulls out her cell from the purse. It is chipped at all corners and its screen slivered with spider cracks.

Jonathan sighs and drives out of the parking lot. On Broadway, rush-hour traffic slows to a standstill every few minutes. Hadeel texts Amina.

"Actually," Jonathan says. "I think you should consider postponing your trip. You should do the surgery as soon as possible."

"Isn't it going to be expensive?" Hadeel says, hoping he'll change his mind. "Don't worry about the cost. I'll take care of that."

"I need to discuss it with Aunt Munira first."

"Of course. You really should."

She's not sure though. The doctor said surgery had to wait a couple of days until the swelling goes down. If she leaves on schedule, why tell Munira and make her worry? She'd rather do the surgery in Kuwait with her mother at her side. So really, there's no reason to tell Munira, or anyone else in her family, Hadeel thinks, shaking her foot nervously, causing excruciating pain which shoots up to her thigh.

Chapter Nineteen

It is after nine at night when Amina finally shows up at St. Julien. Hadeel, glossy-eyed, is slumped in the armchair next to the window. She has just taken another pain killer and feeling numb all over. Jonathan has been pacing around the small room since he brought her back. She begged him to leave but he adamantly refused to leave her alone.

"Hi," Jonathan says, opening the door for Amina.

Amina glides inside towards Hadeel. "How do you feel?"

Is she wearing a mini skirt? Hadeel lifts her head, peering at her friend. A beastly headache, probably caused by medication and lack of water, forces her to drop her head back.

Amina introduces herself to Jonathan then says, "Don't worry, I'll take good care of her."

"Call me if you need anything." Jonathan jots down his number on a hotel notepad and leaves.

"Are you okay?" Amina rests a cool hand on Hadeel's forehead.

"Ready to explode. Please help me to the bathroom." She pulls herself up, shrieks and drops back into the armchair.

"You have to remember not to step on your injured foot." Amina rushes to get a crutch which Jonathan left leaning behind the door. "Here, this might help."

Hadeel struggles to stand, hands pressed on the arms of the chair. She holds the crutch and hops awkwardly. "I can't do this." She drops the crutch.

"Lean on me," Amina says.

"I need to hurry."

"Okay, let's go." She wraps her arm around Hadeel's waist and steers her toward the bathroom.

The bathroom's bright lights above the large mirrors aggravate Hadeel's headache. She grimaces, and limps to the toilet. Then at the sink she scrubs her face with soap and water, wishing she could wash away what happened. She drinks the remaining water from a plastic bottle she'd left there that morning. Amina is leaning on the door, arms crossed, watching her with a friendly smile.

Hadeel wipes her face with a hand towel. "How can you stay so awake and positive this late at night?" she asks Amina.

Amina giggles. "My parents taught me to always look for the positives in a negative situation."

"What's the positive in this case?" Hadeel tosses the towel on the bathroom counter.

"You don't know this, but since high school, I've always wanted to be your friend. Now look at us." Amina spreads her arms wide offering to help. "Let's go."

"Why did you want to be my friend?" Hadeel asks, wobbling back with Amina.

"I'm not sure right now. Maybe you looked so miserable and sad all the time that I wanted to cheer you up." She laughs and adds, "Actually, you might not know this either, all the girls in our class used to refer to you as the richest yet saddest girl in the classroom."

Hadeel lifts her eyebrows in surprise. She wonders if Amina was referring to the time when Ydaida died, or when her father forced her to don the hijab; she's too tired to think. By the time she settles down in the chair, Hadeel feels like she's in the company of her cousin Haya, protected and relaxed. "Thank you, my friend."

"Shouldn't you lie in bed instead?" Amina asks.

"No. I think this will be easier to get out of. You can take the bed." Hadeel examines Amina's tiny handbag on the floor by her chair. Not big enough for overnight necessities. "I hope you can stay with me tonight?"

"Of course! Let me get the footrest for you."

She carefully lifts Hadeel's casted leg and places it on the ottoman. "So who's the old dude?" she asks.

"What?"

"The man who opened the door for me."

"Oh, he's my aunt's husband." Hadeel pauses, realizing she has a lot of explaining to do but feels too exhausted. She drops her head back and closes her eyes. "He wants me to stay for the surgery."

Amina sits at the foot of the bed facing Hadeel. "Did the doctor say you need a surgery soon?"

"He did. He wants me to avoid stepping on my foot."

"Then you really should stay. What's the hurry to go back?"

Hadeel sighs deeply then frowns. "It's complicated. Besides, isn't it so expensive to do a surgery in this country?"

Amina nods. "It is, especially if you don't have health insurance."

Hadeel lifts her head up. "Do you have health insurance?"

"Of course, it comes with the scholarship."

Hadeel shakes her head. "My father doesn't know I'm here."

"Oh," Amina says, obviously surprised.

Hadeel changes the subject. "Did you have dinner? I'm starving."

"I didn't. I came straight from my class. Let me see what they have this late."

She finds the menu on the TV stand, opens it and points at a couple of items. "They've got burgers and fries. Or salad with fruits."

"I'll take a burger with fries. How about you?"

"I'll do the same." Amina drops the menu on the desk, sits on the bed and picks up the phone. She pushes a couple of buttons and waits.

In a flawless American accent, Amina places the order, twirling the phone wire around her fingers. Her short, short skirt reveals chubby thighs and curvy legs. The fact she isn't as thin as most girls Hadeel has seen in Boulder pleases her because of the weight she has gained recently.

"All right!" Amina places the phone back. "Let's shed some light on the subject." She walks around the room flipping on every light switch available then draws the curtains open even though it's dark outside.

"How did you get this perfect American accent?" Hadeel asks.

"I was born here."

"In America?"

"In Boulder. You can actually say I'm a Boulderite," Amina says with a grin.

"How did that happen?"

Amina drops herself on the bed, tugs off her tennis shoes and tosses them on the floor. "My parents met in Boulder when they were working on their doctoral degrees."

"You're joking."

"I'm not. They fell in love, got married, finished their degrees. Just before they went back to Kuwait Mom gave birth to me. Since then we've spent every summer in Boulder."

"Do they teach at Kuwait University now?"

"Yes, both of them."

"I wonder if they were my teachers when I was a student."

Amina giggles. "I doubt it. They're in the science department. You said you were in the English department?"

"Yes." Hadeel peers at her new friend with new admiration. "How does it feel to have such educated parents?" She thinks of her mother whom she's never seen read a book, and her father who's always watching the news on TV when he's not at the *diwaniya* playing cards with his male friends.

"I'm sure they're not so different from yours," Amina

is saying. "But seeing my parents writing, researching, and grading papers all the time made me decide to do something different in life. I mean other than teach, like making movies."

The sound of a doorbell interrupts their conversation. "Must be room-service. I'll get it." After signing the bill, she pushes the wheel-cart into the room and removes the silver domes off the plates. "Here you go." She places a plate in front of Hadeel.

"Thank you. So did you get your B.A. from CU?"

"No, KU." Amina notices the puzzled look on Hadeel's face and explains. "Kuwait University. My parents insisted I stayed home for my BA, promising to send me here for my graduate work. They think it's better for college kids to stay home until they're more mature." She rolls her eyes.

Hadeel picks up her burger. "Better later than never," she admits quietly.

"Is that why you're doing your Master's online?"

"Yes, my father is so strict." Hadeel chews her food slowly.

"I remember you wore the hijab in high school."

"I still do," Hadeel chokes on a piece of food. She takes several sips of Coke to chase it down. "Actually, I've been meaning to ask you a favor."

Amina dabs her lips with the white napkin, her piercing brown eyes show concern. "Sure. What is it?"

Hadeel cannot meet her friend's gaze. Eyes downcast, she explains how she has stopped wearing the hijab just for this trip which no one in the family, except one aunt, knows about. She then mentions the selfie Amina took in the library without her hijab. "My parents don't know

I've removed it. They would be very upset if they saw the picture on social media."

"I can imagine," Amina nods then gives Hadeel a questioning look. "Where would they see it?"

"On Instagram? I've noticed you have thousands of followers. We both know how much Kuwaitis love social media."

Amina exclaims, "OMG! You thought I'd post it there without asking you? You don't have to worry about that."

"And," Hadeel hesitates. She wipes her greasy fingers with the napkin. "The other one you took of me with Yousef just before I fell?"

"Of course!" Amina gasps. "Are you kidding? I hope that's not why you slipped." Hadeel looks away and says, "Well, maybe . . ."

"I'm so sorry."

"It's not your fault," Hadeel mumbles.

Amina leans back on her elbows, keeping her head up, staring at Hadeel. "You need to relax, Hadeel. We're still young, let's leave worrying for older people."

Hadeel's eyes suddenly fill with tears. "I wish I could." She wipes the tears with her hands and tries to smile. "You remind me of my cousin Haya. Do you know her?"

"No, I don't think so. But I'm so curious why you're secretly in Boulder."

"My aunt who lived here, died recently. Jonathan, 'the old dude' you met earlier was her husband. He wrote after she died and said it was important for me to visit."

Amina sits up. "I'm so sorry. How did she die?"

"She was run over during a protest in Denver."

"Oh My God!" Amina yells. "That was your aunt? Amal Al Hamdeen?"

"You knew her?"

Amina tucks her legs under her thighs and pulls the bed sheet over to her waist. "No, but the accident was covered on local news. There were articles in several newspapers. I asked my parents about her, they knew her. They said they met her when they lived in Boulder."

"Really? What did they say?"

"All I remember is they thought she was very kind and very Americanized." She makes inverted commas signs with the word Americanized.

Hadeel shakes her head. "I don't know much about her. The last time I saw her was twenty years ago, when I was five. Jonathan claims she wrote to me regularly, but I never got any letters."

Amina seems to struggle not to show pity. "Your father?"

Hadeel nods. "Anyway, it's all over now." She wants to change the subject, but their words hang in the air like storm clouds.

Amina's mobile rings loudly. "It's Yousef," Amina says, silencing the device. "He's been asking about you. He thought it's his fault you fell. He should have kept a better grip on your hand, he said."

"No. It's not his fault. Please tell him that. I was careless."

While Amina texts, Hadeel checks her own mobile and through the cracks of her screen finds a message from an unknown sender.

"Are you sure you don't want to sleep in the bed?" Amina pats the mattress. "You need to rest before your long trip tomorrow."

"I'm wide awake now. Please feel free to use the bed. I'll let you know if I need anything."

"I'll go brush." Amina picks up her bag from the floor.

Hadeel checks the message. It's Kevin. He has attached the selfie with the message: "My business meeting has been postponed. Another day in Boulder, maybe two. Any chance I can see you tomorrow?"

Hadeel stares at the picture. Ya Allah, nobody would believe he's not Kivanc Tatlitug, the Turkish actor.

"So happy to see you smiling," Amina says walking back from the bathroom. She looks lost inside the hotel's huge bathrobe, its hem sweeping the floor as she walks. "Hope you don't mind me using this robe. There's another one if you'd like."

"No, no. Don't worry about it."

Amina pushes the food cart with the empty plates toward the door. She rolls the cart out into the hallway, locks the door, turns off all the lights except the one next to the bed. "Let's get some sleep. I have a morning class tomorrow." She draws the curtains closed.

"Wait," Hadeel says. "I want to show you something." She turns the cracked screen of her mobile toward Amina. "Who do you think this guy is?"

Amina leans closer to the phone before she exclaims, "OMG! Is that Kivanc Tatlitug? I can't believe it!Where did you meet him? And you're not wearing your hijab there either!"

Hadeel laughs out loud. "So I'm right. He does look like him."

Amina snatches the mobile from Hadeel's hand. "He's not Kivanc? That's hard to believe."

Hadeel ponders the possibility of meeting him again with Amina. Or perhaps having Amina meet him alone. "He's in this hotel, right now," she tells her friend.

Amina gives Hadeel back her cell and plumps up the bed pillows. She props them against the headrest, climbs under the sheets and says, "I want to know how you met him."

Hadeel tells her the story in detail and how they took the selfie outside his room. "You didn't worry about him posting it on social media?" Amina winks.

"No! First, he's American, no one in Kuwait knows him. Second, I gave him a different last name and told him I was married." Hadeel bites her lips.

"What? Why would you do such a thing? Oh, wait, are you married?"

"No."

"So why? He's gorgeous."

Hadeel shrugs. "I don't know. I was nervous. That was the first time I was alone with a guy." She laughs and adds, "especially one this handsome."

"I understand," Amina yawns.

"Do you have a boyfriend?" Hadeel asks, even though not sure if she should have. Amina pulls the bed sheets up to her chin. "No, unfortunately."

"What about Yousef?"

"Him? No way, he's just a friend. Besides, he has an American girlfriend. How about you? Do you have someone?"

Hadeel gazes at Amina wondering if she should tell her about Raj and watch how she'd react to that. She's never told anybody about him, not even Munira. Although she has always wondered how people, especially Kuwaitis, would react to the fact he's Pakistani, a nationality so alien to them. Most Pakistani expatriates in Kuwait do manual work. There's a comforting tone in Amina's voice urging her to tell. She's tired of hiding the truth that she still loves him.

Amina closes her eyes. "With a father like yours, I know your chances of having a boyfriend are dim."

"He wants me to marry my cousin."

Amina doesn't reply, making Hadeel think she's fallen asleep. But after a while she asks, "Do you like your cousin?"

"I like him as a brother."

Hadeel's phone starts ringing. "It's Kevin," she says before she accepts the call. "Hello Kevin. Sorry I have a friend over, and we are about to go to sleep."

"A boyfriend?" Kevin asks.

"No!" Hadeel shouts making Amina jump up in bed. "A girl . . . friend." Then she mouths "sorry Amina." To Kevin she says, "I'm sorry we can't meet tomorrow."

"I don't mind meeting him," Amina says loudly.

"My friend says she doesn't mind meeting you. When do you leave?"

Kevin says, "Not for a couple more days. Let's all have breakfast together tomorrow. Here at the hotel?"

"I'll ask her and text you later. Goodnight Kevin."

When Hadeel puts down the phone, Amina shrieks, "My God you're so stiff! Is that how you talk to someone who's interested in you?"

Hadeel inhales then lets the breath out slowly. "He wants to meet for breakfast. Really Amina, I don't want to get involved. Besides, I have much to do before leaving. Jonathan says there's something important we need to discuss, and I've been putting it off and avoiding him." She shakes her foot and screams, "Ouch! And now this problem."

"You have to stay for the surgery," Amina says.

The time on the digital clock reads 11:50 p.m. Luckily there's a glass of water on the table next to the medicine bottle. "I think I'll take another pain killer," Hadeel says.

Amina clears her throat. "I just got a great idea. If Kevin doesn't mind being a part of my videos, I'll have a million followers."

"I'm sure of that." Hadeel swallows the pill and puts the glass on the side table. "I'll send you his number and you can contact him about breakfast tomorrow. I can't go, you'll have to meet him by yourself. I hope you don't mind."

"Don't worry about that, Hadeel," Amina says softly. "You should worry about your ankle. A beautiful girl like you should not spend the rest of her life with a limp."

Hadeel's heart sinks. Those were the doctor's words as well. She closes her eyes, and tries to focus on what she would need to do if she decides to stay for the surgery. There are many people she needs to contact. First she has to send a message to Aunt Munira. Before she changes her mind, Hadeel picks up the phone and types, "I fell and broke my ankle. I need to stay for surgery. Should I? Please tell me." She taps send.

Next message is for her father, the one her mother persisted about. With heart thumping, she writes, "Baba! I don't want to marry Nawaf. Please wait until I get home." She rereads the message and waits for the pill to numb her worry and fear, then she clicks send.

The words of the third message are easy, she has memorized them for almost two years. It's overdue. Rapidly, she types the words as she has recited them like a prayer every night. Her finger lingers on send as a low-battery signal appears on the cracked screen. The words of her mother's mantra boost her courage, "We should always hope for the best. Who knows what tomorrow will bring?" With a shaking finger she presses send.

Chapter Twenty

AMAL 2001

Living in Colorado with Jonathan often took me back to my teenage years in Lebanon with my father. The fragrance of ancient cedars on sandy hills and miles of mountainous terrain reminded me of my trek with Baba and his history lessons. Treading glaciers and hiking the Rocky trails with Jonathan revived hopes for a better future. During summer, we rented a cabin in Steamboat Springs, Colorado, where we enjoyed the stillness of long summer days together before he had to start work at the university in Boulder.

In winter, while Jonathan was at work and snow fell almost every day, I thrived in the company of Washington Irving. His Knickerbocker's History of New York was a treat! Telling the history of the city from the point of view of a fictitious character was so creative. I loved it and laughed with every page of the book. I was considering writing a similar humorous account of the history of Kuwait when September 11 happened. That event ripped all new hopes and merriment out of my heart. It was during that time that I applied for jobs at universities in Boulder and Denver. That event and my Master's thesis about the Christian Inquisition against Islam might have played a role in diminishing my chances of getting a position anywhere in the U.S.

Then one gloomy day in March 2003, America attacked Iraq. An attack based on false accusations and revenge. Some people rejoiced over Saddam's removal, but I only saw the misery of innocent Iraqis, millions of them. I sank back into depression. Baghdad, once the seat of wisdom and knowledge, was reduced to rubble. Who did that war serve? How could one person have the power to ruin millions of lives? I tried to comprehend the oppression of Muslims and Arabs, imagining conversations with Washington Irving, asking him for an explanation of what happened to the once glorious Muslim civilization. I had nightmares and sometimes long clear dreams that seemed more like visions and revelations.

In one of those dreams, I was running barefoot in Irving's estate in Sunnyside. Birds were just starting to chirp and call from every branch of the tall ancient trees. It was dawn, pink and orange lines gradually erasing the darkness behind the mighty trees, as their branches solemnly swaying, wiping off the dark clouds. I passed the pond that Irving himself created by the main gate, ignoring the pain in my feet from the sharp gravel in the path that led to his house. Cold, wet wind whipped over my skin. I was in my early twenties; my long wild hair covered my bare shoulders in the scanty Spanish-style dress I wore.

I knew where to find him at this hour of the day. I dashed around his two-story house with the green door and turned to the right heading toward the river. There, on the veranda facing the Hudson, Irving sat in his green Voltaire chair. A checkerboard blanket over his legs and old- fashioned binoculars in his hands. He must have been watching birds and boats sailing placidly at this hour of the day.

"Mr. Irving!" I called, breathless. "Mr. Irving!"

When he finally heard me, he placed the binoculars on a table next to his chair and awkwardly tried to stand. He was an old man at that time, with high forehead and gray hair, possibly a couple of years before he passed away at the age of seventy six. I dropped at his feet. "Mr. Irving, forgive my intrusion, but I had to see you."

"Oh, my child." His gentle voice soothed me. "How can I help you? Come, sit next to me." He held my elbow, helping me stand up and take the chair next to him. "Here, put this blanket around your shoulders. It's already cold these September morns, you must be freezing in this rare attire."

I wrapped the blanket around my trembling body and sank onto the iron-cast chair he offered me. Before I could explain the reason for my visit, he exclaimed, "Are you Arab? But you must be, I can tell from the fire in your eyes. You seem to have traveled a far distance and time. Tell me, has your nation regained its glory?"

"Oh Mr. Irving, quite the contrary." I swallowed hard and tried not to sob. "Arabs and Muslims have never been in a worse circumstance in history than they are now."

"Why? What happened?" His cheeks contracted with concern. "Aren't there enough of them anymore?"

"There's no shortage Mr. Irving! More than ever! Busy preparing for the afterlife instead of living this one."

"What about science, philosophy, and literature? Your people gave the world so much—algebra, astronomy, and medical knowledge. You are the nation of 'Read,' the very first word of your Holy book."

"All lost Mr. Irving, all lost! I was hoping you would tell me what can be done before it's too late."

"That's a shame, that's a shame," Irving repeated. Then he held up a book that was resting on his lap. "As a matter of fact, I was reading Percy Shelley's poem, The Revolt of Islam. How brilliant Mr. Shelley was, I regret never meeting him."

"But you met his wife."

He waved his hand. "After Percy died. She's the one who alerted me to some parts of this book, The Revolt of Islam. As well as the parts that he was forced by his publisher to omit."

"I never understood the reason Shelley insisted on this title for the poem when critics insist it has nothing to do with Islam."

"That was an enigma to me as well, until Mrs. Shelley explained." He lifted his forefinger in the air to silence me then picked up the book and opened it to a page marked with a paper divider. "For example, who do you think of when you hear this in Canto 2, number 41?

'. . . I remember now,
how once, a slave in tortures doomed to die,
was saved, because in accents sweet and low
He sung a song his Judge loved long ago'

I gasped. "Bilal, of course! The slave who was tortured because he converted to Islam.

Mohammed and his men freed him and because of his beautiful voice made him the first Muezzin to call for prayers, the *athan*, the 'song his Judge loved long ago,'" I recited, mesmerized.

A smug smile grew on Irving's lips. "It's all in the poem when you read it carefully.

You'll also understand what he meant by the Revolt of Islam."

"I will re-read it. But, Mr. Irving, do you think Muslims have a chance to survive the literary and media war against them?"

Irving shifted in his chair and moved his head closer to mine. "The answer is in the core of Islam. 'Read' is the very first word of the Quran, there must be a reason for that. Loving Earth and what's on it, people, animals, and plants are basic tenets in Islam. By revering Nature, Muslims touch earth with their foreheads five times a day! Their prayers are timed by the movement of the sun. Their calendar is controlled by the moon. There's no greater display of reverence for earth than that. Nature is our essence. When we get drawn away from it, we lose our essence, our morals and creativity."

"Perhaps that's what Shelley referred to by the revolt or reform of Islam?" I whispered in awe.

He nodded. "And think more of Islam's image in Europe during Shelley's time, which was delivered by the Ottomans and their practices around the world."

"Ah . . . I see what you mean."

At that moment, female voices from inside the house drifted toward us. Must be Irving's nieces who cared for him like their own father, ready to call him in for breakfast. "I should go." I rose to my feet and placed the blanket back on his knees.

"Wait!" He lifted his right hand. "Before you leave, tell me about my country. How is the state of affairs in America?"

I hesitated to tell him. But he was a truth-loving man and deserved no less. "Your people, Mr. Irving, have just elected a new President. He's neither a politician nor a poet. He's a businessman. His main concerns are power and money, nothing else."

"Oh," Irving said, the sparkle in his eyes disappeared. "God help us all."

Before I left, I hugged him long and tight. I could still feel the warmth of his embrace and the scent of the vapors he used for his asthma. In his ears I whispered, "Thank you, Mr. Irving, for sending me Jonathan, my *athan*, the love of my life."

Chapter Twenty-One

Hadeel awakes from a deep sleep and stretches her arms. It's the first restful sleep she's had since the beginning of this journey. She finds herself in the brown armchair next to the window, the thick curtains drawn, the room sheathed in darkness except for a dim reading light on the headboard. The details of the previous night slowly stream back to her mind. This is the day she's scheduled to leave Denver and go back to London. How late is it? She leaps up. A splitting pain in her ankle makes her scream and collapse back into the chair.

"Amina!" she calls in distress. "Amina?"

The light over the bed is aimed at a slip of paper where Amina slept. The hotel phone is flashing. The digital clock is blinking 9:20. Hadeel reaches for the crutches by her chair. She picks one up, tries to use it, drops it and hops for the note.

Hadeel,
It's 8 a.m., Gotta run.

Remember? I'm having breakfast with Kivanc :) and then off to my morning class at 9. Let me know if you decide to stay for surgery. I hope you will. You can stay with me.
Later, Amina

Hadeel tosses the paper and grabs the hotel phone. "You have three messages," the automated voice announces. Jonathan's somber voice drones in the first two messages. He offers his help to check out of the hotel in the first message. In the second he asks when he should pick her up. The third message is from his mother. Dorothy's voice, clear and formidable, says: "Hadeel! I'm so sorry about your accident. Wish I could help. Hope to see you again."

Hadeel slams the receiver down. The woman's voice fills her with awe and defiance. "I need to pack!" She yells at Dorothy. She searches for her mobile and finds it on the side table by the chair next to her medication jar. She grabs it, presses the switch button, nothing happens, it's dead. She recalls the low battery signal when she sent the most important three text messages in her life. Her heart throbs. How did everyone react to her messages? Pain crawls up from her ankle to her thigh. She pushes the charger clip inside the mobile but it doesn't fit. The mobile's charging slot is crushed closed. It's impossible to charge the phone. She sits on the bed and mourns the device as if it's a dead corpse. It was her only link to the people she knows, to her world, her family.

Hadeel covers her face with both hands. There has to be a way to communicate with her mother who must now be trying to call her. How did her father react to what she told him about marrying her cousin? What was Munira's reaction and answer to her question about the surgery? And the third message, the one hidden in her mind for two years until she found the courage to finally write and send it. How did Raj react to it when he received it? Was he shocked? Angry? Did he reply? For a moment, Hadeel wishes they didn't receive the messages, knowing that texts are usually delivered even with low battery. So all three responses will stay hidden in the phone, awaiting her answer.

The hotel phone rings. A surge of relief washes away some worry when she hears Jonathan's voice. "Thanks for calling, Jonathan!"

"Would you like me to pick you up?" he asks.

"Yes," she says in a small voice. She clears her throat and adds, "I mean, I need to pack and get ready. Is an hour from now okay?"

"Sure. See you then."

"Thank you."

Using the crutches, Hadeel hops to the bathroom and gazes longingly at the bathtub. She's in desperate need of a hot shower but the thought of making her cast wet prevents it. Instead, she sits on the edge of the tub and settles for a soapy washcloth to clean herself. She's still not sure if she should stay for surgery. How can she without telling Munira? How is she going to reach her? All phone numbers are stored in that little device of hers. She hasn't even memorized her mother's number since she stored it under "Mama." She will have to ask Jonathan to take her to an Apple store to fix her phone.

"Oh my God!" Hadeel exclaims when she pulls the curtains open. A white world outside takes her breath away. Mountains, Flatirons, rooftops, and ground are blanketed in snow.

Feathery snowflakes are tumbling down. Snow in April? The wild wind of the previous night must have brought in the change of weather. Yet, it's sweltering hot in Kuwait according to her mother's last messages the day before. "Yumma, I wish you could see this," Hadeel says, her eyes welling with tears. "*Asfah* Yumma, please forgive me. You will be the first one to face Baba's wrath when he gets my message."

A knock on the door startles her. "Jonathan?" She hops to the door.

"I'm a little early but I need to discuss your surgery," he says at the door.

"Come in," she pulls the door open. "Please excuse the mess." Luckily Amina had made the bed and removed Hadeel's prayer rug from the floor before she left.

"I talked to the doctor this morning," Jonathan says, walking in. "He has an opening for surgery in a couple of days. He said you can leave two days after the surgery if you're careful."

Hadeel sits on the edge of the bed. "What about the cost?"

Jonathan waves his hand. "You don't have to worry about it Hadeel. I'll take care of it. Have you told your aunt?"

"I did." Then on the verge of tears she adds, "My cell is broken, I can't charge it. I can't get her reply. I can't get in touch with anybody." her voice breaks.

Jonathan looks around. "Where's your phone?"

She points at it on the night table and wipes her tears. He examines it closely. "Looks pretty bad."

"Is there an Apple store in Boulder?" "There is, but I doubt if this can be fixed."

"I'll buy a new one."

"I doubt if you can restore your Kuwaiti number here in Boulder."

"I'll ask Amina!" The glimmer of hope vanishes when she realizes she doesn't know Amina's phone number either.

"There must be a way. Let's check out of the hotel first." He takes her suitcase.

Hadeel slips the dead device in her jacket and straps her purse around her neck and takes the crutches. Jonathan watches her struggle toward the door before he hooks his arm with hers and pulls the suitcase with his other hand.

At his house, Hadeel stands by the glass doors and gazes out at the garden. The eight- angled fountain is now covered with white flakes. She thinks of how much she wished as a child to scoop snow in her palms and taste it. She's always wondered if fresh snow tastes different from crushed ice which she liked to crunch on. This would have been the perfect time. She takes a deep breath and listens to Jonathan talking behind a closed door. A weird inkling that Amal used to wait in the living room for her husband to get off the phone makes her uneasy. Had Amal been as lonely as Hadeel feels now? Totally cut off from the world she once knew?

Jonathan startles her when he suddenly emerges by her side. "Your friend is on the phone." He hands her his cell.

Hadeel takes the phone, looking at him questioningly. "What friend?"

"What friend? It's me!" Amina is giggling. "I tried your number but you're not answering. Where are you?"

"Amina, I need your help!"

Amina's voice becomes serious. "Tell me. Jonathan said your mobile is broken."

"I need to call Aunt Munira but I don't know her number! Or anyone else's, not even Mama's. Jonathan wants me to do the surgery but I can't stay without telling Munira. She'll be waiting for me at Heathrow tomorrow."

Amina doesn't respond for a long time.

"Hello?" Hadeel looks at the cell screen to check if they got disconnected.

"I'm here," Amina says. "I was trying to figure out a way to help. I can give you my Kuwaiti phone to use until your phone is fixed. Is Munira your father's sister?"

"Yes."

"Then I know her last name. I will try to find her phone number for you. I'll text it to Jonathan when I find it"

Chapter Twenty-Two

AMAL 2016

Hadeel, I saw you! I saw you! After twenty years of hoping and praying to see you, I finally did. You were with your girlfriends at the Avenues Mall in Kuwait. You looked so happy and beautiful. Ya Allah, how you've grown. I yearned to hug you, talk to you, listen to your voice. The bond I felt between us when you were born, was thriving, filling my heart with warmth and yearning. But Munira wouldn't let me. She warned me against getting near you. She wasn't supposed to let me see you in the first place, she said. "Rashid would be very upset with me if I allow it."

I was in Kuwait for business, had no time or plan for a family reunion. Besides, who remembers me there? However, before I arrived, I begged Munira to arrange a meeting with you, just for an hour. She insisted on doing it "properly." You know Munira, she has to do things "the right way." She told your father. I think her main reason was to restore our family relationship.

She was hoping Rashid would relent and invite me to his house. How naive of her. Not only did he warn her about telling you I'm in Kuwait; he also showed Munira a picture of me at a party having a glass of wine with male friends to prove to her how rotten I am. Shocked, Munira succumbed to his warnings. How can I blame her? I remembered how shaken I was when I saw my father drink alcohol.

At least Munira allowed me see you from afar. You were celebrating your twenty-second birthday with your friends at a cafeteria in the mall. Munira and I met at a coffee shop across from the one you were at. I watched you, tears blurring my vision. I could've run to you, hugged you and left. You probably would not have recognized me anyway. But I didn't want to upset Munira or embarrass you in front of your friends. She watched my movements like a hawk, grabbing my arm whenever I moved to get something from the table. I was amazed at how protective she was of you, as if you were her own daughter. She boasted showing me photos on her phone of you two celebrating every birthday together the last ten years. You two looked inseparable. I was jealous but happy for both of you, for your connection. It was my choice to leave you. She chose to be with you, every single day of your life. I understand.

After you left with your friends, Munira went to the prayer room, so I strolled around the luxurious mall. What struck me most was how crowded it was, how people sat around in coffee shops all day long. Appeasing their senses with the pleasures of food and idleness seemed to me the Arabs' favorite past-time at that moment. I felt as if somehow, I was transported to James Thomson's *Castle of Indolence*, where people's "only labour was to kill the time." I don't remember Kuwaiti society being this idle when I grew up in the seventies. But what saddened me most was seeing Kuwaiti children in the hands of foreign labor while their parents shopped or sipped their drinks. No doubt that would be the case at their home as well. I heard those children speaking broken English learned from their Asian helpers. When I spoke to them in Arabic they did not understand their own native language. What will be the repercussions of such a system? I wondered.

After that trip, Munira's letters and messages became sparse. She dropped me. No more news or updates about you or other family members. But your image that day has remained with me, engraved in my heart. I hope you are still happy. The last I time I bugged Munira for news about you she told me you graduated from Kuwait University and became a teacher. I hope that teaching and learning remain a part of your life forever. Read, read, Hadeel.

At least Munira decided to keep the "womb connection" by sending me Eid greetings twice a year. "Womb connection" sounds funny, doesn't it? Muslims adhere to it thinking they'll gain credit towards Paradise, even if they aren't sincere about it. Just flick a message to a relative and there you are, you've accomplished a "womb connection," and gained a credit toward paradise. How naive is that? It seems as if the majority of people there don't understand what Islam is all about. They think it's nothing more than a bunch of daily rituals which make them content and happy about themselves. Ignoring the fact that Islam means being peaceful with all creatures, especially family members. Islam is about unity and acceptance of all religions and peoples inhabiting this beautiful place we call earth.

Talking about Islam reminds me of a funny thing that happened to me a couple of weeks ago. I was in New York for a few days to work on a research paper. While I was strolling the streets of Brooklyn, looking for Middle-Eastern food, I heard a faint *athan* coming from inside a small building I was passing by. I froze. I haven't heard that call for decades, yet the emotions that overtook me surprised me. My eyes welled with tears and a feeling of longing pierced my heart. The warmth of Ydaida and the *mutawa'a,* our childhood neighbor, swept over me unexpectedly, I almost tumbled to the ground. Then, as if drawn by their hands, I walked inside the courtyard, expecting to find the sidra tree.

The building turned out to be a little mosque. There was no sidra of course—instead a thin mimosa tree stood in the middle of the square yard. People, with their sleeves rolled up to their elbows were rushing toward a room in the back, obviously to perform ablution. To my amazement, I felt a strong urge to go inside the mosque. But at the door, a man stopped me, pointing at my hair. I totally forgot about the rule to enter a mosque veiled. I was walking away when I felt a tap on my shoulder. A young woman, wearing the hijab, handed me a scarf with a smile. She must have seen me turn away, so she voluntarily offered to help. I took the scarf and followed her inside the mosque, to the women's section. Standing next to her in a straight line with other women we performed our Friday prayer. Words I have not uttered in twenty years flowed from my heart to my lips effortlessly. I was stunned. I still am.

Chapter Twenty-Three

Within one hour, Hadeel must decide whether to head to the airport to catch her flight to Kuwait or stay in Boulder for surgery. Jonathan remained in his home office, waiting for her decision. Hadeel is about to put an end to her dilemma and ask him to take her to the airport when he suddenly emerges with a piece of paper in his hand. The white paper, torn from a ringed-edge notebook, has an eleven-digit phone-number in blue ink.

"Here it is," he says. "This is your Aunt Munira's number. I found it in Amal's phone book."

Hadeel looks at Jonathan in disbelief.

"You can use my phone." He gives her his mobile.

"I'm not sure if ...," Hadeel says while calculating the time in London. It's early evening, Munira must be worried sick after receiving her message about the accident. "What shall I tell her?"

"Whatever you need to tell her. It's up to you." He rushes back to his study. Hadeel dials the numbers. If

Munira doesn't answer she'll leave her a message. "Aloo?" Munira answers instantly.

"Ammiti Munira! Ana . . ."

"Ya Allah! Ya Hadeel! Why aren't you answering your phone? I have called you a hundred times. What happened?"

Hadeel waits for her aunt to calm down before she explains the accident and how she lost her phone. "And now," she adds, "I'm not sure if I should stay for the surgery or leave this afternoon. What do you think? Please tell me what to do."

Munira remains silent. Her breathing which was audibly short and quick when she first called, slows down finally. "What did the doctor tell you?"

"He said I shouldn't wait too long. What might be a simple surgery now, could be more complicated later."

"And knowing you, you'll keep postponing and hesitating." Munira exhales a deep breath before she says, "Maybe you should stay and get it over with."

"What about you? How are you going back without me? What are you going to tell my parents?"

"I will tell them the truth. I'll tell them it's all my fault."

"No! Don't blame yourself. It wasn't your fault I fell."

"Hadeel," Munira says in a tone she only uses when she imparts serious news. "When I couldn't get hold of you after your last message, I took a vow. I promised Allah if you come out of whatever it is that stopped you from calling me safely, I will take responsibility for what happened. I will tell your parents the truth about this trip. I will tell them it's my idea, you didn't want to do it but I pushed you to it. I'll do anything to make you happy." She whimpers.

Hadeel remains speechless. Since the day Ydaida died, Munira has never cried or showed weakness to anyone. She took refuge in her prayer rug and kept her head high in face of hardship. As Hadeel mulls over Munira's last words, a burden begins to lift off her shoulders.

The burden of facing her mother with her whereabouts and her father about her trip alone to America.

"So you think I should do the surgery?" Hadeel asks when Munira calms down.

"You have to decide for yourself, Hadeel," Munira's voice is muffled, barely audible.

"I'm done making decisions for you. Do what's best for yourself. I'm taking the flight back to Kuwait tomorrow with or without you."

"Can't you come over here to be with me?" Hadeel pleads even though she knows the answer.

"No. Send me a message if you decide to stay for the surgery. Whose phone is this?"

"Jonathan's, Amal's husband." When Munira doesn't make a comment Hadeel adds, "He offered to pay for the surgery."

Munira hesitates for a second then says, "Thank him for the call. *Ma'asalama*."

Hadeel switches the phone off and relaxes her shoulders. She feels her mind clearing, as if a fogged-up glass gradually clears to allow visibility of what's behind it. It's all up to her now. Like an adult, she should make a decision and take responsibility, instead of letting others decide, then blaming them if things went wrong. She lets out a breath and decides that she will stay.

Jonathan's muffled voice in his study sounds comforting. Hadeel leans back in the leather chair and looks around at her surroundings with fresh eyes. Outside, snow has stopped falling, and the sun is faintly shining through a gray sky. Still, it looks cold, with everything, including the fountain, enveloped in white. For the first time, Hadeel notices a set of French doors, to the left of the patio doors, facing the kitchen. Must be the formal dining room, Hadeel thinks, sitting up to get a better view of the dark room. Amal's smiling face appears behind the glass doors.

"Bismillah," Hadeel gasps. "Is that you, Auntie?"

"Did you say something?" Jonathan appears by her side.

Embarrassed about her hallucination Hadeel shakes her head no. "Can I have a glass of water, please?"

"Of course." He returns with a tall glass in one hand, and a file in his other hand. "Thank you, Jonathan. I've decided to stay for the surgery."

"Good. So we have time to discuss this." He sits in a chair next to the fireplace, placing the file on his lap. "Do you remember the envelope I left for you at the hotel?"

Hadeel gulps the water and wipes her lips. "Please forgive me Jonathan for being so tardy. I didn't get a chance to look at it again. My mother has been bombarding me about something urgent and I totally forgot about it."

Jonathan waves a hand. "It's okay, read this first." He takes out a sheet of paper from the file and watches as Hadeel reads:

Dearest Hadeel,

Jonathan and I had many discussions about what to do with my apartment in Malaga. The flat contains my father's personal history besides books and references. It would be a shame to give it to someone who might not appreciate it. Jonathan and I agreed we should pass it on to you.

Please go there before you make a decision. Go there, feel the presence of your grandfather, and cherish it. I'm hoping you'll learn about him and keep his memory alive. There are books of his own poetry, tapes of his own music, and his voice. I left them all there hoping that one day you might be able to see them. You should listen to him singing his own Arabic translation of Shakespeare's poem "Tomorrow and tomorrow and tomorrow." His voice eerily reflects the meaning of Shakespeare's poem, and Yuba's interpretation of life.

No matter what you decide to do with it, always remember I love you,

Amal
November 2018

Hadeel looks up in astonishment. "I don't understand."

"Amal wrote this six months ago. She wasn't sure about mailing it since you never answered any of her letters."

"Why don't you keep the apartment?"

Jonathan shakes his head. "I have no need for it. Besides, it was her wish to keep it in the family."

Hadeel sucks in a breath. "I can't keep it a secret from my father. I have to tell him, and if I tell him . . ." she bites her lips before she finishes her sentence, the first thing he'd do is trash all the books of poetry and music before anyone could see them.

"You understand how much it meant to her, I hope."

"I do, she was so close to Grandfather." Hadeel rereads Amal's letter. "When was the last time you were there?"

"We were there last December for a whole month. I don't think I'll go there again, not without her." He shakes his head. "So, when you decide what you want to do, let me know. I'll mail you the necessary documents."

"All right." Hadeel glances at Jonathan's cell that lights up then starts ringing. She hands it to him.

Jonathan switches it on silent mode. "The other thing I need to discuss with you is a legal matter. The lawsuit."

"Yes, you mentioned it. I will work on the paper you asked for."

"Thank you. Let me give you some background, though. Amal contributed a valuable literary discovery regarding who urged Washington Irving to write The Legendary Life of Mohammad. She discussed the subject with a colleague, the same one who libeled her. A few months later he published a paper with a similar hypothesis without even acknowledging her contribution. He received literary acclaim and was appointed editor-in-chief of the department journal they both worked for because of it."

"That's terrible!" Hadeel exclaims.

"Exactly."

"How can I help?"

"When we were in Malaga last time, she showed me a journal that published her literary discovery. It was published some years ago in Arabic. She was going to translate it and use it as proof of her own research. I'm hoping the date will prove that she was the original person who came up with that conclusion. My Arabic is not good enough to read and translate the article accurately."

"Now I'm so curious," Hadeel says. "Who did Amal think prompted Washington Irving to write Mohammed?"

"Mary Shelley."

"Really? Why?"

"Mary Shelley was married to Percy for many years. They shared thoughts, writings, and editing manuscripts. When Percy died, his father threatened to deprive her and their only surviving son of inheritance should she think of writing a biography of her husband, especially about his religious inclinations. So she must have looked for someone else who was knowledgeable of the subject."

"Washington Irving?"

"Yes. Biographies of both prove that she earnestly sought to meet him. She finally did. First casually with a friend of Irving's who was an actor in London. Then she invited Irving to dinner with her father William Godwin who wrote 'Political Justice.' Irving mentioned the dinner meeting, but, unlike him, not in detail. The subjects they discussed during that meeting remained a secret."

"Amal thought they discussed a biography of Percy Shelley?"

"Not necessarily." Jonathan shakes his head. "Especially because Irving never met Percy Shelley in person. Amal thought that was a possibility, but more probably they discussed Islam and what it meant for young Shelley. As a result, Irving, who was a diplomat, and knew how to steer clear of conflicts, wrote his book Mohammed and published it a year later. I'm wondering if Mary Shelley had helped with some documents written by Percy himself."

"Do you have the journal that published Amal's paper?"

"Yes, let me get it." He starts towards his office.

"Wait! Jonathan!" Hadeel exclaims. "My Aunt Munira wanted me to ask you something which I found hard to discuss all this time. I'd like to get it off my mind."

Jonathan turns back and takes his seat. "What is it?"

Hadeel tries to select her words carefully so not to hurt his feelings. "I know that Amal wasn't very religious. But, was she by any chance buried according to Islamic tradition?"

Jonathan lifts his eyebrows in surprise, as if he's never heard of such a thing. Then he says, "As a matter of fact she was."

"Really! She was? Why didn't you ever tell me?"

"You never asked." He shrugs.

"Did she ask to be buried according to Islamic tradition?"

"No. But one of the people who joined the protest where she was killed was the Imam of the local mosque. We've known him personally through lectures and research at the university.

He suggested after the accident that we perform the funeral according to Islamic tradition. He believed Amal died a martyr for Islam."

"Oh My God!" Goosebumps crawl all over Hadeel's body. "Ya Allah!" she repeats in disbelief. Amal? A martyr of Islam? In Paradise? Looking down at them, maybe laughing at her? She should tell Munira the good news, well, the sad news.

"So, you see," Jonathan says with a pale smile. "You didn't need to do whatever you did the night you arrived."

Hadeel stares at him. Had he mentioned this in his letter, she wouldn't have needed to take this trip and break her ankle. Munira wouldn't have had to lie to Hadeel's parents and send her on this journey. Hadeel wouldn't have met Jonathan or his mother. But then, Amal would have remained the aunt she'd thought she was, uncaring about her family or background. Hadeel would never have learned the truth about Amal. Ya Allah!

She blinks and gazes at Jonathan. An urge to hug him sweeps over her. "I can't wait to tell Munira," is all she could say for now.

Jonathan gets up from his chair. "Let me get the Arabic journal."

"Wait!" She stops him. "One more question."

"Okay." He halts, scratching his head.

"That oil painting," Hadeel says pointing at it over the fireplace. "Can you explain it?" She holds on to the arms of the chair and lifts herself up. She moves carefully to the mantelpiece and points at the lower right corner of the painting. "Is this a dog?"

"It's a fox."

Hadeel peers closer, sure enough, the fluffy white hair around the face, the shrewd, intelligent eyes. "Why a fox?

Jonathan gives her a keen look. "How do you say fox in Arabic?"

She tilts her head. "*Thalab*. Oh my God! Thalaba!"

For the first time since she met him, Jonathan laughs. "Yes." He points to the figure sitting on the stone bench in the garden where Hadeel likes to sit. "So can you guess who this is?"

"Robert Southey." Hadeel is happy to be able to answer the question. The man has thick eyebrows over a prominent nose and full lips. At his feet is his Thalaba.

"Correct," Jonathan says in a professorial tone.

"Is that you?" Hadeel asks, noticing a resemblance between the tallest man in the group and Jonathan. She looks back and forth between them.

Jonathan nods. "Ah-ha. Who else do you recognize?"

Hadeel examines the woman whose arm is around the shoulders of a middle-aged man standing between her and Jonathan. "Is this Amal?" She asks.

"Yes."

"And that?" Hadeel points at the man Amal seems more affectionate with than Jonathan.

Hadeel is certain he's not her grandfather.

"That's Washington Irving. Or at least what we thought looks like him, based on several drawings of him."

"Oh, so the painting is not a replica of a photograph?"

"No, no. We commissioned a young local artist to paint this based on a popular style lately of painting gatherings of famous people in different settings. We wanted to have fun with it and make it personal, so we included ourselves with our favorite authors. Do you recognize anyone else? You mentioned Mary Shelley as part of your thesis."

Hadeel gazes at the only other woman in the center of the painting. Her light brown hair is tied to the back of her bare neck, her ample forehead shines under a decorative garden lamp. She's holding the hand of a handsome fragile-looking young man. They are walking toward the fountain while looking back at the artist.

"That must be Percy Shelley and his wife Mary."

"Yes. Amal decided on the details. Including these." He points at the writing around the fountain ledge which alternates between Arabic and English. *La ghaliba illah al haqiqa*, there's no victor but the Truth. And of course, there's no conquerer but God.

Hadeel examines the painting closely. It's clear to her now that the attention of Amal and Jonathan in the painting is drawn towards a spot behind the patio doors. There's the vague shape of a couple, arm in arm, on the verge of stepping out to the garden to join the others. "Who are those supposed to be?"

"The artist decided to leave them for the imagination of the viewer. I like to think of them as Mary Wollstonecraft and her husband Godwin."

"What did Amal think?" Hadeel asks.

"She liked to think they're her parents, your grandparents. Who do you see?" he asks, looking at her curiously.

Hadeel shakes her head contemplatively. "I'm not sure."

But if she would tell the truth, she'd say she sees herself, arm in arm with Raj. She's taking him to meet his favorite poet, Robert Southey, and his Thalaba.

Chapter Twenty-Four

Amina's wild hair is pulled back from her face with a teal-green headband, matching her jumpsuit. Her smile glows as she holds open the door of her apartment for Hadeel and Jonathan. "Won't you come in?" she asks Jonathan.

"No, thank you." He places Hadeel's suitcase inside the foyer. He looks at Hadeel and says, "I'll see you in a couple of days. Call me if you need anything."

"Thank you so much, Jonathan." Hadeel waves and waits until he disappears from her view down the staircase.

"Come in, Hadeel. Make yourself at home." Amina pulls the suitcase into the living room.

Hadeel stops to take a breath by the coat rack. "I'd like to leave the crutches right here." She rests them on the foyer's wall and slips off the one sandal in her right foot. "Thank you for taking me in, Amina. I hope your roommate won't mind."

"Why should she? You're staying in my bedroom," Amina says pulling the bag through a sparsely furnished living room. A black coffee table between a gray leather couch and a matching love seat. "Come, I'll show you where it is."

"Everything looks new." Hadeel looks around while hopping and wishing she hadn't left the crutch behind.

"It is. The whole building is new, only three years old. I was lucky to find a space here when it first opened. Over there is the kitchen which Libby and I share, along with this living room."

"Who?"

Amina giggles. "Libby, short for Elizabeth. She's in class right now. The best thing about this dorm is that each bedroom has its own en-suite bath, so we don't have to walk out of our rooms naked."

Hadeel quizzes her friend with a puzzled look and lifted eyebrows.

"Just kidding. Come on I'll show you my bedroom." She turns into a hallway behind the kitchen and pushes a door open. Compared to Hadeel's hotel room this one is spacious and bright with natural light from a large window. Instead of a mountain view though, it overlooks an elaborate fire escape attached to the back of another dorm. Under the window is a brown desk with a computer and a laptop. Facing it is a double-sized bed and a night table. Hadeel stops next to a bookcase with framed photos of Amina and other happy young people laughing, partying, and hugging each other.

Amina leaves the suitcase at the foot of the bed and opens a side door that Hadeel hasn't noticed. "And this is the bathroom."

Hadeel's eyes linger longingly on the shower. "I wonder if I can shower the day of the surgery."

"You can shower now if you want to."

"How?" Hadeel points to the cast.

"I'll wrap it with a plastic bag. You can use the side shower handle instead of the head shower to avoid water over the cast. That's what I did when I broke my leg as a teenager." Amina shrugs. "Come, let me show you something you'd like."

She walks to the desk and waits for Hadeel to join her, then unplugs a mobile that was charging and hands it to Hadeel. "Fully charged. It's my Kuwaiti phone. All yours to use."

Hadeel gazes at her friend not sure if she should accept it. "Really?"

"Really. Don't worry, I don't need it. I've already hooked it to the internet so you can call your mom and aunt with WhatsApp."

"I need to call my mother."

"You can call whoever you want. Sit down, why arc you still standing?" She offers the desk chair on wheels and holds it in place for Hadeel to sit down.

"Can't thank you enough, Amina."

"Would you like a cup of tea? I can't wait to tell you about my breakfast this morning."

Busy examining the phone in her hand, Hadeel absentmindedly asks, "Why? What happened at breakfast?"

Amina giggles. "You forgot! Remember Kevin?"

"Oh, yes! Of course I do." Hadeel leaves the phone on the desk and follows her friend to the kitchen. She sits on a high stool by the kitchen counter. "How did it go?"

Amina fills an electric kettle with water and switches it on. She looks at Hadeel with a face beaming with happiness. "He is so gorgeous."

Hadeel laughs. "I already know that. What else?"

"And polite and smart," Amina blurts out the words. "He didn't stop asking about you.

Are you sure you don't want him for yourself?"

"I'm sure, Amina. Don't worry about that part," Hadeel looks down at her fingernails, the polish on them is starting to fade.

The kettle clicks and the sound of bubbling water gradually stops. Amina pours two cups and carries them toward Hadeel. "Sorry, I didn't ask what kind of tea you'd like. I just made regular Lipton."

"This is great, thank you."

"Shall we sit over there on the couch?" Amina takes the two cups in both hands.

"Sure. So what happened?"

Amina sets the cups on the coffee table and bites her lower lip. "I'm seeing him again this evening."

"La wallah? Are you really?"

"Yes. Would you like to join us?"

"No! Not in this condition." She points at her leg. "Besides, I have work to do before the surgery."

"What kind of work?"

"I promised Jonathan to translate a research paper from Arabic to English."

"I am going to take one of his classes next semester," Amina says, sipping her tea. "I think I can add it as an elective."

"Lucky you," Hadeel says, picking up her cup from the table. "I wish I could, he's so knowledgeable. But tell me, where are you going with Kevin?"

"I wanted to show him the Hill area. There're so many cool places for young people there. Do you know he works for Google? They're expanding their headquarters in Boulder. So he'll be back here soon, he told me." Amina's voice quivers with excitement.

Hadeel smiles. "I hope you'll have a good time tonight. Don't worry about me, most probably I'll go to sleep early."

Amina pats the couch with a flat hand. "I'll sleep here so I won't disturb you when I get back." She lifts her hand when Hadeel protests. "Don't argue, I've done it before and it's fine with Libby." Amina lowers her voice. "She brings her boyfriend sometimes. He stays in her bedroom, and I don't mind him sharing the kitchen."

Amina's nonchalant attitude shocks Hadeel, making her wonder if she could handle such a free-style living. She shakes off the thought and asks, "Do I need a password for your cell?"

"No." Amina jumps up and fetches the phone from the bedroom. "Let me show you a few things though, in case you need to call me."

Some minutes later, noise at the main door breaks the girls' concentration. "That's Libby," Amina says, hunched over the cell, pressing icons on its screen. "Hi Libby! I'm in the living room."

A tall blond girl in a long burgundy parka saunters in. "Hi," she says crossing to the other side of the living room.

"Libby, I'd like you to meet my friend Hadeel from Kuwait."

Libby turns around and looks at Hadeel. "Hello, I'm Libby. How do you say your name?" "Like, her deal." The three girls laugh.

"Nice to meet you. Sorry about your foot. Amina told me."

"I'm having the surgery in two days," Hadeel tells her, just for the sake of saying something.

"Good luck." Libby nods and walks to her room.

"So," Amina says. "If you need to find anyone's number in Kuwait, click on this icon. It's the Kuwaiti phone directory. Hopefully it will include the numbers you need."

"Thank you so much. I need to find my mother's number."

"You haven't memorized it?" Amina exclaims. "Let's try it. What's your mother's last name?"

"Let me do it." Hadeel opens the link and types her mother's name. She waits for a list of similar names to roll down. "I should've known better," Hadeel says, disappointed. "Either my father or one of my brothers got her the mobile and the number. I'll try their names later, otherwise I have to wait until it's morning in London to get it from Munira."

"Okay," Amina jumps up. "I need to shower and get ready to go." She runs to the bedroom and closes the door.

The time on the phone is six in the afternoon in Boulder, one in the morning London time, three Kuwait time. Hadeel finds the note Jonathan gave her with Munira's number in her pocket and adds it to Amina's contacts. She writes the message: "Ammiti Munira, this is Hadeel.

I'm using my friend's phone. I decided to stay for surgery! Please send me Yuma's phone number. I love you."

Hadeel watches the check sign on her sent message. It shows only one signal, meaning her aunt's phone is not switched on, or not linked to the internet. She sighs and tries to calm her racing heart. Her aunt is going back home alone to confront her parents. She can imagine how shocked and angry her father will be when Munira explains. Hadeel wonders if subconsciously it's the reason she's decided to stay for the surgery. Out of cowardice and fear of confrontation. *Asfah Ammiti Munira*, please forgive me. Cold sweat trickles down Hadeel's back, makes her shiver. She places the phone on the table and covers her face with her hands.

"Are you okay?" Libby asks.

Hadeel realizes she's moaning audibly. "Sorry. Yes, I'm okay."

Libby continues to the kitchen, opens and closes cabinet doors. A humming microwave sound then rapid popping like balls thrown on a wall follows. Soon the apartment is filled with the aroma of freshly popped corn. Libby carries a steaming bowl heaped with yellow popcorn to her room and closes the door.

When Amina walks out of the bedroom, Hadeel realizes she has dozed off on the couch.

In corduroy brown pants and a beige turtle-neck top Amina looks smug and cozy. Her bright smile looks brighter with the red lipstick on her full lips.

"Here's a plastic bag for your cast," Amina says. She wraps Hadeel's leg with the plastic and secures it with a large rubber band. "Let me help you take a shower before

I leave." She grabs Hadeel's arm and leads her carefully to the room. "I've changed the bed sheets and left clean towels for you in the bathroom."

The curtains over the window are drawn, and the bedroom smells of soap and a flowery perfume. Hadeel lets her friend assist her in getting ready for the shower she longed for since she fell and broke her ankle.

"Ready?" Amina asks.

"Wait! I need to get my nightgown from the suitcase. And my prayer-mat."

"I'll get them for you." Amina places the suitcase on the bed and zips it open.

Hadeel hesitates before asking, "Do you know the direction of the *qibla*?"

"Of course!" Amina laughs. "But, are you sure you can pray with this cast?"

"I won't prostrate. But I should be able to kneel."

Amina spreads the mat at the foot of the bed facing the window. "There you are."

"Can't thank you enough, Amina, *wallah*." Hadeel steps gingerly to the bathroom with the nightgown. When she walks out fifteen minutes later, Amina emerges with a little tray.

"I made you a cheese sandwich for dinner."

"*Ya Habibti!*" Hadeel exclaims. "How nice. And a glass of milk? I feel I'm at home already."

"Wonderful! Now I can go without feeling guilty for taking your gorgeous boyfriend."

"He's not my boyfriend!" Hadeel shrieks. "Say hello for me."

"I will." Amina throws Hadeel a kiss on the way out.

Feeling positive and hungry, Hadeel gulps the milk and chomps down the toasted sandwich. After praying, Hadeel remembers the most important piece of news she has for her Aunt Munira. How did it slip her mind? She settles between the bed sheets and blankets and writes, "Ammiti Munira. You will not believe this! Not only was Amal buried according to Islam, the local Imam also thinks she died a martyr. So she's in paradise now!! I hope this news will make you happy."

Chapter Twenty-Five

The angelic voice of Fairuz wakes Hadeel from sleep. Motionless, she remains under the covers, listening to the familiar melody and lyrics. "We will return, oh my love, we will return."

Where is the song coming from? Hadeel lifts her head, expecting the music to stop with the motion. But it continues. Hadeel listens intently to the part she, and probably the whole Arab world, love so much, the flowing melancholic tunes of the accordion dancing and swaying to the beat of drums and percussions, ending with Fairuz's long moan, "Ahhhhh, ah . . ."

Hadeel realizes the music is emanating from Amina's desk under the window. It must be an alarm set at half past six in the morning. Except for Fairuz's soft voice, the apartment is perfectly still. Does Amina listen to this song every morning? Wouldn't it make her homesick? It's making Hadeel's heart dissolve with nostalgia for home, and her family. She grabs Amina's cell, hoping to find a reply from Munira. None. Tomorrow morning Hadeel goes to surgery, and it would be nice to talk to her mother before that. But unless Munira sends her the phone number, Hadeel can think of no way to reach her.

She washes and brushes her teeth wondering why Munira hasn't answered her messages. In the meantime, she needs to work on Amal's paper. It's not long, if she works on it all day, she can email it to Jonathan before he picks her up for surgery.

"Good morning," Amina sings, standing at the door. "Did my alarm wake you? So sorry, I forgot to turn it off."

"No, no," Hadeel says, happy to see her friend. "I think I've slept enough."

Amina sits on the edge of the bed and examines her friend closely. "I'm glad to see you look rested."

"Yes, thanks to you. Tell me about last night."

A big smile creeps up Amina's sleepy face. She runs her fingers through her disheveled hair and tucks it behind her ears. "Mom called me while Kevin and I were having dinner. I switched it to video call and introduced her to him. She sent me a text message later at night saying, 'Be a good girl now, Amina. He is very charming!'" Amina laughs and skips toward the window to lift the shutters and bathes the room with light.

Stunned, Hadeel watches her friend. She can't believe there's a parent from her own culture who doesn't mind her daughter dating, let alone dating a foreigner. She can't even dream of it for herself. She wonders how it would feel to get a mother's blessing for a relationship with a boyfriend. Hers gave her hell over a long distance one.

Outside the window the sun is bright in a clear sky. The snow that covered the staircase has already melted. "Do you have classes today?" Hadeel asks.

"I have an evening class. I need to prepare for it at Norlin Library. How about breakfast now?"

"Yes, that'll be nice."

"Scrambled eggs?"

"Sounds good. I'll change and join you in the kitchen."

"Bring Amal's paper and read it to me while I make breakfast," Amina says on her way to the kitchen.

Seated at the counter Hadeel reads in Arabic, "Did Percy Bysshe Shelley Convert to Islam?"

"What?" Amina exclaims over the sound of sizzling eggs in a frying pan.

"That was the title of Amal's paper."

"Never heard of such a thing before. Please, go on."

Hadeel reads, "*On a cold winter day in the year 1812 young Percy Shelley, knocked on the door of Greta Hall in Keswick, England. He was nineteen, seeking the acquaintance of Robert Southey, the author of his favorite poem* Thalaba the Destroyer. *He had written to Southey beforehand and requested the meeting. Southey, thirty-seven years old at the time, had already heard of Shelley. He had consented and scheduled the meeting.*

"*When young Shelley arrived at his home, Southey showed him to his office and closed the door. The details of the meeting remained unknown. However, biographers of the two poets, based on letters of Southey's wife, and later letters by the two men to friends, reported a heated argument between them.*"

"Wow!" Amina interrupts, "I'm getting goosebumps imagining the scene in a movie about Shelley and Southey. Sorry, please read on."

"A few days later, in a letter to a friend, Southey wrote the following about the meeting: 'Here is a man at Keswick who acts upon me as my own ghost would do. He is just what I was in 1794. His name is Shelley, son to the member for Shoreham . . . I daresay it will not be very long before I shall succeed in convincing him that he may be a true philosopher and do a great deal of good with 6000 a year." (footnote#1 Southey, *by Edward Dowden, 1888).*

"But Southey was proven wrong. Shelley, whose ethics and beliefs were more worthy to him than materialistic gains, held fast to his beliefs. In letters to friends he stated that he'd rather live in poverty than succumb to social necessities as Southey did. To Southey he wrote, "I confess your recommendation to adopt the system of ideas you call Christianity has little weight with me, I cannot hope that you will be candid enough to feel, or if you feel, to own, even in your mind, an innocent and a persecuted man, whose only real offense is the holding of opinions you once held." (footnote#2)

"Oh My God!" Amina exclaims. "I'm getting more goosebumps. Toast?" she asks, holding two pieces of bread in her hands.

"Yes, please," Hadeel says without looking away from the paper. She continues, *"In 1818 Shelley published his epic* The Revolt of Islam. *He described it as 'A vision of the nineteenth century.' Before printing it, the publisher Charles Ollier, asked for a meeting with Shelley to discuss changes to the poem. Shelley's wife Mary and his friend, Thomas Love Peacock, attended the meeting. After some resistance to the changes, Shelley succumbed to their demands but insisted that the poem be published with the title,* The Revolt of Islam."

"Wow!" Amina exclaims. "Breakfast is ready."

"Wait! Please, let me finish reading the next two paragraphs. They're very interesting."

"Okay." Amina draws close and looks over Hadeel's shoulder.

"Most critics of the poem insist that it has nothing to do with Islam. However, logically, why would a poem be so titled without having anything to do with Islam? It sounds like a frivolous claim. This paper attempts to prove that Islam is actually the core of the epic and its main purpose. It is about Shelley's vision of a revolutionized Islam, True Islam as it was meant to be. One that is totally different from the version the Ottomans displayed in Europe at that time.

"This paper also attempts to provide yet another example of how the West worked purposefully to cover up any favorable presentation of Islam. A literary inquisition against Islam which has never stopped since the Spanish Inquisition. Thus, they not only encouraged Orientalism but also got rid of, and covered up literary accomplishments by prominent authors who wrote positively about Islam.

"The paper will first analyze historical events during Shelley's life, which might have influenced his vision in his epic, The Revolt of Islam. Second, we will discuss events and facts about Shelley's life which biographers and publishers, under the influence of his father, the Baron, tried to hide and obliterate from history.

"Finally the paper will provide ample evidence of how the sequence of these events led a prominent American

author, Washington Irving, to write a book entitled The Legendary life of Mahomet, *which in recent years has been published simply as:* Mohammed."

Amina gasps. "This is sooo interesting! I'd love to read the whole paper when you finish."

"I will make you a copy of it." Hadeel closes the journal and puts it aside. "Right now, I'm famished."

Chapter Twenty-Six

The morning of her surgery Hadeel gets a video-call from her mother. She grabs the phone with both hands and hits "accept." Her mother's face fills the screen; thin, worried and beautiful.

"Yumma . . .!" Hadeel sobs. "*Samheeni*, forgive me, Yumma, please."

"Hadeel! Binti, *habibti!* What are you doing to yourself?"

"*Ana Asfah,* I'm so sorry, should have told you I was traveling by myself . . ."

"Tell me what happened to you. *Ya waili,* you look terrible! You lost weight. And your hair! It was long and beautiful when I last saw you."

"Just a moment, Mama." Hadeel sits at Amina's desk and props the phone on a pile of books until she gets a proper picture of herself on the top corner of the screen. She hears noises around her mother in the living room. "Is Amma Munira with you?"

"No."

"Has she returned to Kuwait?" Hadeel's mind begins to

offer different scenarios. What if her mother thinks she's still in London with Munira?

"Yes she's back. She told us everything." Yumma looks at someone to her right and says, "Your brothers are here. They want to see you."

One of them turns the phone around and tries to place it on the coffee table so they can all see her. Hadeel notices the familiar objects she grew up with, her favorite rocking chair with the cushion she bought from Zara Home. The silver framed pictures of her family during the last Eid on the corner table. Poignant emotions choke Hadeel and prevent her from speaking.

"*Hadeelo*," Abdullah, her middle brother says. "Where are you right now?"

She swallows her tears. "In my friend's room. How are you, Abboodi? I miss you." Azeez, her youngest brother pushes his head in front of the lens. "Is this America? Doesn't look different from here."

"Yumma, does Baba know?" Hadeel asks, her heart misses a beat.

Azeez answers, "Wait till you get here, he will break your head."

Yumma slaps him on the knee. "No, he won't. Hadeel, when is your surgery? When are you coming back home?"

Hadeel checks the time on the phone. "The surgery is in two hours. I should be back in Kuwait in four days, inshallah." She notices Abbadi, her eldest brother sitting on the far end of the couch. He's resting his elbow on side table, his head on his hand and looks worried. "Abbadi, I miss you, say something."

He shakes his head and takes a deep breath. "We miss you too. Inshallah your surgery will be successful and you'll be back home safely."

Tears flow down Hadeel's face. "Thank you so much. I love you."

"Hadeel!" Mother takes the phone from the table. Her delicate features fill the screen again, the kohl, smeared under her eyes tells about fresh tears. "Take care of yourself. I would have come to be with you if I knew earlier."

"I know," Hadeel whimpers. "Is Baba angry at me?"

"No, he's just worried. He said to wish you the best."

"And to come back soon so he'll break your head." Azeez puts his face in front of the camera lens. Hadeel notices his newly grown mustache. "*Yallah* bye," He waves and walks away.

"Mama, I love you so much."

"I love you too, habibti. Don't worry, everything will be good, inshallah."

"Is Amma Munira all right?"

"She is, don't worry. She was here this morning and explained what happened. She has just arrived from London, you know."

"I know. I hope Baba didn't give her a rough time," Hadeel says. "It's not all her fault, of course."

Yumma sighs deeply. "Can I reach your friend at this number? In case I want to ask about the surgery? What's her name?"

"Amina. I'll send you her local phone number soon. Pray for me, Mama."

"We're all praying for you, *habibti*."

Amina walks into the bedroom as soon as the call ends. Her hair is pulled back in a ponytail, her knapsack is strapped on her right shoulder. She touches Hadeel's cheek. "I have to go to class now."

"Is it okay to give my mom your local number?" Hadeel wipes her tears. "She'd like to call you to ask about the surgery."

"Of course!" Amina hugs her tightly. "Don't worry, it's going to be an easy procedure. I'll see you afterwards, okay?"

Hadeel nods. "Thank you, Amina." She watches her friend leave and recites a sincere prayer for her safety and success.

Later, exactly at the time Jonathan said he'd pick her up, he rings the doorbell. "Shall we go?" he says when she opens the door.

"I'm ready."

In the car, he repeats the doctor's instructions which he has already told her the day before over the phone. "The arthroscopy procedure is less invasive than a surgery, therefore recovery time will be faster."

"Does it require incision and stitches?"

"A small incision, I think. The whole procedure shouldn't take more than two hours, and most probably you can leave the hospital the same day. They'll keep you a couple of hours for observation after you come out of anesthesia, to make sure you're doing well."

"Are they giving me general anesthesia?"

Jonathan stops at a red traffic light on a busy street heading east. The mountains are now behind them. "I don't think so. He said because of your age, he can do it with local anesthesia. Don't worry, it will be all right."

Hadeel squints and bites her lips. "Do you know this doctor?"

"Yes, he's my mother's orthopedist. He did her hip surgery a couple of years ago."

"Oh." The image of Dorothy dragging her legs when she moved around her living room unsettles Hadeel.

At the hospital, she tries to stay calm. What if what's happening is not real, it's just another video game, one she purchased by mistake. She should toss it in the trash-bin after it's over and forget all about it. During preparations for the operation Hadeel cooperates with the nurses who are checking her vitals and asking her questions about her health history. In the surgery room, soon after she meets the anesthesiologist, whose jokes she does not understand, she immediately falls asleep.

When Hadeel comes to, the surgery is over. The nurse who called her name to wake her up is smiling and removing tubes and instruments from her arms. "You're all done!"

"Can I leave?"

"In a little bit. Your uncle is outside, would you like to see him?"

"Oh, yes please." Uncle Jonathan, Hadeel smiles to herself.

He walks toward her cubicle. "Hamdillah 'asalamah," Jonathan says in perfect Arabic, Thank God for your safety.

Hadeel gives him a big smile. "*Allah yeselmak.*"

"The doctor said everything went well. It's important now that you keep your foot elevated for a couple of days to prevent swelling." His phone rings and he answers, "Yes, she's awake. Wait a sec." He hands his cell to Hadeel and says, "Amina."

"*Hamdillah 'asalamah*, Hadeel," Amina's cheerfulness goes straight to Hadeel's heart.

"Thanks, Habibti."

"Your mom left me a hundred messages. Shall I tell her you'll call her in a little bit?"

"Yes, please do!"

"I'm on campus, going home now. I'll see you there."

"Here's Jonathan, he'll tell you what time I'll be there."

Jonathan steps away while talking to Amina. How she wishes she could call her mother herself. An hour later a nurse wheels her to Jonathan's car. Outside the sun is setting behind the mountains, but without the big colorful display Hadeel saw the day before.

A huge vase of red roses on Amina's coffee table is the first thing Hadeel notices when she hops into the living room using the crutches and avoiding stepping on her left foot.

"I better go now," Jonathan tells Amina and hands her Hadeel's purse. "Please call if you need anything."

"I need to make reservations to go back home," Hadeel pleads to him.

"Can you email me your itinerary? I'll work on it." He starts to leave then turns back. "By the way, this coming

Tuesday, is the event in memory of Amal at my department. I'd really like you to attend, Hadeel."

"That's three days from now." Hadeel looks at Amina. "I don't want to be a burden on anyone that long."

"Hadeel!" Amina exclaims. "You're not a burden. I was hoping you'd stay for the whole week."

"Let me think about it Jonathan." Hadeel's phone rings in her purse. "That must be my mom. Excuse me, I need to answer the call."

Amina and Jonathan walk towards the main door.

Yumma's worried face fills the screen. "Hadeel, how do you feel?" "I'm good, Yumma don't worry. The doctor said everything went well."

"*Alhamdulillah.* Did he say when you can travel?"

"He said I need to keep my foot elevated for two or three days. So maybe I can leave after that. Can you ask Munira to book my return flight for Wednesday? She's the one who bought the ticket."

"I will ask her, don't worry."

"Is Baba angry at me?" Hadeel whispers.

"I told you he isn't. Wait, I'll let him talk to you."

"No!" Hadeel's heart tumbles. "Isn't he asleep? It's after midnight your time."

"He wanted to make sure everything went well with you."

"Just tell him I love him."

"Thank your friend Amina for me, zain?"

"Zain, Yumma, goodnight. I'll call you tomorrow morning my time."

"*Ma'asalamah.*"

Amina joins Hadeel on the couch. "*Maskeena*, she's so worried about you."

"She asked to tell you how much she appreciates your help."

Amina waves her hand. "You'd do the same for me, Hadeel, I'm sure. Aren't you going to ask who sent these roses?"

"Who?"

"Don't you want to guess, first?" Amina reaches for the card planted in the middle of the bouquet.

"My mom?"

"No?"

"Jonathan?"

Amina laughs. "No! Yousef! He's blaming himself for what happened." She gives Hadeel the little card.

Hadeel reads it, "Get well soon, Hadeel. I'm sorry for what happened. I'd like to see you before you leave."

"He wanted to come over today but I told him you need to rest."

"Yes, thank you, Amina. I'm so tired."

Chapter Twenty-Seven

AMAL 2018

Habibti Hadeel,

I haven't written to you in a long time since I saw you in Kuwait a few months ago. I returned from that trip heart-broken, we were so close, yet I couldn't talk to you or hear your voice. I succumbed to Munira's wishes against mine, because I was thinking of your welfare. I couldn't decide if my sudden appearance in your life would be of any benefit to you at that moment. However, since then I became less worried about you and your wellbeing. The way you looked, confident and positive, assured me that you'll be able to maneuver yourself through life safely.

The other reason I haven't written to you is because of a new job I accepted at the publishing department of a university in Denver. I now commute between Boulder and Denver four times a week. I have never liked driving; traffic shatters my nerves. So now I'm taking public transportation. That way I can use the commute time to read and work.

Today, all day, I've been thinking of you because of a dream I had of you last night. It was a beautiful dream, almost real. I can't stop smiling when I think of it, how you and I were close, holding hands. My father, your grandfather, was also in the dream. Somehow, we all met in my garden. I introduced you to him and soon you two sat tête-à-tête, talking intimately. You both looked so natural and happy together! Let me tell you the dream in details.

It was dusk, the sky was getting dark. Jonathan and I were switching on the garden lights when Yuba placidly walked toward us. A full moon appeared behind him and brightened the sky. A cool breeze revived our waning energies at the end of the day. Father was his usual self, jovial, talkative, eyes twinkling. He approached the fountain, stooped down, and carefully examined my tiles, the ones that say, *la ghaliba illa alhaqiqa*. When he straightened up, he looked at the moon, closed his eyes and recited,

Don't go crying at the walls of Alhambra,
Heaving over the hills of the valley of the Darro,
Your wasted tears will only blend with the millions
already shed,
Your sighs will in vain seek that of el suspiro del Moro one.
The pain will remain for God only knows how long,
Until the truth becomes clear for everyone.
The narratives will constantly change,
But the truth will stay the same.
The Truth will stay the same.

"That's beautiful 'Ba," I exclaimed. "Who said that?"

"I just did. I got inspired by your work." He pointed at the tiles, melancholy engraved all over his face.

"Here, have a seat." Jonathan brought three chairs and placed them by the fountain. He switched on the fountain water and took a seat next to me. The water's gurgling, and the burbling of the gentle breeze of the evening took me back to the marble halls of Alhambra. "The Mussulman's earthly paradise," as Washington Irving put it in his book, *The Alhambra.*

"I wonder sometimes, Jonathan," my father said, "if it's possible for people to live without religion. Cherishing only reason and compassion toward each other. Wouldn't that be enough for living together peacefully?"

"I wonder about that myself," Jonathan said.

"Just think, religions came when there were no schools to teach people about good and evil. So those were the first schools without buildings. Now that there are schools everywhere," Father makes a sweeping gesture with his hand, "do we still need religion?"

Jonathan pondered for a moment. "I think as long as the afterlife remains a mystery, people will cling to religion to explain the unknown. Some religions, including Islam, give hope for prolonged living in the afterlife."

Father looked at me. "Is that why religions are so popular, Amal? Isn't, *al haqiqa,* the truth, good enough for everyone?"

"Like you just said in your poem, some people seek the truth. By seeking the truth, you encounter uncertainties and doubts before you get to a universal truth. For others, following strict religious rules provides a fixed structure for their lives. They'd rather have somebody think for them instead of using their own minds."

Father nodded. "True. Even though we insist it's the ability to think that distinguishes us from animals."

"Which is one reason, among many others, Islam promotes thinking and learning," Jonathan said. "I regret that this fact is not well emphasized by Muslims nowadays."

"It does not serve those who are in power," I offered.

"True but sad," father said. "Many wars throughout history were initiated for false religious reasons. But what about the 'inward light' within us? Isn't it enough to replace the need for religion? What do you think Jonathan? Have you read *Hayy ibn Yagzan* by Ibn Tufayl?"

"The twelfth-century Arabic novel on which Defoe based his *Robinson Crusoe*? I taught the book in one of my classes a few years ago. Some of my Muslim students got very upset by it."

"Alas. The idea of reason clashing with religion bothers some people of faith." Jonathan smiled. "That class led to another one dedicated to the philosopher Ibn Rushd, Averroes as he's known in the West. It raised so many arguments that I had to invite the local Imam to explain some issues to the most faithful." Jonathan made quotation signs with his fingers while saying the last two words.

Feeling suddenly enlightened, I exclaimed, "Is that why Muslim societies are so stagnant and resistant to change?"

"That's one interpretation," Jonathan said.

"What do you think, Baba?" I insisted. "Is it possible that in the future, people would give up thousands-of-years old rules for a reasonable moral code? A system of rules that is suitable for all peoples to live peacefully together, not just one group of them?"

"People don't have to give up faith, Amal," Father said. "Faith can heal the soul. It's a private relationship between a person and his creator. But it should not be taken out of that context, a private relationship. Wouldn't that solve most problems in the future?"

Like magic, invoked by the word future, you, Hadeel, walked into the garden toward us.

You wore a white dress and a beautiful smile, holding your head up high with confidence. I rushed to meet you and introduce you to my father, but you two acted like you'd already met. You hugged and held hands, gazing into each other's eyes.

"Have a seat, Hadeel," Jonathan said, pulling a chair close to my father's for you. "What do you think?" I asked you. "Would life be better for your generation with or without religion?"

"There's someone," you said pointing at the patio doors, "who's more knowledgeable than I in this subject. I'd like to introduce him to all of you."

You hurried to get that person. I was so anxious to meet him, wondering if I knew that person. Was it your father Rashid? Was it Prophet Mohammed? Or, your beau, Hadeel? I couldn't wait to find out.

Unfortunately, at that moment, my alarm went off. Oh, how I wished I could have met that person. Who was it? Have you already found the love of your life? Are you happy, Hadeel? Munira once, in one of her rare letters, mentioned that since childhood you've wanted to be good rather than happy. Since then I've been praying that you are both good and happy. My dream reminded me of your wish.

Chapter Twenty-Eight

In her friendly, unimposing way, which reminds Hadeel of her cousin Haya, Amina hovers around her like a butterfly. Hadeel, sitting at the kitchen counter, places the journal she's reading down next to her empty coffee cup.

"What is it, Amina? You seem restless this morning."

"I've something to tell you," Amina says, scratching her ear.

"Bismillah, in the name of God. What is it? Is it serious?"

"No, no. But you're going to have a visitor in an hour. And I'm not supposed to tell you who it is."

Hadeel examines her friend's face, trying to figure out something from her expressions.

She tilts her head to the side. "What's going on? Who is the guest?"

"I don't know. But I was told you know that person."

"Who told you?"

"Jonathan."

"Jonathan told you he's bringing a visitor to see me in an hour?"

"Correct."

"Without telling me?"

"Correct."

"But who is it? His mother? I don't want to see her if that's who it is."

"Wallah, Hadeel, he didn't tell me! He just said, someone 'earnestly wants to see Hadeel'. Those were his words."

Hadeel's heart tumbles at a sudden thought. "Is it my father?"

Amina knits her eyebrows together. "Would your father contact Jonathan? Wouldn't your mother give him my number? Wouldn't they contact me instead of Jonathan? Use logic, Hadeel." She taps her head with her forefinger.

Hadeel reaches for her crutches and wishes she could run away. "I don't know anyone else who wants to see me. And I don't want to see anyone!" The image of Dorothy interrogating her about her thesis becomes more bothersome.

Amina follows Hadeel to the bedroom. "Isn't this fun though? It's like a mystery game. And since it's Sunday, I have time to solve it with you."

"What if I don't want to play? And look at me. Do I look like someone who can meet visitors?"

"Well," Amina pulls her lips together. "You have a point there. Let me fix your hair and give you one of my new blouses."

"It won't fit me, you're petite I'm large. Please call Jonathan and say I can't see anyone today."

"Okay, I will." She pulls her mobile from her pocket. "If you're sure of that. Remember, it could be someone you'd like to meet."

Hadeel watches Amina search for the number on her phone. She's right, Jonathan wouldn't bring just anyone over. And, if it was his mother who wanted to see her, there's no reason not to say it was her.

"Jonathan?" Amina says looking at Hadeel.

"Wait!" Hadeel hollers. "Tell him it's fine."

Amina gives her a thumbs-up. "Hadeel agreed to meet your guest. But I have a question. We need a clue, is it a he or a she? Oh, okay, see you soon."

Hadeel sits on the edge of the bed and puffs out air from her lips. "A clue? A he or a she? Why didn't you just ask who it is?"

Amina ignores her question. "It's a he. Therefore, you really have to change those sweats." She opens her closet door and runs her fingers over clothes on hangers. She stops at a white blouse with ruffled sleeves and pulls it out. "Mom sent me this blouse. But I've been avoiding it because it's loose and not my style. I bet it will fit you just fine." She hands her the blouse and reaches for Hadeel's black Eileen Fisher skirt laying on the back of the desk chair. "Together, these will look formal and neat. Now, I need to fix your hair."

"I showered this morning, it's still damp," Hadeel says annoyed.

"Please let me straighten it with a hair dryer."

"Now you're acting like my mother!"

Amina giggles. "I don't mind, she seems like a real loving person." She plugs in the dryer and fashions

Hadeel's bangs and a curl at the back. "Who cut your hair?"

Hadeel suppresses a laugh. "Why?"

"It's not cut straight."

"If you have clips I'll tie it in a bun."

Amina grabs a few hair clips from the vanity drawer. "Here you go. How about some make up?"

"Nooooooo! That's enough! Let me change and get this over with."

"Okay, okay." Amina steps back and checks Hadeel's hair.

"Here's what I think," Hadeel says tying her hair to the back with the clips. "It's going to be an old professor, Jonathan's age, who needs to ask questions for a research paper."

"Questions for a paper? Why wouldn't he call instead?"

"I don't know. So maybe it's the lawyer who's handling Amal's lawsuit."

Amina rushes out of the room. "I'll go tidy up the living room a bit while you change."

Hadeel struggles out of the sweatpants and pulls up the skirt to her waist. During the last two days, she's had her leg lifted on three pillows, according to doctor's orders. It's a relief to be able to move around finally. She grabs the crutches, limps toward the door and stops in front of the vanity mirror. The blouse is a little tight around the chest, and the sleeves are short. She fastens the top buttons of the blouse and pulls the hem down over her skirt.

"Good enough," she mumbles.

Even though it's morning, Amina has switched on all the lights in the living room. The red roses in the vase on the coffee table look brighter under the spotlights. She should text Yousef to thank him, Hadeel thinks. Next to the vase is a box of chocolate in the shape of a heart, and paper plates with red napkins.

"How nice!" Hadeel exclaims. "Can I have a piece of chocolate?"

"Of course!" Amina shouts from the kitchen. The door bell rings. "They're here. Take a seat Hadeel, I'll get the door."

Hadeel collapses onto the couch and drops the crutches to the floor. She listens to Amina's cheerful voice greeting her guests.

Jonathan says something in a low voice to which Amina answers, "Oh, okay." Then everything becomes quiet.

Did they all leave? Hadeel lifts herself off the couch. She sees someone stepping into the living room. A very tall man with dark hair, wearing a beige jacket over black trousers. He halts when he spots her. A large brown envelope is clutched in his hands like a shield.

"Hadeel."

The voice sounds familiar. Hadeel's heart skips a beat. That's impossible, I must be dreaming, she tells herself. "No way," she tells him, louder than she meant.

He hastens to her side. "Please forgive me for surprising you like this. I just . . . I just couldn't take a chance not seeing you before you go home. I was afraid you'll refuse to see me."

Hadeel's head spins. His British accent is music to her ears. His face is younger than she remembers, his cheeks pink and smooth, his eyes are bright but tired.

"Raj. How is this possible?" She blushes deeply.

He takes a seat on the couch facing her. "I tried to reply to your last message, but it wouldn't go through. I was worried about you."

Hadeel buries her face with both hands. "I'm sorry. This is so weird. I can't believe it's really you."

He remains silent until she removes her hands from her face and looks at him. "It's really me, Hadeel." He smiles.

Those dimples are real as well. She tries to say something then shakes her head. They gaze at each other, for the first time since they met online, without computer screens and thousands of miles in between. She can feel his body warmth without touching him.

"How did you find me?" she finally asks, her voice shaking.

"When I couldn't reach you, I texted your Aunt Munira and asked her about you."

"Did I give you her number?"

"You sent me a message once using her phone. I kept it for emergencies."

Eyes downcast, Hadeel whispers, "So you got my last message?" She takes a deep breath and holds it.

"I did. Thank you."

Hadeel exhales and looks up. She searches his face for signs of forgiveness, wondering about his main reason for coming to see her, wondering if there's still hope for renewing their relationship.

Raj must have read her mind, saying, "I was in agony, wondering what happened to you.

I took a chance, even though I don't know if you want to see me."

"Yes, I do," the words slip out of her lips. "I mean, I wanted to end it, to forget you, but now I see how difficult it is."

He waits for her to say more, perhaps waiting for her to explain exactly what happened.

When she doesn't, he asks, "How do you feel?"

At the same time Hadeel asks, "Did you meet my aunt then? Was she all right?"

"She was. When I texted her asking about you she suggested meeting her at her hotel."

"Why?"

"To explain about your accident and that you'll be here alone for a few days. Luckily, it's my Easter break. I asked her if it would be okay for me to visit you."

Hadeel looks at him in astonishment as she hears the most amazing news she ever heard in her life. "And she said it was okay?"

"She didn't exactly say that. She gave me Jonathan's number. She said you called her using his phone because yours was crashed."

"So you called Jonathan?"

Raj nods. "I asked him how to reach you. Turns out Jonathan and I have similar educational and academic background, amongst other things." He chuckles. "By the way, your Aunt Munira asked if I do come to see you to give you this." He places the large envelope on the coffee table between them.

"What is it?"

"I don't know." He pauses then adds, "She also said to tell you she was sorry."

"About what? Now I'm so worried."

"Oh Gosh, I totally forgot." He takes out a small white envelope from the inside pocket of his jacket. "She might explain in this letter."

With shaky hands, Hadeel takes it from him. "Can I open it?"

"Of course, it's yours."

Hadeel tears the flap of the envelope open and pulls out a small piece of paper with the Churchill hotel logo on top. In her familiar delicate Arabic handwriting, Munira wrote:

> *Hadeel, During the last three days, while alone for the first time in London, I realized how wrong I've been the last twenty years. I've hidden a truth from you while trying to decide your life for you. Because of my guilt toward Amal, I sent you on a trip all alone. Put you in danger and through a difficult situation with your parents. The least I can do now, to amend for my mistake, is to give you a chance to decide what you want to do with your life, on your own. Raj seems to be a good man and he loves you. If you decide to stay in England and marry him, I will take your side, fight for you at home, and face the outrage of your father Rashid.*
>
> *Please forgive me, Hadeel.*
>
> *Your Aunt Munira*

Tears are flowing down Hadeel's cheeks. She tries to hide her face from Raj, furtively wiping the tears with her hands.

He offers her a tissue. "Everything all right?"

She nods, shrugs, then whispers, "I'm sorry."

"Don't be."

"I must look terrible."

"You don't. Your eyes are prettier in real life, you know?" His smile deepens the dimples in his flushed cheeks.

Hadeel looks away. "I'm still not sure what Amma Munira is referring to in her letter. But she sounds very remorseful."

"Sometimes things change rapidly and unexpectedly. And often times out of our control," Raj says with a serious voice. He hesitates before he adds, "I remember you wore the hijab once."

Startled, Hadeel touches her hair, wondering if he disapproves of her unveiling. "I decided not to wear it anymore."

He smiles. "See, that's an unexpected decision, I'm sure. Is it?"

"No. I gave it a lot of thought the last few days."

His smile grows bigger. "All right."

She aches to know how he feels about it but doesn't ask. It's her decision, it's her right.

Her eyes roam over his soft curly brown hair and dark eyebrows, then down to his polished brown shoes. He's wearing blue socks. She smiles and looks back at him. "How was your flight?"

"Nine hours of flying can put a dent on anybody." He runs his fingers through his hair.

"Of course, I know. Where are you staying?"

"With Jonathan. We had a substantial phone conversation and he invited me to his home. What a genuine person he is." Raj sits back and tilts his head to the side. "He's hoping you'll stay for your Aunt's memorial service on Tuesday. Are you?"

"Oh, yes. I forgot to tell him. I'm leaving the day after the service."

"So we'll be traveling companions."

Hadeel blushes and tries to think of something to change the subject. "Would you like some chocolate?"

"No, thank you. I think I should leave you to rest."

"Wait, I have a question that's been torturing me."

Raj sits back and smiles at her encouragingly. "Go ahead."

"When you were in Kuwait and," She squints in pain as the episode of letting him down at that critical moment still gnaws at her conscience. "And I didn't show up. Did you actually meet my father?"

"I did."

Hadeel groans. "Was, was he . . ."

"It's all right, Hadeel."

Her eyes moisten. "Was my father . . . rude to you?"

"No. He was civil enough."

"What did he say to you?"

"He said you were engaged and will soon marry your cousin."

Hadeel gasps. "No! I wasn't at the time."

"Are you now?" Raj asks with concern. "Are you engaged to your cousin?"

She looks him in the eyes. "No. I was unofficially engaged. But I made up my mind not to marry my cousin, no matter what."

Raj relaxes his shoulders. "Good."

Hadeel bites her lips. "I don't know how my father will react when I tell him I'm not wearing the hijab on top of not marrying my cousin."

"He seemed to be a caring and logical person."

"He is." Hadeel's voice breaks.

Raj leans forward, his face worried. He reaches for her hand. "If you're afraid for your safety, you don't have to go back home."

Hadeel draws her hand away. "What do you mean?"

"I mean, if you think your father will harm you . . ."

She interrupts him, "My father would never hurt me. Actually, I'm worried about hurting his feelings."

"Hello?" Amina calls and knocks at the main door before she barges in. "Hi! We're back. Jonathan is here too."

Raj rises to meet them. He's a couple of inches taller than Jonathan, Hadeel notices, wishing they'd stay.

"Please stay," Amina must have read her mind. "I can make coffee or tea for everyone."

"Thanks, Amina, but we need to go," Jonathan says and looks at Raj. "Shall we?"

"Yes." Raj looks at Hadeel. "I'll see you on Tuesday then."

"Inshallah." With her eyes still locked on Raj's, Hadeel, says, "Jonathan, I'm staying for Amal's event."

"That's great, thanks," Jonathan replies.

Once the door closes behind the two men, Amina rushes back to Hadeel screaming. "Oh My God Hadeel! I can't believe it! A handsome man like this comes all the way from London just for you? And you haven't even mentioned him once. You have to tell me everything!" She drops herself next to Hadeel.

"I can't believe it myself." Hadeel mumbles.

Amina takes the box of chocolate, hands one to Hadeel and unwraps a piece for herself. "Okay, tell me everything. I *love* love stories."

Chapter Twenty-Nine

Surrounded by dozens of letters and their torn envelopes, Hadeel perch in bed, clutching a couple of them in her fists. "I can't believe this, I can't believe this," she repeats and shakes her head in denial. It's hard to fathom what she has just discovered. Letters Amal wrote to her during the last twenty years, Munira received, opened, read and kept them a secret from Hadeel. Amal had sent the letters to Munira, instead of Hadeel's father Rashid, trusting they'd have a better chance reaching Hadeel. Yet, it was Munira, her pious aunt, not her father, who received them and hid them from her, for twenty years. How could that be possible? How dare she?

It's almost dawn; still, Hadeel can't sleep. She's been reading Amal's letters one by one, then rereading them. The letters she should have read during the past two decades. It feels like an entire life, her own, was stolen away from her. Why did Munira make Hadeel believe that it was Rashid who prevented her from corresponding with Amal? Isn't abstaining from telling the truth the same as lying? Isn't that a sin?

Hadeel re-reads one of the letter she's clutching in her hand and restrains herself from screaming in anger and frustration. Amal was in Kuwait a couple of years ago, only a few feet away from Hadeel and could not approach her. Munira had the nerve to prevent them from meeting. How cruel to deprive her own sister of such a simple request. Why? The longer Hadeel ponders Munira's motives the angrier she gets. How mean of her, Amal's only sister, to do such a thing. She is now remorseful? Now, when it's too late? Is that why she sent Hadeel to bring Amal's body back home? Guilt? Did she think that will atone for her actions?

Hadeel reaches for the phone to call Munira and ask her the questions that are driving her mad. As she looks up her name in contacts, her breath gets shorter and quicker. A voice in her mind says, *what's the point? it's too late now.* Is it helpful to learn Munira's real motive now?

After all, she has realized her mistake and surrendered the letters to their rightful owner. Perhaps she carried the letters with her to London with the intention to show them to Hadeel. Did she forget to give them to her? Or she didn't have the nerve to face her in person? Hadeel lets go of the mobile. She shouldn't call while she's in this state of mind.

Why do people wait for death to happen before they forgive each other? In one of her letters Amal wrote, "We constantly ask God the Almighty for forgiveness, yet we find it hard to forgive each other, especially those closest to us." Would Amal forgive Munira? Can Hadeel forgive Munira? When she looks at her again, would she see the same person she thought she'd known all her life? The loving, gentle, kind-hearted Munira?

Amina's alarm of Fairuz's song, *We will return, oh love, we will return*, sounds, signaling 6:30 a.m. It's Tuesday morning, the day of Amal's memorial on campus. Hadeel wonders how to face the world with the new information about her aunts? One, 'the fallen woman,' emerging as a martyr. The other, the pious one, coming out as a liar. Should she list her in the category of 'fallen women?'

The last letter Amal had written to Hadeel about her dream of her grandfather amazes her the most. It reminds Hadeel of the painting on the fireplace in Jonathan's house, and the way she's been drawn to it every time she was there. Hadeel wants to believe that Amal was giving

Hadeel her blessings to accept Raj as a husband. That is if he's still interested, of course. The thought of that possibility changes the course of Hadeel's thoughts. She collects Amal's letters and places them back inside the big brown envelope. She should stop looking backward and start planning her future. What if Raj is not free anymore? Would she reconsider marrying Nawaf?

No! She shakes her head. But if Raj isn't still interested in her, if he has someone else, why would he come all the way here to meet her in person?

When Jonathan picks up Hadeel and Amina at four-thirty in the afternoon the weather has changed from sunny to cloudy. Raindrops tap on the windshield of his Tesla. Jonathan is driving to campus, solemn and deep in thought.

Next to him in the passenger's seat is Raj, seeming at home in this London weather. In the back seat, next to Hadeel, sits Amina, all smiles and contentment. When they get closer to campus Jonathan comes to life and explains the program. He tells them that Raj, to Hadeel's surprise, will be one of the speakers.

"Is that why you're in Boulder, Raj?" Amina asks and winks at Hadeel. Raj looks over his shoulder at Hadeel and smiles.

"As a matter of fact," Jonathan says, "it's a last-minute decision. I'm so grateful to Raj for accepting my request."

Once parked, Jonathan leads the way. For Hadeel's sake, they stroll slowly through campus grounds, avoiding puddles of water on the smooth concrete paths. Campus looks completely different to Hadeel now from last week's visit. The trees are green, full of blossoms and promises of blooming flowers in the days to come.

Hadeel takes Raj's offered arm and hops lightly on her right foot. He's holding an umbrella over their heads with his free hand and is keeping an eye on her. He has suggested she uses a wheelchair, but she refused.

"We're almost there." Jonathan turns and points at an old tall red-brick building with white window trim.

"Old Main," Amina announces. She's taking shelter under Jonathan's umbrella, keeping both hands deep in her yellow rain jacket. She looks so tiny next to Jonathan's tall frame. Amina looks back at Hadeel and Raj. "That was the first building on campus."

At the entrance, the men hold the doors open for the ladies and shake water out of the umbrellas. Inside, it is warm and cozy. Just like its name, the building is ancient, but beautifully maintained. The wooden floors creak under their tread. A little winding stairway leads to the doors of a small theater. Hadeel clutches the railing to avoid being dependent on her friends.

She's glad she left the crutches in the car. They would have been cumbersome in these narrow hallways.

Once inside the theater, Hadeel stops to take in the scene. The walls are covered with thick black fabric for sound effects. There's a mezzanine with extra seating which Amina did not recommend for Hadeel. In the main floor most seats are already occupied, only a few in the back remain vacant.

"There's Yousef." Amina points and calls, "Yousef!"

"Hi!" Yousef rushes to greet them. "I saved two seats in the front for you," he tells Amina and shakes Hadeel's hand warmly. "Good to see you, again."

Amina looks at Jonathan. "Shall we go with him?"

"Go ahead," Jonathan nods. "I need to take care of a few details on the stage."

"I'll join you," Raj says and follows Jonathan.

"Hadeel!" an authoritarian voice calls as Hadeel and her friends approach their seats. "Very glad to see you." Dorothy, Jonathan's mother, is looking at her from the middle of the front row.

"Excuse me," Hadeel tells her friends and hops toward Dorothy.

"Marjorie," Dorothy says to a white-haired lady sitting next to her. "This is Amal's niece. She had an accident recently and broke her ankle. Hadeel, Marjorie was a colleague of Amal's before she retired."

"Very pleased to meet you," Hadeel says, shaking Marjorie's hand.

"Oh my," Marjorie exclaims. "Same voice and accent."

Dorothy nods somberly. "Yes."

"Excuse me," Hadeel says. "I'll have to go back to my seat."

A few minutes later, the curtains open to reveal a large photograph of Amal in a blue suit and a big smile holding a certificate. To the left of Amal's photo is another familiar one. It's a photograph of a white and blue tile that has Arabic letters that translate to: There's no victor but the Truth.

Hadeel hears scattered voices reading the Arabic words of the tile. One of them is Yousef who adds, "It looks like the script on the walls of Alhambra. But that one says, there's no victor but God."

"Yes," Hadeel explains. "Amal has both texts on the fountain in her garden. This is actually her handwriting."

She finds herself fighting tears. A memory of herself as a five-year-old, begging her aunt not to leave becomes vivid.

A knock on the microphone on stage brings the attention of the audience to Jonathan. At the same time lights are dimmed except for the spotlight aimed on him. Tall, thin, and solemn in a black suit and a black tie, Jonathan looks out at the audience.

"Thank you all for attending," he says. "We are here today to honor the work and life of Professor Amal Hamdeen. To those of you who don't know Arabic, Amal means hope, Hamdeen means the thankful. And during her life Amal was both. Those two qualities are always enforced throughout her work and extensive research, which is, by the way, listed on the back of the pamphlets in your hands. She firmly believed that seeking the truth leads to uncertainties which lead to more research, and ultimately, hopefully, to the truth.

"The most important accomplishment that I, as a fellow professor and her husband, credit Amal for is shedding light back on a prominent American writer, Washington Irving. Irving in recent years has fallen out of favor in the literary scene. Some of his work was either forgotten or scoffed at by some critics. Sometimes this was done intentionally, for different motives, if I may add. Let me give you an example. How many of you have heard of Irving's book, *The Legendary Life of Mahomet*?"

Jonathan covers his eyebrows with a hand to shield his eyes from the glare of the spotlights. "I see a couple of hands, thank you. That original title by Irving, *The Legendary Life of Mahomet*, was changed by publishers to 'Mohammed'. You'd think at a time in America, when Islamophobia is spreading all over the continent, a book by a prominent American writer would be in the spotlight and discussed. But unfortunately, that hasn't happened, not even in academic or in intellectual circles at the least.

"Amal was a firm believer in Edward Said's theory of Orientalism. Her Master's thesis, written years before Said's valuable book, dealt with a similar topic. Amal was energized and thrilled with Said's theory and speculations. In one of her last published papers, she sought to prove yet another aspect of Orientalism, that of the intentional covering up of works by famous Western authors who wrote positively about Islam. For example, works by celebrated Romantic poets like Percy Shelley and the British Poet Laureate Robert Southey.

"By pursuing that path, Professor Hamdeen was seeking the truth. Amal was not proselytizing Islam or advocating for the Shari'a law as a colleague of hers accused her. She was only seeking a hidden truth." Jonathan points at the photo of the tile behind him. "Anyone who knew Amal knows that this accusation is totally unfounded. For one thing, Amal did not believe in the compatibility of politics and religion. Therefore, one wonders if the real motive of this unfounded accusation was to prevent Amal from uncovering the truth. Or, to block a promotion she was entitled to."

Murmurs arise in the theater among the audience while Jonathan pauses for a breath. "What a shame," someone in the back yells.

"Yes, really," Jonathan says. "What a shame, because these allegations were claimed by an influential person who had an agenda." Jonathan's eyes search around as if looking for that person in the audience. "However, those false accusations came out after two literary discoveries that Amal revealed in papers that got published at that time. One of them discusses an interesting character who might have instigated Irving's writing his book about the Prophet Mohammed.

"The other is the discovery of the original Thalaba, who might have been the basis of Southey's Thalaba in his epic, *Thalaba the Destroyer.*

"Tonight we are lucky to have a professor from England who's been researching and teaching *Thalaba the Destroyer* for the last ten years of his young life. Professor

Raj Sharafuddin." Jonathan points at Raj and pauses for an applause before he adds, "I will now leave the floor for Professor Sharafuddin to explain how his work and Amal's coincided in the most amazing circumstances."

With a fluttering heart Hadeel sits up. She folds her arms around her chest and watches Raj walk to the stage and shake hands with Jonathan. Raj brushes a lock of hair from his forehead, clears his voice and brings up the microphone to the level of his mouth. He looks at the audience and says, "Life sometimes presents us with unexpected gifts, miracles if you will. Unawares, some people miss these chances. Others like me, accept them with awe and let them take their place into existence, because, in a metaphysical sense, everything in life is connected.

"Last year, I happened upon a paper published in a British anthology that discusses why Southey might have chosen the name Thalaba for his epic, *Thalaba the Destroyer*. A question that has baffled me ever since I discovered that lovely poem and made it part of my career.

Finally, the question has been answered. The fifteen-year-old Arab Thalaba in Southey's epic became real. Not only that, but he, the original Thalaba, the same age and span of life, had lived with the Prophet Mohammed, learned from him, worked for him. He died with his head resting in the Prophet's lap, seeking forgiveness. The author of the paper of this discovery was Amal Hamdeen. I contacted her by email and invited her to an annual symposium on British Romantic Poetry and Islam. She accepted and we were supposed to meet three months from now."

Raj waits for sounds of regret and disappointment emanating from attendees to subside. He continues, "That's exactly how I feel. But what's more astounding than that is the fact that speaking at her memorial today is a total coincidence. As a matter of fact, I did not know of Professor's Hamdeen's passing away until I arrived in Boulder for personal reasons." He pauses, looking in the direction of Hadeel and smiles. "Another example of life's unexpected surprises, and the intricate way we are all connected."

A couple of heads turn to look at Hadeel, including Yousef's with an understanding smile.

While perspiration trickles down the back of her neck, Hadeel takes a couple of deep breaths to slow her heart beats. How could this be happening? Her head spins, she holds on to the chair's arms. She can't concentrate on Raj's ongoing speech. She loses track of the lecture while trying to put pieces of the puzzle together, how they were all connected by Thalaba, until laughter by the audience at something Raj has said forces her to gather her attention back.

"In conclusion," Raj is saying, "The main premise that both Amal and I agreed on is that Southey in his epic displayed a hope for a better world for the unity of Christianity and Islam. How punishment and reward in Christianity was actually influenced by Islam's. And that Southey's informed knowledge offers a prophetic message through the plot of *Thalaba the Destroyer*. A message we should all heed. Thank you very much."

Amidst the loud applause Jonathan walks back to the stage and offer the audience a chance for questions or comments. A cordless microphone is delivered to those who raise their hands to comment. Most of them are students who want to share their experiences meeting Amal, or their thoughts regarding her work. One of them, a girl in a blue hijab, and an ankle length white dress, seemed determined to speak her mind. She walks to the front and takes the microphone. Her milky white complexion, clear blue eyes and flawless American accent assure Hadeel that the girl is an American Muslim. After introducing herself as Jameela, the girl asks Professor Jonathan to take a few minutes to discuss the term 'Islamophobia' which is what caused Amal's demise.

"I for myself resent the term," Jameela says, looking defiantly at the audience. Her face is now flushed pink, her lips red. "Unlike the terms racism, terrorism, or Antisemitism, terms that put the blame on the attackers, *Islamophobia*, the fear of Islam, on the other hand, provides an excuse for attacking and harming Muslims because of fear and misunderstanding. Why isn't it called anti-Islam? Or terrorism against Muslims, for example?"

The audience applauds in approval. Someone in the back calls, "Yeah! I agree!"

"Very good point," Jonathan says. "Let's discuss this topic in class. Thank you, Jameela."

Hadeel glances at Raj, wondering what he thought of Jameela's comments. She can only see his head bent over his broad shoulders in the front seat, he seems absorbed in jotting down something.

Without previous intention or plan Hadeel lifts up her arm. In the other hand she's clutching a letter she brought with to give to Jonathan after the event. Why is she doing it now? She quickly lowers her hand. But it's too late.

"Yes, Hadeel!" Jonathan calls, causing heads to turn back to look at her.

With sweaty palms, Hadeel reaches for the mike which Jameela rushes to give to her. "Thank you. I'd like to read a paragraph from a letter my Aunt Amal wrote to me a few months before she was killed. In the letter she said, and I quote: Let me make myself clear, Hadeel, I am not defending Islam. Islam can defend itself as the Quran tells us. My wish is to defend Muslims, who are recently been under attack around the world. Just like all other humans, Muslims are worthy of respect and protection. People should work for justice for all, not just the privileged.

Why don't we learn from history? Why do we have to wait for another holocaust to take place before we act?"

Hadeel looks up from the letter, swallows and clears her throat. "I believe that anyone with such an opinion should not and cannot be accused of being in favor of promoting Sharia law. This letter should refute any allegations against Dr. Amal Hamdeen. Thank you."

Jonathan waits for the applause to stop. "Thank you Hadeel for sharing your letter. Now, I'd like to announce a trust fund for graduate scholarships offered by my mother, Professor Dorothy Walton, in Amal Hamdeen's name for female students in need. At this time, let's take a moment of silence to remember Amal."

As Hadeel sits in silence with the rest of the audience in the antique hall, she thinks how strange that she has finally found Amal amidst strangers. Of course she would have preferred to find her alive, but perhaps by celebrating Amal's life and work would serve to remind people that no matter how different we are, we are similar in more ways than we think.

Chapter Thirty

Raj's hazel eyes remind Hadeel of honey. The phrase, "swimming in honey" pops into her mind whenever she looks at him. It must be describing her feelings at the moment, where pain, fear and worry all melt away in his gaze. They are standing in front of Amal's painting over the mantelpiece in Jonathan's living room.

"Sorry to interrupt, guys," Jonathan says. "Hadeel, can I borrow you for a minute?" "Yes, sure." Hadeel takes one of the crutches Jonathan is offering her.

"Can I talk to you in my office?" Jonathan asks Hadeel. "Excuses us, Raj."

"Yes, of course." Raj steps back.

After the reception at Amal's memorial Jonathan asked Hadeel, Amina and Raj to join him at his house. He wanted to discuss something important with Hadeel, he said. Bubbly Amina accepted with no hesitation. She'd never been to a professor's house before, she claimed. Hadeel reminded her that both her parents are professors, which is where she grew up. Hadeel appreciated Amina's company to Jonathan's house until Yousef called and picked her up to join him at another event on campus.

In his office Jonathan closes the door and offers Hadeel a chair. He takes a seat behind his desk which is swarmed with books, piles of paper and several pen-holders and letter openers.

Hadeel guesses he wants to discuss Amal's letter which she quoted at the event. She pulls it out of her pocket and offers it to him. "I hope it will help in the lawsuit."

"Thank you, Hadeel." He takes it and reads the writing of his wife. He then looks up and says, "Tell you the truth I'm not sure I want to pursue this lawsuit anymore. If that professor issues a letter of apology, that would be good enough for me."

"I understand," Hadeel nods. "Did you get a chance to read the translated version of Amal's paper that I emailed you?"

"I did, thank you."

Hadeel waits for him to dismiss her from his office. She wonders what Raj is up to at that moment.

Jonathan clears his voice. "I've been thinking a lot lately of something very precious to me and Amal." His gaze resting on his folded hands on the desk. "I'm certain that Amal would agree with my decision."

"The Malaga apartment?"

"No, no. That is settled, she and I discussed it in person. This we didn't think of." Jonathan clears a path on the desk between them and pushes a blue velvety case toward her. "Please open it."

Hadeel opens it and gasps. "This is a *shabka!*" she exclaims. Pinned to the blue satin interior is a bracelet and two earrings, surrounded by a sparkling diamond necklace. Rubies in the shape of pomegranate seeds are studded intermittently in the necklace and the other pieces. She looks up at him. "I cannot accept this."

He's wiping tears with a handkerchief. It reminds Hadeel of the first day they met at the airport, a week or so ago, which feels more like a year. Only this time, her heart aches at his grief. "I'm so sorry," she whispers.

"I got it for Amal when I proposed." He places his glasses back over his eyes. "Please, consider it a gift from both of us. A wedding gift."

"What wedding?" Hadeel sits up with a jolt. Why is everyone suddenly talking about her getting married?

Jonathan shrugs. "I'm sure, one day, you will get married. As for now, I cannot think of anyone more appropriate to pass this to."

Dumbfounded, Hadeel gapes at him, then at the jewelry. When she looks up again her eyes stop at a framed photograph of Amal on the desk, to Jonathan's left. "Is she wearing the *shabka* in that photo?" she asks.

"Yes." He hands her the frame. A picture of pure joy. Amal is laughing as she shows the earrings to the camera, the twinkling in her eyes matches the sparkling jewelry. On her finger is a matching wedding ring.

"I left the ring on her finger," Jonathan chokes. "That's why it's not in the set." Hadeel finds no words to assuage his pain.

"Thank you, Jonathan. I'll cherish it."

"Thank you. I have a small carry-on bag you can use. It would be better if you carry it with you onboard."

Shocked at the unexpected gift, Hadeel remains in her

seat, staring at her feet. A *shabka* and a flat in . Her grandfather's apartment and Amal's *shabka* would make her independent from her parents if Raj asks her to marry him again. Would she say yes now? Would she stay in London and avoid confrontation with her parents? Would she break her father's heart for her own happiness?

Jonathan returns with a cloth bag and places the jewelry case inside it. Hadeel straps it on her shoulder and with Jonathan's help hops out of the office.

They find Raj in front of the painting where they left him.

Hadeel rests the crutches on the mantelpiece and looks around the living room that now feels like home. Will she ever be back here? Will she ever see Jonathan again? The thought makes her sad.

"Is everything all right?" Raj's eyes roam all over her face as if to find an answer.

"Yes. I'm just thinking of how lonely Jonathan will be when we all leave."

Raj nods. "I know. But it was very nice of you to visit him."

They both stare at each other awkwardly. Hadeel is too embarrassed to tell him how much she resented taking the trip initially.

"Hadeel," Raj says after a heavy silence. He clears his voice and says, "Hadeel, will you marry me?"

Her eyes well with tears as a sense of relief fills her heart. Her shoulders relax and she looks deep into his gentle eyes. She has hoped for this, longed for it, but she hasn't prepared herself for an answer. Her tears roll down her face.

He steps closer and takes her hand. "Will you marry me, Hadeel?"

"I'd like to, Raj," Her voice breaks and she tries hard not to sob. "But I don't think I can. I cannot say yes at the moment."

"Tell me why." He wipes a tear from her cheek with his thumb.

"I can't do it without my father's blessing. I have to get his approval."

"What if he says no?"

"Then I won't marry you, Raj, or anyone else." She swallows her tears, lifts her chin, and looks at him in the eye saying, "I will not marry anyone else if I can't marry you. But I cannot build my happiness with you over my family's misery. Please understand."

"I do." Sadness fills Raj's countenance. "Would you let me know, though?"

"I will. I promise."

Chapter Thirty-One

The captain asks his crew members to prepare for landing at Kuwait International Airport. Hadeel gathers the scattered letters around her seat and stashes them back inside the cloth bag Jonathan gave her. During the last six hours of the flight from London to Kuwait, she has re-read all the letters that Amal had written to her, wondering if she would learn from her aunt's experience in leaving home and living abroad. She compared Jonathan's love for Amal to Raj's love for her. "Trust is the most important ingredient in a relationship," Amal wrote in one of her letters. "As much as you ask for it from your partner, you have to be worthy of his."

During the flight from Denver to Heathrow Hadeel and Raj avoided discussing marriage.

They talked about their childhoods and growing up, education and work, universities, and job opportunities in England and elsewhere. She tried her best not to bring up the issue of love. But no matter what subject they touched upon, love always infiltrated. She explained her passion for video games, and he told her about his attempts at poetry. She playfully pressed him for a sample, and he read a poem that he wrote for her shortly after his trip to Kuwait. He had it saved on his laptop.

> Snow fell softly through the dark night,
> Pure white, as silent as my heart.
> This morning the golden sun came out
> And melted the snow out of sight.
> My love for you will never melt, though.
> It will keep us warm in winter's snow
> Even in the summer it will glow
> If only in our hearts and souls
> My love for you will never dissolve.

While her heart pounded with every word he uttered, Hadeel tried to keep a straight face. She did not know how to react. Should she thank him? He kept smiling at her while she avoided meeting his eyes. Finally, she managed to say, "it's beautiful," and asked him to forward it to her.

Preparing for landing at Kuwait International Airport, Hadeel's fingers grope for the jewelry box, making sure it's still there before she stashes the bag under the front seat. How is she going to explain everything to her parents? Hopefully, Munira has already taken off half of the burden. They haven't talked since. Hadeel remembers how Munira cried with remorse the last time they communicated.

As the aircraft begins descending, Hadeel inhales deeply and peers out the window. The familiar sights of her homeland look different now. The sinuous man-made roads cutting through the gray sand dunes seem alarming. The shoreline of the Gulf looks narrow and short. Dry stringy bushes stoop down painfully under the jet-wind force and perhaps another approaching dust storm. When the plane touches down and rolls closer to the terminal, the old control-tower appears, looking flimsy. The paint of its facade peeled, uncovering the cinder blocks beneath.

Hadeel switches on her mobile the moment the plane halts at the gate. Amina has kindly insisted that Hadeel keep her Kuwaiti phone during the trip. "You will need it, believe me." When Hadeel wondered how to return it to her she said, "Don't worry, there are many ways to send it back. One of them is to give it to my mom. She's coming to see me soon, during summer vacation."

Ten messages pop up on the screen. "Waiting for you at the airport," Yumma texts. Then another: "*Yallah!* Where are you?" Hadeel giggles at her mother's impatience. She imagines the shock on her face when Hadeel walks out without the hijab. Her plan is to stay home for a couple of weeks to heal and deal with her father, as well as to avoid relatives who are used to seeing her with the hijab. Then what? She doesn't know yet. She only knows she will not let other people decide for her anymore.

With nostalgia, Hadeel gazes at the pictures of Amina with Kevin. "He's already a star on my Instagram!" Amina has written. "Just for a brief clip, Kevin became a star. The big news is he agreed to be in my dream movie, The Palestinian Exodus!! Actually, it's my mom's dream movie since childhood, to show how her Palestinian grandparents, and hundreds of thousands others, were forced to leave their homes in Palestine when Israel was created."

Hadeel smiles as she thinks of Raj's dream movie, *Fearless and Forgiving*, based on Southey's *Thalaba the Destroyer*. A science-fiction-style film that he discussed when she told him about her video games. Kevin would also be a perfect Thalaba, Hadeel giggles at the thought that she and Amina are converting him into a movie star. Before she vacates her seat on the plane she takes a long look at a selfie of herself with Raj at Heathrow. He is the movie star, the star of her life, the glimmering light of her dark nights. It was hard saying goodbye to him in London, especially, knowing they might never see each other again. But her duty as a good daughter of good parents took precedence.

"Where are you?" Another message from Yumma pings.

"At the passport check."

"Welcome home," the customs officer says. She smile at Hadeel before she stamps her passport.

Three Years Later

MALAGA, SPAIN

The ocean is calm today. The waves barely raise their heads above the surface as they rush to the shore with millions of frothy kisses. Hadeel lifts her face and closes her eyes hoping some of the moisture would reach and touch her cheeks. She's resting on one of the wooden dining chairs she dragged from the kitchen, the only thing that fits in the narrow balcony. The bulge in her midsection is getting bigger lately and feels alive. She folds her arms around it protectively and inhales the fresh scent of the sea.

Way down below, people are strolling barefoot on the sandy beach. The sand must be warm from the sun's heat all morning, but the December chill can still be felt all the way up to the balcony. The time on her watch says 3:45 p.m. He should arrive any time now, she thinks, bending down to look for him through the railings. A sudden stab under her arms forces her to gasp and straighten up. She sits still and feels a slight kick under her hands for the first time. Mama should know.

In the living room, Hadeel picks up her mobile from the coffee table. “Yumma! The baby’s kicking!” she chuckles.

“*Mashallah*!” her mother says. “It’s still early but it can happen. Has your husband arrived?”

“Not yet. He should be here soon. Don’t worry.”

“You should’ve stayed longer with us until today. But you were in a hurry.”

“I wanted to change the furniture before he arrived.”

“How does it look? I hope everything looks like they show online. Does everything fit in that dingy place?”

Hadeel laughs. “The place is small, yes, but it’s not dingy, Yumma. You should see it now.”

“Remember, your father offered to buy you a bigger one as a wedding gift.”

“I don’t need a new place, Yumma. I love this one.” Hadeel glances at a photo of her grandfather smiling from the top shelf of the bookcase. “Besides, we don’t live here, it’s only a vacation spot.”

“Make a video of the new furniture and send it.”

“I will. Oh, there’s a knock on the door, I have to go.”

Hadeel drops the phone and rushes to the door. She doesn’t have to look through the peephole to check who it is. She swings the door open to the tall, smiling man waiting with a dozen red roses in his hands.

“These are for you.” Raj offers the roses. “Happy anniversary.”

"Thank you! They're beautiful!"

He places his suitcase inside, locks the door, and pulls her to him in a tight hug. "Be careful," she whispers in his ear. "Thalaba is kicking today, for the first time."

He kisses her lips. "Good timing, on our anniversary."

A message from her mother says, "Your father is still trying to hide his happiness to be a grandfather. Hadeel, please plan to deliver and spend the first forty days after delivery with us in Kuwait. That's our tradition, don't forget."

The memory of her father meeting Raj at Uncle Bader's house brings a thrill to Hadeel's heart. She'll never forget that moment, the moment she planned for with her mother and Haya for a whole year. However, it couldn't have happened without Aunt Munira's help. The three angels, as Hadeel calls them, worked tirelessly on her father to accept Raj as part of her family. But, ultimately, it was Raj's sincerity, and humble behavior that charmed everyone who met him. Rashid, Hadeel's father, seemed content when he accepted him as her husband.

Happily, Hadeel translates her mother's message to Raj who's leading her by the hand to the balcony. "Let's think about it later. All right?"

"Where's Jonathan?" she asks.

"I dropped him off at the Malaga hotel."

"How was the conference in London?"

"Excellent." He slides the balcony doors open and helps Hadeel step outside carefully. "Jonathan's paper on 'Washington Irving's Mohammed' raised a heated debate. Some zealous Muslims didn't like Irving's conclusion."

Hadeel looks at Raj with worry. "How did Jonathan handle it?"

Raj chuckles. "He's used to it. That gives him a chance to discuss faith versus reason."

"Ahh," Hadeel sighs. She remembers Amal's dream in one of her letters, how they gathered around the fountain discussing that same subject.

Raj puts his arm around Hadeel's waist and draws her close to him. "I like the title of your new paper, by the way."

Hadeel recites, "Percy Shelley's Vision of Islam?"

"Right"

"Do you think it would raise a heated discussion as well?"

"No, I don't. It's your analysis of Shelley's The Revolt of Islam, which basically calls for adhering to the essence and deep philosophy of Islam. I can't wait to see it published."

Hadeel grins. "It will soon, I received an acceptance from a journal I sent it to."

He kisses her forehead. "Congratulations. I'm proud of you."

"Thank you." She pecks him on the cheek. "When is Amina arriving?" Raj asks.

" A week from today. Christmas Eve."

"And Kevin?"

"The same day," she laughs. "I can't wait to see them after all this time."

They smile while their gaze travel out to the waves building up on the surface of the Mediterranean, and rest at the ocean together. In Hadeel's ears, Aunt Amal's voice, the way she remembers it from childhood, rings with the words Hadeel memorized from the last letter Amal wrote to her:

> *We are in this beautiful place for a brief period of time. Our purpose is to enjoy it and preserve it for the next generations to enjoy. It is that simple.*

GLOSSARY OF ARABIC WORDS MENTIONED IN THE BOOK

Ahlan: Welcome. A formal way of greeting someone. Ahlain: Welcome. An informal way of greeting.

Alhamdulillah: Praise be to God.

Alhamdillah Alasalameh: Thank God for your safety. Usually said to someone who has just arrived from a journey.

Alheen: Right now.

Allah: Arabic word for God.

Allah Yerhamha: May God have mercy on her (usually referring to a dead person.)

Alhaqiqa: The truth.

Athan: A call for prayer. In Muslim countries, Mosques announce the call for prayer five times a day.

'Amma: A paternal aunt. 'Ammiti: My paternal aunt.

Asfah: I'm sorry, said by a female (a male would say: Asif) Astaghfirullah: I ask God for forgiveness.

'Aza: A period of mourning. It's usually three days in the house of the family of the deceased. Members of the family and friends gather and read the Quran.

Bidoon: Without nationality, stateless. In Kuwait, the word refers to people who crossed Kuwaiti borders at one point in the past and lived in the country but were not granted citizenship because they lack official identity papers.

Binti: My daughter.

Bismillah: In the name of God.

Bismillah Arrahman Arraheem: In the name of God most Gracious most Merciful. These three words are the opening of all prayers and sometimes ceremonial speeches.

Diwaniya: A meeting place, usually a large room attached to someone's house, for men to socialize and discuss social and political issues.

Dishdasha: Men's traditional attire in the Arab Gulf Countries. An ankle-length loose shirt, usually made of white cotton in the summer and dark-colored wool in winter.

Elmuhim: What's most important.

Fedwa: Something believed to have happened to eliminate something worse that could have happened. A small price for what happened.

Ghoozy: A huge dish of lamb meat served over rice with spices.

Habibi (male) and **habibti** (female) mean 'my dear' or 'darling,' both are common words of endearment.

Haboob: A strong sandstorm. In recent years it's become part of the American English vernacular.

Hadeeth: A documented saying by the Prophet Mohammed. Haqiqa: Truth.

Hamdillah 'asalamah: Informal way of thanking God for safety. Haram: Forbidden by religion.

Hasafah: What a loss, or what a shame.

Hijab: A veil around the face to cover the hair and neck. Ibn: the son of.

Imam: A Muslim cleric. Usually, he leads prayers in the mosque.

Inshallah: God willing. It's mostly used to mean hopefully.

Katb-el-Kitab: The official ceremony of marriage agreement before the wedding can take place. Usually, male members of both bride and groom sign the document (marriage contract) with the marriage officiant, *al ma'thoon.*

Khalas: That's it, or that's enough. Khalah: Aunt, the mother's sister. Khalti: My maternal aunt.

Kosheri: An Egyptian dish made of rice, lentils, macaroni, topped with onions.

La Ghaliba Illa Allah: There's no Conqueror or victor but God.

La Ghaliba Illa Alhaqiqa: There's no victor other than the Truth. La Wallah: Really.

Ma Ajmala ellail: How beautiful is the night. Ma'asalamah: Go with safety. Usually said as a goodbye.

Mashallah: Whatever is God's will. Usually uttered to avert the evil eye.

Maskeenah: Poor thing, said about a female. A male would be Maskeen. It is said to show sympathy.

Muhram: A male chaperon for Muslim women when they travel. The Muhram has to be an immediate relative, i.e. father, brother, uncle or nephew.

Mutawa'a: A title for religious female teacher in the Arabian Gulf.

Ommi: My mother.

Oud: A lute. An Arabic string instrument similar to a guitar.

Questioner: In Islam, when someone dies two angels come to question him/her in their grave asking three questions: Who is your God? What is your religion? Who is your Prophet?

Rubbi: My God.

Samheeni: Forgive me, addressed to a female. If addressing a male, Samihni.

Sidra: A popular tree in Kuwait. It's a desert tree whose botanical name is 'Ziziphus Spina-Christi.' It is a revered tree because it's mentioned in the Quran.

Shabka: A set of jewelry given to the bride by the groom before the wedding to be worn on the wedding day. It usually consists of a ring, necklace, earrings, and a bracelet. The word 'shabka' is a derivative of the word 'shabak' meaning to connect.

Salat elesha: Night prayer, after the fifth 'athan,' call for prayer.

Thoub: A loose garment worn over regular clothes to cover uncovered parts of the body when praying. In the old days it was used as a traditional attire for women.

Wallah: By God. I swear to God. Wahsh: A monster.

Ya Allah: Oh My God.

Yallah: Let's go.

Ya Waili: Woe is me.

Yeseer Khair: We'll see. Hopefully all is good. Yuba: Father.

Yumma: Mother.

Zain: Okay.

Acknowledgments

So much gratitude to Nancy Hayes Kilgore, the angel who came my way and showed me the path to the light. Nancy, your encouragement and faith in my work gave me a boost and kept me going. I am so grateful.

Professor Layla Almaleh, your insight, expertise and professionalism were indispensable during the last phase of working on my novel. I can't thank you enough for your time, patience and passion.

Professor Yusur Almadani, thank you for including me in the circle of your family and friends since the very beginning. Your kindness and generosity are endless and matchless, and are always appreciated.

Many thanks to Laura Lippman whose skill in creating suspenseful plots, apparent in all of her novels, helped shape mine. To Ann Hood and all the fellow writers in the Spanocchia Writers Workshops, you were all an inspiration. Can't wait to see you again in Italy.

My friends Jennifer Heath, Carol and Tom Brock, and Annie Hedberg, your comments, feedback and conversations were invaluable and deeply appreciated. Many thanks for your time.

And finally, Sam, the first and last reader/editor of every work I venture on. Sam, you are a role model of dedication, optimism, and perseverance for everyone who knows you, and I'm lucky to be one of them. Thank you for Raj's love poem, which I used in the novel, after all, you are my Raj, Kivanc, and Jonathan, and I am forever grateful.

www.ingramcontent.com/pod-product-compliance
Lightning Source LLC
Chambersburg PA
CBHW021716070925
32138CB00004B/12
9798992398830